**Also available from** ~~Philip~~
**and Carina Press**

*The Hideaway Inn*

**Also available from Philip William Stover**

*There Galapagos My Heart*

# THE BEAUTIFUL THINGS SHOPPE

**PHILIP WILLIAM STOVER**

carina
press

carina
press®

Recycling programs
for this product may
not exist in your area.

ISBN-13: 978-1-335-94088-9

The Beautiful Things Shoppe

Carina Press
22 Adelaide St. West, 40th Floor
Toronto, Ontario M5H 4E3, Canada
www.CarinaPress.com

**Printed in U.S.A.**

For my great romance, my husband, WBC.

Dear Reader,

If this is your first time in New Hope, please be aware that something happens when you cross the Delaware River into this quirky river town halfway between New York City and Philadelphia. New Hope has a way of making people feel comfortable in their own skin and helping them find their heart's desire. At least it does in the stories I write. I wanted to create a community where everyone is welcome and everyone feels seen.

The very real town of New Hope, Pennsylvania, has been a haven for inclusivity for the better part of a century. In the late '60s, Joseph "Josie" Cavallucci, who had previously served in the US Army, hosted mock gay weddings alongside the canal. "Mother Cavalucci's" elaborate events often attracted mainstream media and became the cause célèbre of the town.

I never met Mother Cavalucci but I sometimes wonder what she would think about *Obergefell v. Hodges* and the advent of marriage equality across the country. I remember the first time I called my partner of twenty years my husband. It seemed so strange and foreign. I felt like maybe I was just playing a part in one of Cavalucci's fantasy nuptials. It took some time for it to feel real. Now I use the term *husband* the way it has been used for centuries—to name the man I love and have chosen to spend my life with.

I'm thrilled that I'm able to write romances that not only feature LGBTQ characters but also the unique stories that make up our HEAs. I'm so honored that you have chosen to read this story and I'm proud to be featured as one of the #ownvoices in the Carina Adores line. Please find me on Instagram or at my website, www.philipwilliamstover.com. I'd love to hear from you.

Welcome to New Hope. I'm so glad you made it across the bridge.

*Philip William Stover*

# THE BEAUTIFUL
# THINGS SHOPPE

# Chapter One

*Prescott*

"What is that hideous object doing in the window of *my* store?" I turn my head away from the large section of plate glass to avoid looking at the horrible tchotchke. The tiny mounds of dirty snow on the sidewalk offer more visual appeal than whatever that thing is. Bravely I push through the cerulean blue–trimmed door and enter the shop. A man is standing behind the counter wearing a hoodie the color of a traffic cone and a T-shirt with some sort of bear in a polka-dot tie and tiny hat.

I need my move-in to go smoothly today so I can be ready to reopen the shop for business at the Winter Festival next week. This is my opportunity to become a serious antiques dealer and I don't need a detour through the Island of Misfit Toys. "Who are you and why are you putting such vile merchandise in the window of *my* store?"

"Excuse me. Did you say *vile merchandise?*" the man asks, walking over to the window and grabbing the offensive object. He holds it in his hands like a newborn infant. "I'll have you know this is a genuine *Muppet Show* lunchbox with the Kermit the Frog thermos in mint condition." He inspects the object for a moment. "Somebody will fall in love with this and cherish it as much as I do."

I'm about to move in some of the finest antiques from the nineteenth century and this confused man is putting a *lunch box* in the window of my new retail space. There must be some mistake. I take out my phone.

"Who are you calling?"

"I should be calling the police to let them know a deranged criminal with horrible taste has broken into my shop but I'm calling the man who leased it, Arthur." This was his shop for years but he invited me to take over so he could finally retire.

The confused man goes back to unpacking a parade of items from a grade-school show-and-tell in hell. Somewhere in this quaint town on the river there must be an empty store waiting for his horrible toys. Does he have the wrong address or wrong town? A quick glance at the things he's unpacking makes me think he might be on the wrong planet. I begin to dial when the vintage brass bell above the door rings and Arthur, the man himself, walks in carrying his cane.

"Uncle Arthur, I'm so glad you're here," the man with bad taste says.

"Uncle?" A sinking feeling descends. "Arthur, you know this man? You're related?" I ask.

"Oh, it's an honorific. Many young people in the queer community call me Uncle Arthur. Frankly, it makes me feel old." He smooths his white beard.

That man walks over to Arthur and kisses him on the forehead. "You aren't old. You're cherished."

I've known Arthur only a few years. We'd seen each other at estate sales and auctions and he'd always been very kind to me as a fellow lover of antiques. Eventually he noticed I keep to myself at these events and made gentle, repeated attempts to coax me out of my shell. I eventually felt comfortable enough with him that I looked forward to our exchanges. Knowing he was going to be at big events made tackling the social aspects of them much easier. When he asked me to take over the shop I was thrilled. I had always wanted a shop of my own so I could establish myself as a serious collector. I left the entry-level position at Fisher Fine Arts Library that I'd had since finishing graduate school, gathered my growing collection of antiques and moved to this charming town on the banks of the Delaware River—not far from the spot depicted in the Emanuel Leutze painting of Washington's crossing.

I was more than ready to leave Philadelphia after half a dozen years as a student and almost as many at the library. The Georgian stone farmhouses with painted wooden shutters and stunning view of the river made moving to New Hope an easy decision, but clearly I should have pressed for more details about how the lease would work.

"Arthur, would you mind helping me understand what's

going on here?" I try to smile and remain as pleasant as possible. This can't be Arthur's fault. But then he gives me a look that says I'm not going to like what comes next.

He takes off his vintage bowler and puts it over the silver Labrador head that tops his cane. "Prescott, I would like to introduce you to Danny Roman. He has been running an online shop for a few years, selling all sorts of fun collectibles from midcentury to kitsch."

"I have a large inventory of Beanie Babies if you have any holes in your private collection," this Danny says. If the situation is making him nervous he isn't showing it.

"What on earth is a Beanie Baby?" I ask.

"Sure, play it coy like you don't have a Dinky the Dodo you sleep with every night," he says, that confident grin returning.

"Dinky the…" I start but Arthur cuts me off.

"Gentlemen, please," Arthur says. His warm voice is kind yet firm. "Now I apologize that I didn't have the opportunity to explain the arrangement in greater detail but I was quite busy moving my things out and getting the shop ready so the two of you could move your collections in. I want nothing more than for you to put your own marks on this place." Arthur looks around the mostly empty store. The freshly painted white walls and barren space must be difficult for him to take in, considering the decades he spent operating one of the finest shops in the region.

"Arthur, I don't understand," I say. How could comic-book-in-a hoodie fit into his plan?

"The Beautiful Things Shoppe has enough space to accommodate you both. You each signed a lease that allows you half."

"You're telling me that I have to share the shop with *him*?" I say, scanning Danny from head to toe.

Danny looks back at me, unfazed by my dig. He looks at Arthur. "Where did you find this one? He's wound more tightly than the corset on Lady Footlocker at gay bingo." He then turns to me and says, "Look, you uptight snob, I'll have you know that my collectibles are some of the hardest to find items anywhere."

"Maybe your things need to stay hidden." I've raised my voice just enough to make my point but this guy takes it as an attack. He raises his finger and is about to jab back when Arthur interrupts.

"Gentleman, please. Both of you. I just came by to make sure you were settling in nicely and make a formal introduction but I see that isn't needed. I realize this is a bit unconventional, but Prescott, you are one of the sharpest antique appraisers I've ever met and Danny, no one understands how objects can bring people joy more than you. How you two divide the shop is entirely your decision. I do suggest you be ready for Winter Festival next week. The streets will be filled with winter shoppers." Arthur puts on his hat and grabs his cane. "After decades in this business I can tell you both one thing. People come in this shop thinking they're looking for one thing and walk out loving something different entirely."

He leaves and I am alone with Danny.

We stare at each other in silence, each of us sizing up the other. This guy barely looks like he has the maturity to run a paper route let alone half of an established antique store. He's my age or maybe a few years older than me. I'd guess at least thirty-five but he's dressed like he's late for homeroom and forgot his homework. In addition to the weird T-shirt and hoodie, his jeans are too big in the waist and too short in length. He has a thick brown scruff and even thicker hair sticks out from the collar of his T-shirt above his chest.

My eyes linger there a moment longer than they should before I realize this person is going to destroy my chances of being taken seriously in the fine art world. I will not let that happen. I stare him down and smile with a sense of determination.

*Danny*

Just keep smiling, I tell myself. Ignore his blue eyes and the flecks of gray-green sparks that circle his pupils. Just pretend they don't exist. I move my gaze up to the severe side part in his perfectly combed blond hair. He looks like he's about to start his first day of prep school in his blue blazer and khaki pants. I begin to wonder what his body is like under his crisp white button-down when I gather my senses. This man had the audacity to insult my Muppets lunch box. Is Miss Piggy not a sacred diva? Still, Uncle Arthur seems to have given him his stamp of approval. How bad can he be? Maybe we got off on the wrong foot.

"Let's start over," I say and extend my hand. He looks like he expects my palm to have a gag buzzer lurking. Slowly he extends his arm and we shake.

Big mistake.

His hand is thinner and more delicate than mine but just

as strong. I look down and see my hairy knuckles against his golden smooth fingers and suddenly I'm wondering what mysteries might be lurking under those perfectly ironed khakis. You know what they say, the firmer the crease...

I pull my hand away as quickly as possible so I can re-focus.

"I'm Danny Roman," I say gathering as much formality as I can—which for me is not very much.

"I'm Prescott J. Henderson," he says. His voice reminds me of Fred Astaire dancing lightly across the silver screen—smooth elegance and refined precision.

I chuckle, glad that he has made a small joke to lighten the mood. "No, what's your real name?"

"That *is* my real name," he says so firmly the words almost come out as a growl.

"Oh, I'm sorry. It's just... I mean... Prescott J. Henderson? It sounds like a hoity-toity character in a comic book. Like Scrooge McDuck or something."

"You think I sound like a duck?" He's clearly annoyed.

"Well, I didn't say you sound like a duck, but to be fair I haven't heard you quack yet." This guy is so uptight that any physical charm he may or may not have is completely pointless. Arthur knows how much I hate these pretentious poseurs who think taste is reserved for the privileged. How could he do this to me?

I've known Arthur for years and when he told me he wanted to lease out the shop I jumped at the chance. I needed a change. A big change. After getting dumped on my birthday by a guy I thought was serious about me, I realized I needed something to help me take my focus off romance. I've learned I have great instincts when it comes to vintage collectibles and lousy instincts when it comes to men. I'd love to turn my collectibles into a thriving business, but having something to ground me is just as important. The whole reason I took on this lease was so that I could stand on my own two feet.

"Listen, you're going to have to move these boxes. I have a van arriving with some of my things in just a few minutes." Prescott is talking to me as if I work for him. I ignore the tone.

"What time?" I ask.

"Noon," he says like I just challenged him to a duel.

"Well, I hope your van can find a place to park," I say nonchalantly and move back to unpacking, knowing it will eat him up.

"There's a loading zone right in front of the shop. Obviously the van will park there," Prescott says, falling into my trap.

"I don't think so. That's where my truck will be." I take a short yet dramatic pause. "At 11:45."

Prescott blinks, slowly and steadily, then breathes in. "I have some very fragile and valuable pieces. I'll need a clear path and don't want the movers spoken to or otherwise distracted in any way."

"Spoken to? You don't want the movers *spoken to*? Who do you think you are, the Queen of England? Cher?"

"I just mean don't distract them. They are serious about their work." Prescott opens the door and a rush of cold air sweeps around the store. Arthur usually had the potbelly stove keeping the place toasty warm and without it the shop is chilly.

Prescott starts measuring the doorway. "I don't have time to argue with you. I need to make sure the Chippendale can fit through the door."

"Chippendale? Here I am, thinking you're a stuffy prude. I stand corrected. I hadn't thought of bringing in male strippers but it's not a bad idea—and if you're worried his piece might not fit through the door then it's beginning to sound like a great idea," I say in my best impersonation of Fozzi Bear, who just so happens to be on the shirt I'm wearing.

"I suppose you're trying to make some type of vulgar joke. I'm assuming you know full well *Chippendale* refers to a neoclassical style of furniture from Yorkshire, England." He rattles off the description without hesitation. He certainly knows his stuff. "Excuse me for not laughing but I am unaccustomed to such crass humor in a place of business." His tone is all serious, but I can tell there is a chip in his polished exterior from the way the corners of his mouth have to fight moving upward. This is the kind of guy that wants to belly laugh but thinks it wouldn't be proper. Just because he looks like he should be playing the lead in a Merchant Ivory film doesn't mean he needs to act like the Dowager Countess of New Hope.

I hear a series of screeches from the street so loud they can most likely be heard on the other side of the river. They're followed by hissing, a jangle of chains and the grinding of gears. I look out the window and see a truck that looks like it has just competed in Thunderdome and in the driver's seat is my old pal and current roommate, Lizard.

# Chapter Two

*Prescott*

"No, no, no," I say firmly as I run outside, waving my arms in a rather undignified manner. I need this sad excuse for a truck to leave the loading zone so that my van has a place to park. "You *cannot* park there," I screech at a tattooed woman with green hair that's shaved on one side.

"It's the loading zone. Of course I can park here," she says as she hops on the back bumper of the truck to take a seat.

"Hi, Lizard. Thanks for helping me out." Danny comes out of the shop. He's wrapped a white scarf with pink polka dots around his neck. It looks like an exact replica of the one the bear on his shirt is wearing. "The truck is fine there. Don't listen to this guy. He just escaped from the prep school down the river."

This woman's name is *Lizard*. I can't even pause to reflect on the reality of being named after a reptile. "My van will be here in less than thirty minutes. Where are they supposed to park?"

"Not exactly a problem solver are you?" Danny says needling me. "If you help us unload we can be done before your van even arrives." Lizard tosses Danny the keys and he throws open the back door of the truck with one arm. What he lacks in charm this guy certainly makes up for in strength.

I look inside the truck and let out an uncontrollable gasp. "What is all this stuff? Are you sure you got the right truck? Maybe this one was going to the circus and got lost." There are clear plastic bags with brightly colored stuffed animals, racks of clothes that look like they were featured in *Saturday Night Fever* and a box the size of a wine cask labeled Beanie Babies.

"This *stuff* as you call it is the merchandise that's going to sing to people as they walk past the window. Like a siren's call, it will boost our foot traffic." Luckily there are two distinct display windows; one on each side of the entrance. I'll approach the shop from only my side of the store.

I hop on the back of the truck and grab a lamp that has a hula dancer in a grass skirt as the base. "This is going to call people into the store? Are you sure you don't mean scare people away? There's no way we are putting that in either window."

"Of course we aren't," Danny says grabbing the lamp from me, and I have a second of relief. "This is Shirley and she goes right next to me at my desk. She's been with me forever."

"At least if it was for sale I could buy it from you and throw it out myself," I mutter. For a second I consider a hostile takeover. What if I purchased all of his merchandise and bought him out of his lease? That way I could have the store to myself. How much could all his stuff cost?

The reality is I'm not sure I could even buy the lamp from him, let alone everything else. My finances are in a bit of a transitional period. I put what little money I had left after signing the lease into acquiring a few very special pieces for the store, and the rest of my small savings is going toward the rent for the next few months and filling the holes in my collection. I was grateful to Arthur for giving me this place at such a steep discount...but now I realize how he was able to do it.

"I realize penny loafers aren't the best shoes for physical labor, but the faster we get my stuff unloaded the easier it will be for your van to have this spot," Danny says to me. I look down at my perfectly polished loafers and then over at his...oh, dear lord. I was assuming I would see some type of sneaker or athletic shoe but it's worse, so much worse. I grab the side of the truck to steady myself.

"What are those things on your feet?" I ask. I wonder if I'm hallucinating.

"Fabulous, aren't they? They're limited edition Crocs that were made to look like cheeseburgers. They even have layers of lettuce and tomato. So cute and comfy. I'd get you a pair but they're a real collector's item. The shipping from

Japan cost more yen than my entire collection of He-Man action figures."

"I'll pass," I say. I pick up a box.

"Careful with that one," Danny says. "It has some of my more priceless pieces."

"I'm almost scared to ask." I put the box down on the floor of the truck so I can hop off.

He opens the moving box and pulls out a smaller brightly colored box shaped like a barn covered in cartoon characters. I know exactly what it is but I can't imagine any reason someone would pay money for it. "This is a vintage Happy Meal with the original Fry Kids toy," he says smiling as if he just unboxed the Crown Jewels.

I close the flaps to the box and lift it off the floor of the truck to carry it into the store. "There is absolutely nothing happy about these things."

*Danny*

Prescott walks away from me and I can't help staring at his behind under the double side vents in his blazer. First I check to see if he has removed whatever he has stuck up it that makes him so uptight, but the only thing he has up his ass is more ass. I mean it's beautiful and round, like two small pumpkins are trapped in there. As I'm imagining what this guy might look like out of his khakis, Lizard jumps into the truck with me.

"Ah, no. That's an *N*, followed by an *O*. Both capitals," she says taking a bandana out of her back pocket and tying it around her forehead so her green bangs stay off her face.

"I love the new dye you're using…" I say casually.

"Don't change the subject." She wags her finger at me.

"What subject?" I ask, going to the back of the truck and innocently opening a box.

"The subject in the tight khaki pants and button-down shirt inside the shop."

"Prescott? He might be the most annoying person I've ever met. The way he talks to me like I'm some kid." I scan the back of the truck quickly. "Hey, did you make sure I packed the Snoopy cookie jar? I want to make sure to put that on the pedestal."

"Yes but…"

"And the Amore hot chocolate tin?" I ask looking around the back of the truck with concern. "It's really old and beat up but it's the most important piece here. I can't start a business without that tin. I need it for receipts and paperwork. It's…"

"Yes, yes," she says cutting me off this time. "I have the hot chocolate tin. Stop changing the subject." She stands in front of me like a palace guard. "I know your type. Pretentious pretty boys you get lost in as you lavish them with gifts and attention."

It's impossible to disagree with her. She's right and she knows it. Paul was the one who I thought was different. He seemed so perfect, always laughing at my jokes and taking an interest in everything I did. He loved it when I took him out to the most expensive restaurant in town and he was absolutely amorous when I surprised him with trips to the city to see a show. I thought I was headed toward a real future until I found out he had maxed out my credit cards and was cheating on me with the personal trainer—

that I was paying for—who could have been his twin. I still haven't recovered from finding him on his knees with that protein shake come to life.

"Lizard," I say picking up a box. "I told you I've reformed."

"I know but, come on, that guy. He's gorgeous."

"Is he? I hadn't noticed, since it's impossible to see around his ego." I take a box off the stack and hop off the truck. Even though it's an early January day, it isn't freezing. I pause before I go into Beautiful Things and admire the most charming storefront in the entire state of Pennsylvania. The name of the shop is painted in gold script on the glass front door. Each side of the door has a large bow window perfect for displaying merchandise. All of the trim is painted either royal blue or a bright yellow and a blue-and-white-striped awning allows window shoppers to peek in without having to worry about a stray winter squall or rain shower. The shop looks like it belongs on the set of *Meet Me in St. Louis* or maybe *The Harvey Girls* or some other Technicolor Judy Garland epic.

Before I open the door, I watch Prescott walking around the store trying to find a place to put the box he carried in. Even though he's clearly no fan of my stuff I notice he's careful with the box and treats it with respect. But Lizard is right. I can't let this guy distract me.

Five years ago I left my family's company to step out on my own and pursue my life's passion. I knew managing a team of employees and meeting quarterly projections at an international food company wasn't for me. Also, when you work at a place where everyone knows you are the heir to the family fortune it makes the people around you treat you differently. The only problem was I didn't really know what my passion was. I went to San Francisco where I thought I would write a book but I never found a focus or a font that really spoke to me. Instead I found a guy who needed a free proofreader and a boyfriend. I started watercolors in Santa Fe and then started dating a local chef until I noticed I was painting more pictures of his daily specials than lonesome cacti.

When I discovered New Hope a few years ago I knew I had found a home even before I found an apartment. This place is small-town America but on the corner of Quaint and Queer. Before I landed, I was buying little things like toy cars or action figures as I traveled because they made me happy. They reminded me of simple childhood things. I've been poking around in Arthur's shop for years, looking for treasures. I love finding that special something that I know will bring the right person joy. I started selling online but that lacks a personal connection. I enjoy browsing and chatting with someone as we search for that special something together. A physical store gives me the opportunity to really connect with people. I've been excited to get started but that was before I found out I was going to have to share the place with this snob.

"I'm putting all of your boxes on that side," Prescott says as I walk in. An ancient potbelly stove in the middle divides the more or less symmetrical sales space inside The Beautiful Things Shoppe. A counter with a cash register is centered behind the stove, and there's a small kitchen pantry in the back next to a storeroom.

"Fine," I say. "Everything on this side of the door will be my space," I say gesturing like a flight attendant showing the emergency exits. I use two fingers to point to each of the corners in front of and behind me. "Remember in case of an emergency landing to secure your air mask first before helping others and thank you for flying Beautiful Things Airlines." I shine as artificial a smile as I can at him, expecting a scowl in return. Instead he tightens his mouth intensely, as if he's fighting back a small giggle. Could I have made this stuffed shirt laugh just a tiny bit?

# Chapter Three

*Prescott*

After two days of unpacking I still have no idea how I'm going to share the shop with that tasteless, brash, *occasionally* humorous ringmaster. I walk from my apartment in Lambertville over the bridge that spans the Delaware River to the center of New Hope and I can't stop thinking about how this guy pushes my buttons.

I've never been good at sharing. I understand the concept, but as a practice it's never been an area in which I excel. The truth is, I've never really had to. I'm an only child so the usual experiences of sibling cooperative play weren't part of my upbringing and at school none of the other kids were interested in the things that captured my attention. I'm not sure why the other sixth graders had no interest in my burgeoning collection of Victorian era fountain pens but it meant I spent a lot of time alone, which was fine with me. When I went to college the pattern repeated itself for the most part, though I had a few acquaintances or even dates here or there. Keeping to myself isn't something I consider to be a problem. In fact, whenever I think I need to connect with people more it always backfires. Case in point: the pretentious narcissist I casually dated before I left Philadelphia.

I met Jefferson Worthington, Worth, at a fundraiser for the Barnes Foundation. A former professor had an extra ticket and the event included an exclusive showing of a rare piece of tapestry from the collection, so I went. I was admiring the fine detail of the weave when Worth started relentlessly flirting with me and trying to impress me with his wealth and affluence. When he asked me out I agreed because he made it so difficult to say no. Worth looked good on paper; he was a connoisseur of the arts so I convinced myself that I just needed to be more open and stop being so standoffish. But after a few more dates I realized it was definitely him not me. He never listened to a word I said and he was always trying to get me to sleep with him. He's a handsome guy but I had zero interest in pursuing a physical relationship. I used the fact that I was moving out of Philadelphia and starting the shop to avoid having any confrontation about ending whatever it was that he might have thought was developing. It never really got off the ground so I didn't see any point in making a big deal out of stopping something that barely started. Maybe I should have made things clearer, but it's sometimes easier just to let a relationship fade into the murky waters of time passed.

I stop at the center of the bridge, take a deep inhale and let the cold air fill my lungs. I remind myself that this is a new beginning. I shrug off any uncomfortable memories of Worth.

I can see New Hope in the distance and a light haze dulls the colorful buildings making them look like a fine piece of Impressionism. Having an apartment across the river in Lambertville allows me to be close enough to New Hope to walk to work but far enough away to be outside the social scene. I prefer to appreciate it from afar. I'm able to be home and in bed before the bars and cafes begin to operate in full swing. Being a little removed makes me feel more comfortable.

Another benefit of living on the other side of the river is that my commute to the shop takes me across the stunning New Hope–Lambertville Bridge. The beams have a rich bright greenish-aqua patina and the south side of the bridge has a cantilevered walkway for pedestrians. I love feeling the strength of the river under my feet and the endless expanse of water to either side of me as mini-icebergs glide peacefully by.

New Hope is still quietly asleep under a fresh coating of newly fallen snow. Winter Festival is only a few days away and the street corners are already set up with unlit lanterns, bonfires waiting to be ignited and rustic pedestals that will hold various forms of ice sculpture sponsored by area merchants. I fell for New Hope the moment I laid eyes on it. I came to visit Arthur at his shop a few years ago and as soon as I started exploring the crooked streets and unique shops I knew I was in a special place. Community and inclusiveness are an integral part of the fabric of the town. People think small towns mean small minds but that's not what I found in New Hope. I found an openness, an inclusiveness and the best cranberry pecan white chocolate scone that exists.

The Honeysuckle Bakery and Cafe is just a few doors down from the shop and I've been looking forward to reacquainting myself with this exceptional treat. Inside, small tables are full of shoppers and locals warming up with a hot beverage or pastry before the day begins.

I spot the object of my affection all alone under a glass dome. The woman behind the counter asks what I would like and I order a coffee and point to the treat. My phone rings and I realize it might be a notice about a delivery I'm waiting for so I excuse myself and head to the alcove in the back of the store to take my call.

As soon as I finish I head back to the counter and see that the glass dome is empty. I assume the woman behind the counter has plated the scone for me or put it in a bag to go. I walk over to the register to pay and *he* is standing there.

"Good morning." My tone is crisp, even and cold. Yesterday we'd had a twenty-minute argument about which way to hang the toilet paper in the bathroom. If I say something is up, Danny says it's down. This man is the most stubborn, obstinate human being I've ever met.

"Good morning," he says in his normal chipper tone. His voice is deep and masculine but always punctuated with this playful cadence, even at this hour of the morning.

The woman who was behind the counter when I ordered has been replaced by a different person who is much younger and maybe working while high school is still on winter break. "Excuse me. I placed an order before I had to take a call." The young man looks at me, confused. I notice a coffee with my name written on the cup next to him. "I think that's my latte," I say pointing. "And there's a cranberry scone waiting for me."

"Oh, yeah, sorry," he says handing me the coffee. "This latte is yours but I'm afraid I sold the last scone. Can I get you something else?" Out of the corner of my eye I see Danny gently dangling a small paper bag in front of his face. "You!" I say like I just accused him of stealing the Hope Diamond.

"Yes," he says smiling smugly. "Me." He takes the scone out of the bag, tears off a corner and pops it in his mouth, chewing with delight like he's auditioning for a food commercial.

"That is my scone," I say pointing toward his mouth. "I ordered it before I had to take a very important call. You must have come in after me."

"Your scone? If it is *your* scone then why is the deliciousness still lingering on *my* lips?" He licks each of his fingers in spite.

A few people turn their attention toward us and the young man behind the counter looks very uncomfortable. "We'll have more tomorrow. I think?" he says, his voice cracking either from fear or puberty or both.

"You think I saw you from the window and hatched this elaborate plan to steal your scone?" Danny asks, raising his voice just a bit. It's almost as if he likes the audience. He takes the rest of the scone and shoves it in his mouth. It barely fits and little pieces of it fly off and land back in the bag underneath his mouth. How anyone could ever want to buy so much as a paper clip from him is beyond me.

"The least you could have done is share it," I say to him as he struggles to chew the enormous bite he took.

"The only thing I'm sharing with you right now is your bad attitude," he says and walks out of the cafe.

*Danny*

As soon as I get to the shop I check the bag from the bakery to make sure there isn't a crumb left for Prescott to even smell. How dare he accuse me of stealing his scone? The scones belong to no one. The scones are free to offer their delicious goodness to anyone who wishes and today the scone was mine.

I smash the bag into a ball and throw it into the trash in the back pantry area. There are only a few days left until Winter Festival and so much needs to be done—unpacking, arranging, pricing—getting the store ready for the big event and my new future. It's a huge job, but that's what I signed up for when I signed the lease.

Of course, I didn't know I would be sharing the shop with The Little Prince. Why couldn't Arthur have found someone I would be compatible with? There's a lovely woman in Doylestown who has a huge collection of vintage Barbies. She thinks God talks to her through her dentures, but she keeps them clean and she's never lonely. She would be better than having to deal with Prescott. I hate snobs and I always have. I dealt with them growing up and I've built my entire world around not having to be around the high and mighty. New Hope is without pretense. It's simply a friendly, inclusive community where it doesn't matter how many zeros are in your bank account or what kind of car you drive or any of that nonsense. That's why I'm here and Arthur knows that, so I can't figure out why he would spring this guy on me.

The shop is closed but I see someone through the gold script knocking on the window. I open the door and a handsome guy in a red parka and rainbow-striped knitted hat says, "Hi, I'm Martin Cho. Did Uncle Arthur tell you I was coming?"

"Uhm, no," I say, not ready for whatever surprise is next.

"I'm from Frozen Dimensions, the company doing the ice sculptures for Winter Festival. The Beautiful Things Shoppe sponsored one for the pedestal next to the shop. Arthur arranged it but he said that the new shopkeepers would choose the subject. I brought a gallery of our designs." He holds up a tablet.

"Sure, come on in," I say and open the door widely. "I'm afraid it's freezing in here. I haven't had a chance to get the potbelly stove going."

"Oh, that's alright. I'm used to creating in our refrigerated studios so this is absolutely toasty to me."

Instead of getting the wood from out back I pull up a chair on the other side of my desk so Martin can sit down. He starts up his tablet and begins to swipe through images of glossy crystal masterpieces that look like they are constructed from diamonds.

"Very nice. Do you do all of these yourself?"

"I'm just an apprentice. I'm still learning but I'm getting pretty good." He clicks to the next image and a saucy mermaid with a mysterious smile catches my eye. She is surrounded by a raw bar of oysters, shrimp and lobster.

"She's a charmer, but I assume the seafood is not part of her usual entourage."

"I'm afraid not. That was for a party in Doylestown but we could do the mermaid alone. People always love her." Martin smiles and I'm just about to pull the trigger when Downton Crabby walks in.

"Enjoy your breakfast?" Prescott snaps at me as he goes to put his coat in the pantry.

"Every last crumb," I say making sure my spite comes through each syllable.

Martin suddenly looks scared. He might want to form a support group with the guy at the counter who witnessed us battle over the scone. "Hello, I'm Martin Cho," he says standing up to introduce himself.

Prescott shakes his hand formally. Everything this guy does is like there is someone watching making sure he's following proper etiquette. It's super annoying. "Yes, Martin. We've been expecting you. To select the ice sculpture?"

"Exactly," he says.

"Well, I've already chosen something so we can check that off the list." I point to Martin's tablet. "A delightful sassy mermaid. Isn't she adorable? I have a Pucci-inspired bikini top in purple, orange and pink that I might put over her seashells. She'll look fabulous."

"A mermaid? Absolutely not," Prescott says making a

face like he licked an ashtray. "That might be fine for a seafood buffet at Disney World but it makes no sense at Winter Festival. I've already perused the catalog online. I think it's sculpture A-21, if I'm correct."

Martin flips through the tablet images and lands on one marked A-21.

"A snowflake?" I ask. "Are you kidding? It's Winter Festival. There will be snowflakes up the wazoo. Who needs to see another one?" I say spitting my words at Prescott and then turning to Martin. "No offense Martin. It's a very lovely snowflake."

"Thank you?" he says his voice cracking in the same way the young man's at the coffee spot did.

"A snowflake fits in. It makes sense precisely because it *is* Winter Festival and look how elegant the design is. It's simple and refined not some half-naked lady with her arms holding up her hair."

"A snowflake is so boring. Just like you. I already told you I would put a bikini top on her so it will be very tasteful." I can feel the anger rising in me.

"Tasteful? You wouldn't know good taste if it walked through the door with a sign around its neck saying, 'Good taste'!"

That's it. The limit. The absolute limit. "How dare you insult me and…"

"You just called me boring. You started with the insults…"

Martin is furiously flipping through images on his tablet when he suddenly stops and holds up the screen.

"Here. Sirs. This. How about this?" He displays a picture of a snowman with a crooked smile and a body made of three sparkling globes of ice. It's cute but also refined. "A snowman would fit in with the Winter Festival theme but it's a bit more exciting than just a snowflake."

"It's a very nice snowman. It's a classic," Prescott says with a slight, approving nod.

"He's as cute as a button," I say making sure all of my enthusiasm goes toward Martin and not Prescott.

"Great. One snowman for The Beautiful Things Shoppe." Martin packs up his tablet and runs out of the shop like it's on fire.

I stare at Prescott and he stares at me. We don't need ice sculptures. The looks on both our faces are so cold we could just sit on the pedestals ourselves. I don't see either one of us melting in the near future.

# Chapter Four

*Prescott*

While Danny and I agree on almost nothing, we are on the same page about being ready when the sleepy riverside village transforms into a winter wonderland with ice sculptures along the river walk, bonfires at the intersections and skating races on the canal. Even the weather forecast has been in on the planning, with enough of a dusting scheduled to make the eaves and windowsills uniformly white but not enough accumulation to inhibit travel.

Inside the store, the boundary lines are clear. Danny and his jamboree of forgotten TV memorabilia have exactly half the store on the north side and I have the other half on the south side.

I've grouped all of my objects by decade, style and artist. It's a tasteful display of some very fine pieces including a Chippendale side table, a Japanese Satsuma tea storage jar and my most prized possession: my Cartier LeCoultre desk clock. A simple gold circle a few inches high, displaying a cream watch face with elegant black lettering. The base has an intricate pattern of gold filigree with jade accents. I purchased the clock as a present to myself when I graduated with my MA in Decorative Arts from U Penn. I had been working three part-time jobs to pay for tuition, room and board and during the last week of classes I saw the gorgeous object in a shop window. After some intense bargaining I was able to negotiate a price that made it a steal. I have no intention of selling the clock. It tells customers they have arrived at a place that signifies class and elegance. That is, as long as they keep their backs to the other side of the shop, where Danny is setting up a collection of what looks like plastic blue mice that live in some kind of red plastic mushroom.

"What in the world are those mice doing?" I can't help but ask. We have been mostly working steadily in silence today in order to be ready for the festival.

"They aren't mice. They're Smurfs. This one is called Drummy because he's playing the drums and this one is delivering mail. He's called Posty," he says, holding out the blue creatures so that I can inspect them. "You've never heard of Smurfs? Where did you grow up? Under a rock?" He looks me up and down and I remain silent.

I keep my personal life to myself as much as possible. I'm well aware that it makes some people think I'm cold or stuck-up. I've never been someone to openly engage with the world. Given the choice between a room full of chatty people and a room full of dusty antiques and I'll choose dusty over chatty every time. Chatty people judge you for being quiet or saying the wrong thing. I've never once gotten a dirty look from a gilt-decorated parlor lamp.

"Just because I don't recognize your little blue Smarf mice," I say.

"I told you. They're not mice. They're Smurfs!" Danny is getting visibly agitated.

"Whatever they are, make sure they stay on your side of the store and don't crawl over here."

Danny walks over to my side and stands next to the glass display table I have set up. "You're telling me to worry about my things crawling away when you have *that* on display." He reaches his arm across his body and makes a face that looks like he is about to enter a haunted house. Everything is so dramatic with this guy.

"That is a Victorian fan made out of a bird wing. Women used these to communicate and they were seen as a sign of wealth and prestige in the late nineteenth century. It's worth hundreds of dollars."

"Hundreds of dollars? A dead bird? I really should call the Board of Health to see if selling roadkill is allowed in a retail establishment." He's all sass and charm. And funny, but I'm not about to let him know I think so.

"Roadkill! Now listen here blue mouse man, this is an absolutely authentic…" A truck in front of the shop honks, cutting me off.

"That's the wood delivery for the stove. I'll go help with

it out back and leave you to your carcasses." He walks out the back door to the alley where Arthur had always kept his wood supply. I want to chase after him and deliver another dig but as soon as he's gone there is a knock at the front door. I turn to see who it is and as soon as I recognize the face I think about heading out the back door to help with the wood. I'd rather risk a handful of splinters than deal with this person.

"Knock. Knock. I hope you don't mind a visitor," Worth says as he opens the door.

"Why Worth, hello," I say trying to register a pleasant welcome rather than the disappointed surprise I actually feel. I have no idea why he drove his vintage Jaguar all the way from Chestnut Hill in Philadelphia and I'm not interested in finding out. I guess my hope that he would fade away was ill-conceived. I slap a smile on my face and welcome him in.

*Danny*

After helping stack the firewood in the alley I'm covered in sap, stray wood chips and sweat. I carry a few pieces inside to help keep the stove going but before I enter the floor of the shop I hear Prescott talking with someone.

I walk in with my arms full of firewood and the guy he's talking to comes over to me to shake my hand. I'm not sure what he thinks I'm supposed to do with all this wood in my arms, but I put it down next to the stove so I can at least be polite.

"Hello," he says. His voice purrs condescension. "I'm Jefferson P. Worthington but everyone just calls me Worth. Please feel free to do the same."

I shake his hand and say, "I'm Danny."

As soon as our palms connect his face looks like he just swallowed a spider. "Oh, dear," he says, pulling his hand away with disgust.

"Sorry about that. I was just stacking wood for the stove." I grab a rag I was planning to use for dusting and hand it to him. He wipes his hands like Lady Macbeth after a night on the town. It's just some sap and dirt. What's the big deal?

Just when I thought there couldn't be anyone more up-tight and snobby than Prescott Henderson, this guy walks in. He speaks like he's narrating an episode of *Masterpiece Theatre* and is conventionally handsome in a way that bores me. Prescott is also handsome but in a totally different way. Prescott is distinctive. There's a small bump on the ridge of his nose and his eyes are definitely in a category of their own in terms of intensity and color. Not that I've noticed. Not that I've noticed at all.

"Well, anyway," Worth says, dropping the rag on the counter like it is radioactive. "It's nice to meet you and so sweet of you to help Prescott with his store. I know setting all this up is hard work. I'm glad he's got someone to haul wood. Every job is important." His smile is all polished pearls and his voice is as sincere as a telemarketer. I can't really even respond so I look past him and speak to Prescott.

"Is this guy for real? He's trolling me, right? I'm being trolled by this guy." I look around the shop as if there are hidden cameras spying on us.

Even Prescott realizes the situation is uncomfortable enough to interrupt. "Worth, Danny doesn't work *for* me."

"No, I do not," I say.

"We're sharing the store. Arthur thought this was a good idea. A variety of merchandise might appeal to more people and we could capitalize on the crossover aspect."

"Oh, dear," Worth says as his gaze moves around the room from Prescott's side to mine. I imagine it's like that scene in *The Wizard of Oz*. Prescott's stuff in drab black-and-white and my area like Munchkin Land, full of vibrant color.

I've found vintage gingham in a variety of colors to line the shelves and display tables. Colorful floral bunting hangs over the area with some of my earlier pieces like Pyrex bowls from the 1950s and a beautifully preserved Big Bird doll. Further toward the back I have all of my midcentury items and I found a gorgeous Formica boomerang table to display some teak bowls and a tension pole lamp with three orange lanterns made of lava-looking plastic. Near my desk in the back I have smaller items from the seventies and eighties including a Bionic Woman doll with the original jumpsuit and a *Good Times* lunch box that has so many dents it's clear that it has seen some bad times. My Smurfs and Beanie Babies are arranged on two displays on either side of my desk where Shirley illuminates my hot chocolate tin.

"Can't decide what you want to buy, Worth? Or are the prices a bit too high-end?" I can't figure out what this guy's relationship is to Prescott. It's not intimate but I get the feeling they might have been once. I wouldn't be surprised. Prescott is probably the type of gay man who only dates men who look a certain way.

He simply sneers at me and turns toward Prescott.

"I didn't know your orbit made it this far out of Philadelphia," I hear Prescott say. I go back to work cleaning my favorite cookie jar so it will be ready for the opening but the shop is so small it's impossible not to hear them.

"I had some business in the area and my mother has an estate in the country not very far from here." From the corner of my eye I see him vaguely gesture as if he is working undercover. Prescott doesn't push it and they start talking about his favorite pieces and I tune out for a bit until I hear Worth say, "Press, everything here is absolutely exquisite." I notice Worth's gaze lingers on Prescott in a lascivious way that makes me uncomfortable. Prescott seems to escape by walking over to some boring chair that looks like it could be in the lobby of any midscale hotel in any midsize city. It's cherry stained, highly polished with a back as stiff as the two men admiring it.

"This is really special. It's French walnut Louis XVI. The person I bought it from thought it was of English origin. Can you imagine?" Prescott says in almost a whisper.

They both laugh and I do my best not to throw up on anything, and ignore the rest of their conversation.

My ears perk up as Worth begins to leave. "I really can't tarry," he says. I think about texting Lizard to tell her that this guy just used the word *tarry* without irony, but she would never believe me.

"Thanks for stopping by," Prescott says but something in his voice makes me wonder if he's all that grateful.

I quickly return to my cookie jar. Who doesn't love Snoopy? The adorable black-and-white pooch is sleeping on the top of his bright red doghouse. It looks like a simple piece, but this is a first edition from the Peanuts collection and very rare. I had Lizard help me make a special pedestal so I could display it all on its own right when customers walk in. It's the absolute perfect piece to feature.

I carefully place the cookie jar on the pedestal. Then I hear Prescott say, "Worth, you forgot your gloves." Worth is already out the door but Prescott grabs what he left behind and tries to catch him. In his rush, his foot catches the leg of the pedestal and with a sudden loud boom my prized cookie jar comes crashing to the floor like a ceramic piñata with nothing inside.

I stare at the floor feeling one of those very rare moments when I am at a loss for words. My most favorite piece is now in pieces. It was one of the first collectibles I ever purchased and now it's destroyed. I look up from the floor at the man who shattered it.

"I'm so sorry," Prescott says. His voice is sincere and a bit shaky. The crash was a shock to us both and now we are standing in the center of a ceramic junkyard. "Let me clean this up." He runs to the pantry and returns with a broom and dustpan. He kneels on the floor. "Maybe I can fix it," he says.

"Fix it? It's in three hundred pieces. I can't believe you're so clumsy. You must know what it's like to have a favorite piece."

"Yes, of course," he says sweeping up Snoopy's remains.

"I was planning on putting actual cookies in it tomorrow. I have an order placed at the Honeysuckle and everything."

"You could use one of my urns," he says with a crooked smile.

"Who eats a cookie out of an urn?" I yell. I look down and see poor Woodstock broken in half. My very favorite piece shattered by this thoughtless jerk. "Do you have any idea how special this piece was to me? I loved it. I can't believe you could be so thoughtless."

Prescott finishes sweeping the dust remains into the dustpan and gets up. "Well if you loved it so much maybe you shouldn't have put it in the middle of the store. I could have broken my neck."

"So it's my fault you broke my favorite piece?"

"I said I was sorry. What else do you want me to do?" he asks and dumps the remains of the cookie jar into the trash bin. I glare at Prescott. I pick up the pedestal that he knocked over and stare at the empty spot where my cookie jar should be. Any cease-fire that might have happened is officially over. The shop is officially a battle zone.

# Chapter Five

*Danny*

While brightly painted colonials dominate in New Hope, there are also quirky additions that give the town the feeling that everyone is welcome. There's a tiny log cabin up Ferry Street that has sold maple syrup products for years, a cafe in a former church that hosts a Mardi Gras drag brunch every weekend complete with shiny beads and frozen drinks, and a building made out of recycled trash that sells art that's also made out of recycled trash. The Beautiful Things Shoppe is a gorgeous orchid in the center of a slightly overrun garden. The morning of Winter Festival, I'm thrilled to start my first day as chief gardener—or at least co-chief gardener.

Then I remember I have to pick up the order of cinnamon snaps that I placed when I still had my favorite cookie jar. It was too late to cancel and I didn't want Mona to have to suffer the financial loss anyway. I'll find something else to serve them in, but that's not the point. How could Prescott be so careless? The way he acted afterward just shows how insensitive he is. He thinks things are only valuable only if they appraise at some astronomical figure or have some artistic pedigree. I loved that cookie jar and that's what made it special. It makes my blood boil to think about the way he just dismisses the value of emotional attachment.

"Hey, Mona," I say as I walk in and try to shake off the cold and my anger at Prescott. "Are you ready for Winter Festival?"

She looks down at her flour-covered apron and then back at me. "My apron looks like it, don't you think? I've been up baking all the night. I've got your order in the back. Let me just finish with these cupcakes." She grabs a tray of white beauties with spun sugar on the top and starts placing them on a pedestal.

"Thanks," I say and start drooling over all of the baked goods on display.

"You're lucky I'm not making you work behind the counter today," she says as she keeps moving pastries from the tray to the display.

"What's that supposed to mean?" I ask grabbing a paper cup for the self-serve coffee.

"Timmy, the new counter help I hired, said that two men were arguing yesterday over a scone and he didn't know what to do and that maybe he should work in the kitchen. He said one of the men was a handsome blond and the other was wearing cheeseburger Crocs and a *Star Wars* T-shirt."

"Damn, my incredible flair for fashion. I could never get away with robbing a bank. I'm too stylish," I say surveying myself ostentatiously to amplify my joke.

"What happened? Who was the guy you had the argument with?"

"It's not *an* argument. It's arguments. Plural. He's the guy I'm sharing Arthur's shop with. I had no idea I was only getting half the shop. That part's fine. I guess. But this guy is unbelievable. He's formal and fussy all the time and the things he sells are even more formal and fussier. Not to mention that he shattered my most favorite cookie jar." I shudder at the thought of it in pieces on the ground. "It's like, ugh, I hate to use the cliché but oil and water."

She places the last cupcake on the pedestal and then looks directly at me. "Hey, Danny, I got news for you. You know what's in these cupcakes? Oil and water. And I think they come out pretty great if I do say so myself. The key is adding the right amount of sugar. It helps things emulsify." I stare at the small white clusters of frosting and cake and wonder how long she has to beat the ingredients together until they behave.

"Anyway, I talked Timmy down but it took a chunk of time. You want to make it up to me?"

"Sure," I say.

"I got my brother to agree to run the bakery this spring while I go walk the Camino de Santiago. Help me out by introducing him to some nice guys. He needs to settle down."

"I follow his Insta. He's a hottie. Sure, no problem. I'd put myself on the list but I'm taking a break from dating."

"Why?"

"I want to focus on making the shop work and guys complicate things."

A bell from the kitchen goes off. "I'll be right back. I got a batch of Kitchen Sink Muffins ready to come out. Let me deal with them and I'll get your cookies."

Mona leaves and I walk down to the end of the counter. I gaze at the cupcakes and think about her oil and water remark. Prescott and I are worse than oil and water. We are fresh-squeezed orange juice and minty toothpaste. Try making that into a delectable dessert? I see the scones under the dome. This morning there are plenty of them. When I saw Prescott order the last scone through the window I don't know what came over me. I swooped in and bought it out from under him just like he suspected but I would never let him know that. I can't help pushing his buttons. It's like a turn-on but not really because I can't stand the guy. It's more like a spark, but the kind that happens just before the oil refinery explodes.

Mona comes back out with my order and for a second I think about making a truce and celebrating our first day with a pair of scones but what would be the point? Prescott would never appreciate the gesture. Our battle lines have been drawn and maybe it's better if I just stick to them. I walk away from the scones and any thought of a cease-fire.

As I approach the shop I grab my keys out of my pocket

to unlock the door but stop dead in my tracks at what I see through the window. If I were a religious person I would get on my knees and cross myself twice in front of the vision before me.

I walk inside and shout, "What is that?" so loud I wonder if a few icicles shake on the awning outside. Prescott is warming his hands in front of the potbelly stove that he has already got roaring.

"What is what?" he responds with a pretend nonchalance.

I walk over to the pedestal that was empty when I left the store last night and gently pet the beautiful red-and-white Snoopy cookie jar with Woodstock joyfully teetering on the top of the dog's nose. "Where did this come from?" I ask, wondering if it's some type of mirage. I should see if my hand can pass right through it.

"That came from a Ms. Polly Snavely," Prescott says.

I put my hands on the jar and I'm about ready to turn it over when Prescott says, "Best not to disturb it. The next closest one is in Tennessee and I'm not up for another long drive." He goes to his fancy desk and sits as if the subject is closed.

I walk over to his desk and stand in front of him. He smells like Ivory soap and is all freshly scrubbed for the day wearing a perfectly fitted tweed blazer with elbow patches. "You are going to have to explain this. How did you? What did you? When?"

"After I left the shop last evening I mailed back the gloves and then went online and found an original first edition cookie jar exactly like the one that I accidentally damaged.

The woman was willing to part with it after some intense negotiating. I gassed up the delivery van, drove out to Harrisburg last night, came back and put it on your pedestal this morning. There really isn't that much of a mystery surrounding it. Although there might be some intrigue with the van. It was making a strange rattling during the last twenty miles. Arthur has already agreed to get it checked out for us." Prescott goes back to his laptop like he just explained how to boil water.

"Harrisburg? That's like two and a half hours away. Five hours round trip. You drove all the way to Harrisburg? Last night? Are you out of your mind?"

He looks up from his computer and rolls his eyes. "You know a simple thank-you would suffice."

"Thank you," I say immediately. He's right. "Thank you, thank you. I'm just so shocked that you did that. That you went through all the trouble to find it and then went to all the trouble to get it here in time for the opening."

"It was my accident and my responsibility. It was the least I could do," he says, still not looking at me.

"Actually, it was the most you could do," I say swallowing hard and feeling guilty about not picking up a scone for him when I had the chance this morning. I'm touched by his gesture and regret my attitude yesterday. I look him squarely in the eye and say as sincerely as I can, "Thank you."

"Thank you, for shopping with us, ma'am. You have a *beautiful things* evening," I say, opening the door to the shop to let the last customer out and turning the sign from Open to Closed. Our first day is officially over.

"Have a *beautiful things* evening?" Prescott asks raising his eyebrows.

"It never hurts to lean into the brand," I say and walk over to my desk. I take out the old hot chocolate tin I use for my receipts and add the final few sales to it before plopping down on the overstuffed chair in the corner. "I think we had an excellent opening. I wrapped so many Scooby-Doo glasses in newspaper I think my fingers have a permanent black tint to them."

"Business was brisk," Prescott says as he starts to go through his own receipts for the day. He stops before he gets to the end of the pile and sits down at the chair at his desk. "I'm exhausted too. Exhausted and starving. I didn't even have time for lunch."

Prescott is resting his eyes, leaning back in his chair in recovery mode and it gives me a chance to really look at him. He is impossibly handsome. Even after a long hard day he has these classic features that remain so exquisitely arranged on his face that nothing can really distract from their appeal. Then I get a terrible idea that I know is a terrible idea in every part of my body but for some reason my mouth is not on speaking terms with my brain so I hear myself saying, "Hey, The Hideaway Inn is having their Winter Festival Burger Special. Let's grab something." Prescott looks at me with a bit of suspicion. "Dinner is my treat. The Snoopy cookie jar was a great conversation piece and the cinnamon snaps tasted even better out of that jar. I want to thank you. What do you say?"

I hate eating alone and both of us are hungry. We were so busy today that we forgot about hating each other. Why not keep things trending in the right direction?

"I am starving but I'm sure that place is packed with tourists," Prescott says.

"You're in luck. I happen to know the chef, Tack, and the house manager, Anita. Tack makes this incredible veggie burger if you're into that sort of thing, but they also get all of their meats locally. Have you been in there yet?"

"No, but I've been wanting to try it since I moved here." I can see him weighing the decision in his head.

"We could talk about the store, maybe plan a promotion or something. That would make it a business meeting. Tax deductible even."

"I mean a business meeting after the first day makes sense. Why not?"

"Great," I say and get up so I can start turning off the lamps and straightening up the area where I check people out. Prescott does the same thing on his side of the shop and then we both head to the back of the store at the same time. "I just want to make sure the pantry area is tidy."

"That's what I was going to do," he says. "I'm a bit of a neat freak in case you haven't noticed." His tone is warm and sincere, like he is making a confession.

"Actually, I hadn't noticed," I say. "Because I've probably been too busy tidying up myself. I'm a neat freak too," I say.

"I think we finally found something we have in common. Let's go argue over who gets to wipe down the counter," he says and we tidy up quickly and begin to shut down the store. Once we're ready to lock up and head out

I switch the lights from the bright day mode to overnight where only spotlights illuminate a few corners of the shop.

One of the lights shines directly on the Snoopy cookie jar. I still can't believe he drove all the way across the state to replace the original. I look at Woodstock sitting on top of Snoopy and I wonder how an aloof and unflappable black-and-white beagle became so close with a sputtering and fluttering yellow bird. Prescott opens the door for me and I take one last look at the ceramic duo and then head out of the shop beside him.

# Chapter Six

*Prescott*

The winter sun has already set so any fleeting warmth has been replaced by brisk cool air. The streets are still crowded with people enjoying the ice sculptures illuminated by the period street lamps. Soft pools of flickering light dot the street. Danny is bundled up in a sherpa-lined corduroy jacket. A wind snaps around the corner and I'm surprised by my desire to snuggle between Danny's fur and that sherpa lining. I tell myself it's the cold that's making me have crazy thoughts. It's not like this is a date. It's a business meeting. I make a mental note to remind myself to get a receipt.

The Hideaway Inn is just a short walk from the shop. I've passed by the converted stone farmhouse plenty of times, but I've never been inside. As we approach I notice a line of tourists waiting to be seated.

"We can go someplace else," I say to Danny.

"Nah, it'll be fine. There's always room for locals," he says and walks over to a woman in a wheelchair with some menus in her lap. "Anita, sweetie, how have you been?" He bends down to kiss her on both cheeks and she returns the gesture.

"Danny, how did it go? I saw people going in and out all day from here. Were sales good? Did that stuffed shirt give you any problems?" she asks, not realizing I am the stuffed shirt and I'm standing next to Danny.

"The stuffed shirt," I say, "did not give him any problems."

Anita laughs and looks me up and down. "And you said he had no sense of humor."

"Prescott, I would like you to meet Anita Patel, the manager of The Hideaway," Danny says. I smile at her and nod, showing them both I'm able to take a joke sometimes.

"Come on, Stuffed Shirt," Anita says. "I've got a great table for you overlooking the river in the side dining room." Danny and I follow her and as soon as we enter the smaller dining room I'm taken by the view of the river. It looks almost purple-violet in the moonlight and the snow on the banks looks like dollops of frozen whipped cream. We take a seat and Anita says, "Clayton is a bit overwhelmed tonight so if he doesn't come by to take your order someone else will."

"Got it. Poor Clayton. He stresses on busy nights," Danny says, opening the menu. "He's been the server here since as long as I can remember," he continues, "but he's not really good with crowds and this place has been packed since Vince bought it. Vince is the owner and Tack, his boyfriend—or I guess I should now say fiancé—is the chef. They had a big party celebrating their engagement just before the holidays."

"Is there anyone here you don't know?" I ask Danny. He looks up from the menu and scans the room.

"Don't think so," he says and then he looks more closely at the table right next to us. "Oh, wait." He puts down his menu and turns to the man and woman sitting at the table next to us.

"Hey, there. Sorry to bother you. I'm Danny Roman and this is Prescott Henderson. We are the proprietors of The Beautiful Things Shoppe down the street. I don't think we've met." He says all of this without a hint of embarrassment or hesitation. I am, of course, mortified. There are burlesque performers more reserved than Danny. He jumps into everything. He jumps into life without so much as a second glance. I think through everything, analyze every detail. There is a part of him that scares the crap out of me but if I'm being honest there is another part that charms me. I wonder what it would be like to live in the world so carefree.

"Well, isn't that mighty friendly of you," the man says with an accent I quickly identify as being from the Carolinas. "We were told Northerners were unfriendly but everyone we've met here has been so nice."

"Just a charming place," the woman says. "I'm glad we

decided to take a little vacation here for Winter Festival. I'm Taylor," she says.

"And I'm Taylor," the man says.

I look at Danny who looks as confused as I am. "You're both Taylor?"

They laugh. "We know. We get that reaction all the time. Yep, we are both Taylor. It causes a great deal of confusion," he says.

"But it's also a lot of fun. Might be what has kept us together over thirty years."

"Thirty years? That's impressive. Enjoy your evening and the rest of your time in New Hope. Check out our store while you're here. We'd love to have you visit."

"Mighty kind of you," Taylor says and Taylor nods.

Danny turns back to me. "Well now I can say a confident yes. The man and woman seated at that table are Taylor. Do you want me to introduce you to everyone else?" he asks. The very thought of talking to a roomful of people makes me shut down a bit. I could never talk to people the way Danny does.

"There are at least twenty people seated in this room. Do you mean to tell me you know each one of them?"

"Yes. I mean I just met Taylor and Taylor, but everyone else I've already met. It's a small town. People know each other." He waves to a table of people who raise their drinks and wave back. He does know everyone and everyone seems to like him. I've never been great at that kind of thing. I can talk for hours about porcelain manufacturing or trade patterns but small talk with a stranger about things like the weather or current events? Forget it. I always say the wrong thing and regret it for hours after. I try to just keep to myself to prevent embarrassment. I guess people think that's being standoffish.

Danny pops up from behind his menu. "The veggie burger. It's out of this world. Tack mixes beans with fresh herbs and then grills the whole thing before putting it on a brioche bun. Heaven."

I'm starving and it sounds like a veggie burger will hit the spot. "Sounds good. I'll have one too."

Danny drops his menu and holds his face with both hands, imitating the Munch painting. "I'm shocked," he says with over-the-top fake surprise.

"Why? It sounds delicious," I say, not sure what has prompted his reaction.

"Of course, but maybe we should order a bottle of champagne. That's only the second time we've agreed since we've met. Neat freaks who like veggie burgers." He raises one eyebrow and throws me a grin-laced smile that lands right in my gut. A warm feeling of comfort rises in my body, but I quickly convince myself that it's hot air from the stone fireplace.

*Danny*

"Delicious. Absolutely, delicious," I say as I wipe up the last bit of homemade spicy ketchup from my plate with my last garlic sweet potato fry.

"Well, I'll let Tack know you enjoyed it," Vince says, taking my plate away. His deep voice has so much gravel in it you could drive across it in a blizzard. "I told him you were here, but we are slammed tonight so he can't get out of the kitchen. He wanted me to tell you that he loves your dad's butternut squash soup. It's his new favorite."

"Oh, is your dad a cook?" Prescott asks.

"Sort of," I say quickly. "He loves working with food." I don't tell Prescott that when Tack says he likes my dad's soup he means the new line of organic soups from Amore Foods Incorporated, part of the international food empire my family has built over multiple generations. Saying my dad loves working with food is an entirely accurate statement and I did see him cook an egg once. I'm not unaware that it is also entirely misleading. I don't want Prescott to know about my family right away. It always makes things weird. I'll tell him when the time is right. I quickly change the subject.

"What did Jules think of Strawberry Shortcake?"

"They love it," Vince says.

"You cook too, Danny?" Prescott asks, assuming Vince is referring to some confection.

"Me? No, I use the oven for overflow storage of my Crocs. Strawberry Shortcake is a vintage doll. Her friends were Apple Dumplin' and Huckleberry Pie. Tack's kid is obsessed with them," I say like it's common knowledge, but Prescott gives me a blank stare. "Sorry, they were made in 1980 not 1880 so no reason you would know them. Vince, I'm afraid my colleague is more interested in the nineteenth century than the one we are currently living in."

"Hey, don't knock the nineteenth century," Vince says gathering more plates. "Some of my favorite poets come out of the pastoral movement." Prescott lets out a short laugh to acknowledge Vince's retort.

"I sometimes forget that underneath all that muscle and business sense is the heart of a poet," I say rolling my eyes and with a slight chortle. "Tell Jules I have my eyes open for a Purple Pie Man doll. They're rare but I'll find one."

"I know you will. I'll tell Jules and they'll be thrilled. Oh, before I forget. Tack and I are having some people over for a potluck to recover from Winter Festival. It would be great if the two of you could join us. Anita and Toula will be there and Kevin and Evan. Let me know," he says and heads back inside.

There is a short but deeply awkward silence once Vince leaves. Tonight's dinner was really nice. I assumed that tomorrow we'd go back to our corners and come back out fighting as usual, but maybe we don't have to.

"Tack is a great chef, but they go all out when they host in their home." Of course Prescott will want to go. He's new in town and doesn't know that many people. I know we haven't exactly gotten along but we got through opening day and since he's new here he must want to meet everyone he can. I know I would.

"I don't want to intrude. It was very nice of Vince to offer but...it's not really my thing," he says, moving his napkin from his lap and putting it on the table. "I should get going. It's getting late and I have a lot to do at the shop tomorrow."

"What's that supposed to mean?" I ask.

"What's what supposed to mean?"

"It's not really my thing," I say echoing his clench-assed response to the very warm invitation he was given. "Do you prefer to hang out more with people like you? Like that Worth? Is that more your speed?"

"Stop it. You don't know him. You don't know me for that matter," he says. I can see the muscles tighten in his neck and jaw.

I can't believe I was letting my guard down with this guy. "Do you only mingle with high society? Not enough prestige to slum it with a bunch of working queers in town? You know…" For a second I think about telling him the truth about my family. That their wealth and social position would make Worth's look like dollar store merchandise on clearance. But I don't want to win the argument that way. I don't want Prescott to start treating me differently. Actually, that's not true at all. I do want him to start treating me differently. I just don't want him to do it because he thinks I come from money.

"It has nothing to do with that. You're so quick to make judgments, aren't you?"

"I call them as I see them," I tell him.

"No you don't. You call them as you *want* to see them. You don't listen. You have no idea why I don't want to go."

"I heard every word you said," I say. Prescott grabs the check off the table and pulls out a credit card. I take out my credit card and say, "I'm paying. I suggested dinner." I take his credit card off the bill and place it to the side.

I go to pick up the bill again but instead of grabbing the check I grab his hand. He looks up immediately. My hand is on top of his. I don't move it. I can't. A feeling so intense shoots through me I think I'm frozen. I want to rub my fingers over his smooth knuckles and gently move my fingers around to the palm of his hand and feel the softness of his skin. His beautiful eyes have such a sharp focus on mine I wonder if he somehow knows what I'm thinking. Does my face show my curiosity in finding out more about the man under the overly starched shirt? What would it be like to rip the Brooks Brothers off him and find out what makes his pocket watch tick? How can I even think that when I dislike this guy so intensely? I sharply pull my hand away.

"I asked you to dinner," I say again, and stand up. I put my credit card back in my wallet and pull out enough cash to cover the dinner, a generous tip and maybe even a night in one of the newly opened rooms here at the inn. I put the money on the table. "You're right. It's been a long day. I'll see you at the shop. Good night." I turn away from the table and walk away from him, feeling my heart beat faster and faster.

# Chapter Seven

*Danny*

"You will not believe what I heard this morning," I say walking into the store. Prescott already has the potbelly roaring so a wave of dry warmth embraces me softly. With Winter Festival at least a week behind us and the bulk of the tourists long gone, New Hope is back to its usual winter calm barring my recent alarm over a troubling bit of news.

Prescott is carrying a small porcelain teacup in his hand. "Would you like some green tea?" he asks. I can never tell if he is being simply polite or trying for nice. There's a difference. *Cordial* might be the best word to describe how we've been acting since our ill-fated dinner at The Hideaway.

"No thanks," I say remembering that the last time I

accepted a cup of tea from him it tasted like boiled dirt. "You won't believe what's happening down the street," I repeat and shove my hand into my pocket and pull out the notice I ripped off the telephone pole on my way to the shop. "Look at this!"

He looks it over and then hands it back to me. "Looks like they are doing some construction. So what?"

"It's demolition. They're tearing down the First Bank of Bucks building."

Prescott shrugs. "I repeat, so what? Who even uses a drive-through anymore? I never thought that building fit in here. It's so different from everything else in town." He wriggles his nose.

"Ugh," I say, verbally punctuating how I feel inside. The bank is beautiful. It was built in the midsixties and I'm sure it was a modern marvel when it was constructed. "How could you say that building doesn't fit in here? This is New Hope, for crying out loud."

Prescott puts the papers he's working on at his desk in a drawer and closes it firmly. "That's precisely my point. This is New Hope. Look out the window. What do you see?"

I humor him, walk over to the bow window on my side of the shop and turn my head from side to side. I see gorgeous painted ladies with porches that swing out to greet the sidewalk, the stone farmhouse that is now The Hideaway down the street and the wintery barren cherry trees that stand in front of Toula's bookshop. "Main Street is adorable. What's your point?"

"It's adorable because it's cohesive. There's a certain aesthetic." He walks to a shelf where he has the ugliest, grayest collection of metal cups and candle holders I've ever seen. "All of the pieces in my pewter collection are from the Cunningham Studio. And when I get my hands on that elusive pear-shaped tankard it will be complete. It's more valuable as a set than it is as individual pieces because everything fits together."

"I hate matchy-matchy. And fitting together is not what makes this town great. New Hope is a place where all different people come to be a part of something. It's about diversity and inclusivity at its core. It's the fact that a building like the bank can stand next to all the old crap that you like."

"Oh, so it's okay to speak maliciously of things I like but heaven forbid anyone say a bad word about that eyesore."

"Eyesore!" I shout, my volume greater than I had planned. I flip the sign on the front door from Closed to Open and walk back to my desk. "I'll have you know I consider that bank to be one of the most beautiful buildings in town."

Prescott laughs. "You would," he says, and he rolls his eyes.

"Listen here you pompous little prince…" I start in on him and he's ready for the sparring. He comes right back at me and we are full on yelling at each other and in each other's faces when the front door opens and we both freeze.

"Oh, no. Did we catch you in the middle of something?"

Two trim women wearing yoga pants enter the store. They both have tightly pulled back ponytails. One woman has curly blond hair and the other's is straight brown.

"The sign said Open, so we just came on in. We hope that's okay?" the woman with the brunette ponytail says.

"Absolutely, ladies," I say smiling and grateful for the distraction.

"We are happy to have you in our establishment," Prescott says stiffly. I'm beginning to notice how tense he is when a customer pops in. Once he gets started talking about one of his objects he's a different person, all color and light, but he's always a bit awkward in the beginning.

"My uncle has a birthday coming up," the blond one says. She walks over to a small silver pill box on Prescott's side. It's simple, small and boring. "Tell me about this?" she asks holding it out to me.

"I'm afraid I wouldn't know," I say, turning toward Prescott.

He jumps in. "That is actually a snuff box. It was used by sea captains who sailed from Nantucket. They kept various recreational, shall we say, vices in..." As soon as he starts talking about the thingamajig his voice is smooth and inviting. The slight tremble from his greeting has vanished.

"Oh. My god. Is that a Nyform troll?" the other woman asks leaping toward a shelf on my side. She gets within inches of the doll but clearly knows enough not to grab something so valuable.

"Why yes, it is," I say. "Amazing. Right? I love these little guys. This one is very special."

"My anniversary with my wife is coming up and she would totally flip if I brought home a Nyform troll. Do you have any idea how rare those things are?"

"I do," I say with a sly smile. I look over at Prescott who is deep in conversation with the other customer. He gets this intense look when he's explaining the history of one of

his pieces. His face gets all serene but very focused. I wonder if this is what he looks like when he is having sex. For a
second I get lost in the thought of unbuckling his khakis...

"Do you have any more trolls?" the customer asks.

"Yes, of course," I say turning my attention back to her.
I walk over to the shelf where I display the trolls, but I can't
help but keep an eye on Prescott. I've tried everything I can
to either stop hating him or stop lusting after him. How
can someone so infuriating also be so sexy?

*Prescott*

"Mars?" the customer holding the cylindrical telescope
says, examining it carefully. He's looked at multiple items
from tear bottles to candle sticks but the small brass object
used for finding the Red Planet has captured his attention.
Customers are often surprised to find out the Victorians
were not so different from us.

"Around 1877 Giovanni Schiaparelli believed he had
spotted artificial waterways on the planet. He used his telescope to spy on the Martians. Ideas about extraterrestrial
life were very popular and like so many things at the time
they were linked to technological advances. Improvements
in optics made it possible for people to get a better look at
the heavens. It was taken very seriously and people often left
money in their will for plans to make contact with aliens."

"Absolutely fascinating. I'll take it," the older gentleman
says and I feel a short burst of pride knowing I was able
to use my knowledge to convince him. I carefully wrap
the telescope and thank him for his purchase as he leaves.

Danny was busy on his side of the shop all morning

long. After the yoga women came in a group of seniors on their way to a matinee at the Playhouse marveled over some pieces of his that seemed completely mundane to me. I think they were prizes from the bottom of a box of Cracker Jack or some other such thing that most people usually throw away. Still, to hear Danny talk about them you would think they belonged in the Smithsonian. He can talk to anyone about anything. While my conversations are limited to the merchandise at hand, Danny has this ability to open up to total strangers about almost any topic, from the tonsillectomy he had as a child to the fourteen reasons he no longer eats licorice. And the people involved in his conversations listen to every word and then open up to him about their gall bladder surgery or why they don't eat salmon. It's a raw openness that's impossible to avoid. He was gabbing with a customer today while I was eating lunch at my desk and pretending to be deep in research. I overheard every word of his explanation and I even stole a few glances at him when he wasn't looking.

Sometimes I wish I was more like that, able to say whatever I'm thinking or feeling. Why couldn't I have told Danny last week at dinner that it wasn't that I didn't want to go to the party at Vince and Tack's, it was more that the thought of socializing with a bunch of strangers who were already his friends gave me so much discomfort that I couldn't say yes. Maybe a small town isn't the place for me. Maybe I should have stayed in the city where I don't have to worry as much about getting caught in social situations that make me unsure of myself. In Philadelphia I didn't feel pressure to extend my relationships beyond the professional level.

I wanted to tell Danny all of that. I had a feeling this curious mixture of cruise director, children's television host and Sexiest Bear of the Year would actually understand. But he had to go and insult me and pick a fight. It's infuriating. How dare he assume that I think I'm too good for his friends? Even though my work brings me in contact with some people who might think that way, I do not. You can love fine art and still be a person who believes in equality and justice. He just made assumptions about me and it pushed my buttons.

Still, there are other buttons he's also pushing. When he put his hand over mine at the restaurant last week I felt something electric pass through me. I fantasized about ripping off his ugly Hawaiian print shirt, putting on a more tasteful one, and then ripping that off. I was grateful he walked out of the inn when he did because I wasn't sure what I was going to do. I went home and couldn't stop fantasizing about him. I lay in bed and started running through inventory stats and then the image of his furry forearm would appear or that big hearty laugh. I've never met anyone with so much joie de vivre. His energy is generally like that experiment with the Mentos and two-liter bottle of Coke. He just sort of explodes whenever something catches his attention.

Danny comes in from the pantry talking on his cell phone. "They are planning to demolish it. We have to save this building. The Bank of Bucks is too important. Talk soon." He puts his phone back in his pocket.

"Have you become a preservationist in the span of a day?" I ask.

"I care about beautiful things just as much as you do. I happen to *not* have such a narrow view of what makes something worth saving."

Usually he makes a jab and it just rolls right off me but sometimes he says something that stings a bit more than it should. Am I really narrow-minded? Do I have a limited sense of what makes something beautiful? "I doubt there is anything you can do about the demolition anyway," I say.

"We'll see about that," he says opening a notebook and jotting something down. "You'd be surprised how much a community can do when it pulls together."

"But that bank isn't even historical," I say.

He closes his notebook and walks over to me. "I'm not sure who taught you that history is something that happened only over a hundred years ago, but the fact is history is happening now."

He wants a debate about history. Bring it. "That may be, but you think history extends only as far back as your childhood. You're only willing to honor history when it's a part of your memory."

Danny walks over to the front door and flips the sign to Closed. "Grab your blazer. We're going on an educational field trip."

"Now?" I ask. There are a few more hours until we are officially closed.

"Of course, now. I'd say there is no time like the present but I'm sure you would say that 1850 or 1903 were equally as good as the present so I'll just say, 'let's go.' There's always an afternoon lull anyway." He walks over to the door and holds it open and I can't help but follow him on this adventure. I don't have any choice. He smiles at me triumphantly as I throw on my blazer and wrap a Burberry scarf around my neck and begin to put on my gloves. Danny really does have a radiant smile, all warmth and confidence. I walk past him and since I sense a bit of flirtation in his request I make sure my arm brushes against his chest. The sensation is thrilling. It feels like taking a risk, but the pay-off was seeing Danny respond with an expression of excitement tinged with confusion. I'm a little confused myself but only to the extent that I can't figure out which of us is the Mentos and which is the bottle of soda.

# Chapter Eight

*Danny*

I try to ignore the sensation from Prescott's arm brushing against my chest and focus on showing him the buildings. There's still snow on the ground, but the sidewalks are clear enough for us to walk side by side. The air is cold and clear. We walk a few blocks past Bridge Street until we're standing in front of the First Bank of Bucks.

"Isn't it wonderful?" I ask, admiring the gorgeous mid-century marvel. Four tall windows make up the facade. They are uninterrupted by adornment—pure open glass that reflects the snowy street. Between each massive window is a stone and cement pillar. Each one creates a simple but perfect rectangle. A straight flat roof sweeps from the center of the windows out beyond the building creating the entrance awning and drive-through window. It looks like something from an episode of *The Jetsons* or a pavilion at a World's Fair from the last century. It's a vision of the future that never was, straight from the sixties. I adore everything about the look and feel of the structure. Modern. Exaggerated. Hopeful.

"*Wonderful* is not the word I would use," Prescott says.

I smack him gently on the shoulder. "I know you're just saying that to make me mad. You can't possibly be blind to the beauty of this building." He tilts his head from side to side and his bangs flop in such a cute boyish way that I almost have to look away.

"Aesthetics are only one piece of it. I'm not against mid-century design. I suppose I just don't get it. It seems so random. That movement never embraced all that came before it. It didn't just rebel against the Beaux-Arts. It ignored it."

No matter what I say, Prescott finds a way to disagree or criticize. It's exasperating but I want him to see what I see for once so I work harder to convince him instead of argue. "But that's the idea. The buildings are about the future. They say we can create the world we want and not be the result of what came before. We can be free to be whatever we want."

He looks carefully at the building again and I watch him thinking. "I guess I never thought of it that way." The words creep out in a momentary surrender.

"See that steel girder that holds up that roof over the drive-through?" I say pointing. "It's not adorned with sculptures of pretty birds or painted to look like a Greek statue or covering up anything. It is what it is and that's enough."

"But your stuff in the store. It's covered in color and texture and pattern."

"Right, but no one has told me that stuff is supposed to be beautiful. I collect what I love because it makes me happy. It brings me joy. Do things in your collection bring you joy?" I ask him because I truly want to know. Prescott takes a few seconds to answer.

"Yes, they do. But not for the same reasons. I like knowing the history of each piece and understanding where it fits in." He looks at me very seriously for a second as if he is sizing me up and figuring out if he wants to go deeper. "Were you teased much as a kid? You know, for being gay?"

I'm surprised by his directness about something so personal but my gut reaction is an honest one. Mercilessly, I want to say. I want to tell him about having to change boarding schools because of bullies and how I would do anything to redirect their aggression. Instead I say, "Yeah, I was. It sucked." I'm being truthful but not overly candid. I wonder where he's going with this line of questioning.

"Me too. But when I started studying antiques and learning about them, it gave me an expertise. I think some gay men become experts in things because it gives them a sense of power and control that they might not feel in other parts of their lives. That's how it was for me. Knowing the provenance and art historical background of something makes me feel safe because it makes me feel in control. I guess that sounds silly."

"Not really," I say, thinking about how I always had an

ability to make people laugh and how I used that in the same way he's describing. If I could make the bullies laugh it made me feel in control and that made me feel safe.

"Excuse me," a woman wearing an orange safety vest says as she places stakes in the ground in front of the bank. "You're standing where I need to put my next marker."

We both politely move on impulse. "What are these markers for?" I ask even though it's pretty clear they aren't just decoration.

"Demolition." She says the word as if it does not signify catastrophe.

"They *cannot* tear this bank down," I say as if plucking the markers from the ground might stop it.

She looks at me like I'm on her last nerve. "You think I have a say in what happens? I got a job to do so they know where to plan the explosion." She continues down the road toward the corner, putting markers every few steps of the way. Prescott turns his attention from the bank to the woman. She puts down a stake and then walks a few feet, but when she gets to the edge of the bank she continues.

"What's she doing?" Prescott says with a sense of urgency.

"I guess she's marking the places where they'll start the demolition. That's what she said." It's not like him to be so obtuse.

"No, I mean she is well past the bank now. She's in front of—" he swallows hard "—the Yardley House." He can barely get the words out of his mouth. I look over at the building next to the bank and even though I've seen it a thousand times, seeing it through Prescott's eyes in this moment I understand it in a different way. It's classically proportioned, elegantly designed and although a bit genteel in its demeanor, it does have some charming details when you look closer.

Come to think of it, so does Prescott.

*Prescott*

"Ma'am, excuse me," I say to the woman in the safety vest. I'm sure there is some explanation for everything that will make sense. "May I ask what you're doing?"

She adjusts her orange vest before cocking her head to the side and giving me a look that is certainly more pissed off than the look she gave Danny a few minutes ago. "Like I just told the other one—marking boundaries for the demolition for the new parking facility."

I'm getting more nervous by the second. "Are these markers in front of the Yardley House here so it won't be damaged?"

She laughs and then goes back to her work. "Damaged? I think fifty pounds of dynamite and a few bulldozers will do damage enough, you betcha. The bank only needs twenty. This building will take thirty pounds and it should be flatter than a pancake from Sweet Sue's in eight seconds flat."

"I thought they were only demolishing the bank?" I ask with one last bit of hope.

"They're both going down. Can't do just one. They share the same support structure since they're on the river. If one goes down then the other has to go too."

I've followed her down the street asking questions and

left Danny back at the bank. I walk back to him and ask, "How could anyone tear down such a beautiful building?"

"Why do I think you're not talking about the bank?" Danny rolls his eyes.

"No," I say to him and then point at the end of the block. "That beautiful building, the Yardley House. It's a stunning example of nineteenth-century craftsmanship in the Second Empire style."

"Remind me again. What was the first empire?"

"City Hall in Philadelphia is in this style. I'm sure you've seen it. This was built about the same time in 1871. See the dormer windows and mansard roof?" I point to the sloped tiled roof on the top floor, which is covered in simple gray tile.

"Is that what that's called? A mansard roof. Looks like it belongs in Paris."

"Good eye. Pierre Lescot is credited for creating this style. The most famous example is on the Louvre in Paris, *bien sur*. I did my master's thesis on the Second Empire Period in the decorative arts of Eastern Pennsylvania and the Yardley House was one of the finest pieces I have ever seen."

"You mean that dull, boring building where that woman is putting down stakes," Danny says and I can tell he is teasing just to push my buttons.

"Yes, that dull, boring building—as you say—is one of the most important historical monuments to American aesthetics ever built on the Eastern Seaboard. Who in their right mind would tear down something so beautiful and so extraordinary?"

"Apparently Bridgeton Construction," Danny says,

pointing to the notice on the side of the building that indicates the plans for construction. "I knew the bank was in danger. I didn't know about that building." He says it plainly and without malice.

"The Yardley House is as special to me as that bank is to you." As I say it, I realize what the bank must mean to him.

"I get that," he says and I think he means it.

"According to that woman, both buildings share a support system. I imagine there are pylons dug close to the river—"

"—so if the Bank of Bucks goes down so does the Yardley House." Danny's expression is pained.

"Yes, and if the Yardley House goes down, so does the Bank of Bucks. I don't know if there's much we can do." The thought of the Yardley House being razed to the ground makes me shudder.

"Nothing is a done deal. Ever. If we get enough people to protest we can make a difference. We can save both buildings. I've already gathered a list of names of concerned citizens and started planning what we need to do."

"It's only been a day," I say incredulously. I've observed him working hard in the shop, but I've been just as focused on making my collection a success that I haven't noticed how determined he can be. It's impressive. I know he has a lot of energy, in fact more than I can handle most of the time, but when he focuses he can be a real dynamo.

"The truth is I could use help. So far we have started a group online to share information and get people involved but there will be city council meetings to attend, protests to plan and glitter to buy."

"How will glitter help you save the building?"

Danny sighs. "You have so much to learn. Glitter can save a lot of things."

I have no idea how glitter works into the equation but I guess I'm willing to find out. "One of the first things we need is a teach-in to let people know how important these buildings are. I was already planning on talking about midcentury architecture and you could talk about the mansion roof."

"It's called a mansard roof and it's very special," I say looking up at the stunning craftsmanship of dovetailed tiles. "But I don't know. I've never really done any social action sort of thing in that way. I'm more a behind the scenes person."

"Don't be silly. I've seen the way you talk about the things you love in the shop like with that man this morning when you were talking about that telescope. He was enthralled."

"You heard all that?" I ask.

"Yes, I mean, I guess so. Any mention of aliens makes my ears perk up. Anyway, he bought the thing didn't he?"

"I suppose he did," I say feeling my defenses weaken. Danny has a way of pushing me out of my comfort zone. Usually he does it by making me angry but he's also able to find other ways.

"The Yardley House is something you love. You're a great speaker about all of that historical stuff. I'm sure people will listen to you."

"Did you just pay me a compliment?" I ask.

"Don't get used to it," he says, but the fact is I could get used to it.

I could get used to it very easily.

# Chapter Nine

*Danny*

Serilda is the president of the New Hope LGBTQ Historical Society, an elected position, but they are nonetheless treated like local royalty. They have lived in this area for decades and rule the political conscience of the town with equal parts sugar and spice. With Prescott on board and a list of community members interested in participating, sitting down with Serilda seems like the next logical step. When I asked Prescott to join us he agreed, and we didn't even argue about it. In fact, we haven't had one of our blow-out disagreements in days.

Prescott has gone from indifference to sustained enthusiasm since finding out the Yardley House is part of the demolition. Even though we each have our own agenda and reasons for wanting to stop the destruction the fact is we are working on this together because we don't have a choice. The fate of each building is tied to the other so this is shaping up to be a team effort more than I thought it would be.

After a busy morning in the shop we put the "We'll be back shortly" sign in the door and head over to the Honeysuckle for our meeting. Serilda is ready and waiting seated at the same table they always sit at in the back of the cafe. It's like their throne. If someone is sitting there and Serilda enters, that someone moves and does it quickly. It's a healthy mixture of fear and respect.

Today, Serilda is wearing a black-and-purple houndstooth pantsuit and a white faux-fur hat that's almost like a crown on the top of their head. In addition to always being fashionable, Serilda can smell b.s. from across the river so it will be interesting to see how they react to Prescott.

"Serilda, so nice to see you," I say, giving them a kiss on the cheek. "May I present Prescott Henderson?"

"Danny, always nice to see you," they say.

Prescott extends his hand and Serilda shakes it gingerly. "Your broach is stunning," he says, admiring the pearl-encrusted crescent moon on their lapel. "It looks like it's from the Aesthetic Movement. Late 1860s or possibly 1870s I would say, without a more careful examination."

Serilda looks Prescott up and down. They are serious and we both anxiously await their verdict.

"To be exact, 1866. It was my great-great-grandmother's. She purchased it after her first year teaching at a school during the Reconstruction era," Serilda says, moving their fingers over the pin.

"Sounds like she was a trailblazer, like Mary S. Peake," Prescott says and Serilda's eyes open and warm.

"Please sit down," they say, studying Prescott. We both pull up chairs at their table. "How do you know about Mary S. Peake?" Serilda asks. "My great-great-grand-mother corresponded with her when she was a student. They became friends and colleagues."

I'm not sure who they're talking about but it's clear that the mention of this woman's name has given Serilda and Prescott a keen interest in each other.

"Really? I'd be so interested to see any letters if you have them and are comfortable sharing. I studied Mary S. Peake in graduate school. There is a famous engraving at the National Portrait Gallery."

"The one by Lewis Lockwood. Yes, I know it," Serilda says. They are one of those people who seem to know everything, like a human Wikipedia. I've begged them more than a number of times to try out for *Jeopardy* but they think game shows are crass.

"Who is Mary S. Peake?" I ask not wanting to feel left out.

"She started a school for formerly enslaved people. She was one of the first Black teachers to work in a private school. Like my great-great-grandmother," Serilda says.

"She was an incredibly important figure in education in the nineteenth century," Prescott adds.

"Sounds like it," I say and notice that Prescott is smiling. I know he was nervous about meeting Serilda since I described them as a somewhat intimidating figure.

"This one is not only handsome but also a scholar," Serilda says as if I should be paying more attention.

I don't tell them "this one's" been trying to ruin my life for the past few weeks, since we are here to work together, after all. Fortunately, they don't wait for me to answer. "Now, we can use your knowledge to help educate the community about those wonderful historic buildings. That's the first step in a social action. Educate people and get them fired up. A teach-in."

I knew Serilda would be able to give shape to this action. I've listened to them tell many stories about being on the front lines of social justice movements from the March on Washington when they were a kid to organizing the float for the Trans Peer Support Group last Pride. I'm grateful they feel passionately about these historic buildings.

"I was thinking we could do something at the store like a community forum. I can talk about the bank and Prescott knows a great deal about the Yardley House," I say.

"I've been thinking about that," Prescott says slowly. "Instead of doing a talk I could write something up sharing my research about the building. That way people could look at it when they wished." His chin drops a bit and his eyes are just slightly downcast. I know he was hesitant about talking in front of a group, but I thought he had agreed to.

"It's good to have something like a website as a backup but we need you live and in person. Both of you," Serilda says, their eyes sharpening at Prescott's resistance.

"What do you think, Prescott?" I ask holding my breath and realizing I might want him to be a part of this more than I'm letting myself realize.

*Prescott*

I take a sip from the now-cold coconut latte sitting in front of me to buy some time. I know the other night I told Danny I would speak about the Yardley House but that was the result of his flattery. The truth is, anything over a crowd of two and I tend to freeze up. I don't have the big personality that Danny does. He doesn't seem fazed by any type of public speaking. The other day a busload of tourists got an impromptu lesson on making shadow puppets that ended with cheers and applause. When I had to defend my graduate thesis I practiced for weeks and even though the room contained only scholars I had studied with for years I still threw up the night before.

"I don't know. I think a carefully researched website could have more detail than I could give during a talk. Or Danny could take my notes and do it," I suggest.

I look at Danny, expecting him to be pissed that I'm hedging my bets with all this. He has every right to be. I study his face and notice that he doesn't have a hint of the anger that he has displayed during the last few weeks in the store. He looks almost sympathetic, like he understands.

It's Serilda who gives me an out. "I think Danny should focus on the bank. Prescott, it would be wonderful to have you speak. The community is very warm and welcoming but if you aren't comfortable…"

Danny looks at me, his gentle eyes persuading me but not forcing me. "We'd be doing it together. It wouldn't be like you're speaking alone. We would be like a team," he says. It's easy to piss him off dusting some forgotten toy or ugly needlepoint pillow in the shop, but right now his

eyes are gentle and kind. He's giving me options and asking for my consent in a very lovely way.

"Yes," I say. "We'll do it together. A team." The words
just sort of waltz out of my mouth. I can't believe I agreed
to talking in front of a group, but I remind myself that it's
for a good cause and I won't be doing it alone. I'll be doing
it with Danny.

# Chapter Ten

*Danny*

We host the community forum in the store after shop hours. Prescott goes out to get the refreshments and I'm unfolding chairs we borrowed from Toula's bookshop when Lizard walks in wearing her usual leather-studded motorcycle jacket. Her green hair is straight up in the air as a result of the gravity-defying hairspray that almost asphyxiated me the other day.

"Where is The Little Prince?" Lizard asks seeing that Prescott isn't in the store.

"He went to the Honeysuckle to pick up some snacks for tonight." I grab a chair from the stack and unfold it and Lizard goes to hang her leather jacket in the pantry. "And please don't call him that," I say.

"The Little Prince? Why not?" she asks walking back from the pantry. "You gave him the name anyway. I'm just using it."

"I know. It's just that it's not a very nice nickname and…" I trail off. It's not just that the nickname is mean, it's that I don't see Prescott in the way I did when I first met him. He cares about things deeply and he's not the superficial pretty boy I used to think he was.

Lizard sits down in the chair I just unfolded and looks at me with her mouth wide open. "Daniel Pawel Roman, you like him!" Lizard is one of the few people who knows my full name let alone remembers every syllable of it. I'm also one of the few people who know her given name is Darlene.

"I do *not* like him," I say. "Not in that way. It's just that I don't hate him. We've been working on this event together and I just want it to go well. That's all."

She gets up off her chair and stands directly in front of me. "You look me in the eyes and tell me you do not like him in that way."

"Fine," I say. I draw in a short breath and suddenly I can't help thinking about how his eyes dance when he is talking about something he finds beautiful or how he always bites his lower lip when he's trying to figure something out. I'm about to force myself to say the words, but I can't seem to get them to go from my brain to my mouth. Lizard knows exactly what's going on.

"Danny just be careful, okay?" Her tone is suddenly serious and concerned. "Don't let him take advantage of you. Like…"

"Actually," I say cutting her off before she can say the name of the gold-digger who humiliated me. "That's what's sort of funny about the whole thing. Prescott has no idea about my family."

"That's impossible. How could he not know? Surely he's Googled you."

"Do you know how many Danny Romans there are online? Anyway it sort of came up the other day and I sort of didn't exactly tell him the truth about it. He thinks my dad works with food, not that he owns an international food conglomerate. I sort of liked not having to explain the inner workings of my family's dynasty."

"That's your business, Danny. You don't have to tell him anything. Maybe it's not a bad thing you haven't told this guy your family could buy the entire town with their pocket change. Maybe the entire state of Pennsylvania."

"That's not true at all," I tell her. "Not the *entire* state. Maybe just a few of the smaller counties." I'm proud that my family has a tradition of valuing philanthropy over profit, but still I often make jokes about the massive wealth. It helps alleviate the pressure and guilt I can't help feeling about it. I did nothing to earn it yet it's attached to me and a part of who I am. Maybe not telling Prescott is actually about keeping a part of myself hidden and protected. "Shh, he's back. Not a word."

Prescott is standing at the front door, both hands holding boxes of donuts from the Honeysuckle Bakery and Cafe. "We can't leave him standing outside. He needs help with the door," I say and walk right past her to grab the handle and let Prescott back in.

"Thanks," he says, walking in and putting the treats on the table. "Hello, Lizard," he says formally.

"Yo!" she says in the opposite tone.

Prescott carefully opens the lid on one of the boxes to reveal over a dozen freshly made doughnuts with blue-and-white icing and silver sparkly sprinkles that make them look like snowflakes.

"They're so pretty," I say admiring them.

Lizard looks at me and says, "Yeah, Danny *definitely* likes what he sees." I give Lizard a look that lets her know she is going to be wearing these doughnuts home if she goes a step further.

"Hey, guys," Tack says, walking in with Vince. Luckily The Hideaway is closed tonight so they can both join us. I walk over to introduce Tack to Prescott. "This is the man who created that delicious burger you had the other night."

"Nice to meet you," Prescott says stiffly, like the words are hard to get out. A short while ago I would have thought it was pretension and not apprehension. I'm becoming more aware of how hard it is for him to interact with people he doesn't know well.

"You too. Vince told me you two were there on a date the other night," Tack says.

Prescott's face registers clear surprise but he doesn't correct Tack. I know Tack. He's incorrigible so I'm sure this is his way of stirring the pot. I wait for Prescott to at least make a face refuting the date label. He doesn't so I assume he misheard it. Then he says, "You make an excellent veggie burger," darting his eyes to the side. "We enjoyed it very much."

We? There is a we? First he doesn't recoil at the word *date* and then he uses the word *we*. "Please, allow me to take your coats," Prescott says formally and gathers them in his arms before heading to the back pantry.

I walk over to Tack and smack him on the arm. Hard.

"Hey, what's that for?" he asks throwing me that cocky farm boy smile.

"You know full well what that's for, Tack O'Leary," Vince says. "I'm sorry my fiancé is such a troublemaker. I'll try to keep him in line."

"I just want Danny to find the love of his life like we did," Tack says, his voice still full of playfulness. Vince bends toward him and kisses him on the nose. The two of them are so sweet together that if they weren't so nice I'd be uncontrollably jealous.

"He's coming back. You two knock it off!" I say sharply.

"Me? I didn't do anything," Vince says, but they are both silent when Prescott comes back. He gives me a look like he knows we were talking about him, but he just smiles. "I have a few images I'm going to project from my laptop. Excuse me. I want to make sure everything is perfect." Prescott ducks away to prepare his talk, I know he's nervous but I also know he has been preparing like crazy with pages and pages of notes. I plan to speak off the top of my head about the bank, so I don't need that much preparation. I'm better greeting guests and he's better giving the formal lecture. It feels good to complement each other's skills in this way.

Prescott goes to his desk and opens his laptop as more people come through the door, followed by even more people after that. I greet each guest with a warm hug or friendly handshake. Occasionally I catch Prescott looking over at me like I'm diffusing a bomb. Through the shop window I see Arthur approaching with Serilda.

Arthur opens the door for Serilda and they walk through making a statement entrance as always. Serilda is wearing a red toggle coat with a huge red hood trimmed in white faux fur that perfectly frames their weathered yet well-preserved face.

"It never got this cold in Atlanta," they say.

"Nice to see you, Serilda," I say, kissing their cheek. "Uncle Arthur, hello. I'm so glad you're both here."

"Nights like this I wonder why I ever left the South," Serilda says with a shiver. Arthur helps them take off their coat and he hands it to me. "How is your crush going on Prescott? I hope you haven't been distracting him while he's been researching," they ask, pretending to whisper but definitely not whispering.

"Serilda!" I admonish them. "Please keep your voice down. I do not have a crush on him. Arthur what did you tell Serilda?"

"My dear boy," Arthur says to me, "no one tells the charming Serilda anything. They speak their own mind."

"Thank you, Arthur," Serilda says giving Arthur a sly smile. The two of them have known each other for years and I've never thought there was anything between them, but something about that shared smile makes me think things might have changed.

"If you do not have a crush on him why do I need to keep my voice down? And do not blame this wonderful man," they say, putting a gentle hand on his arm, making me more suspicious. "I saw it with my own eyes at the Honeysuckle. Everyone is talking about it. I heard from Toula that you two had a very romantic dinner at The Hideaway the other week. You were seen canoodling."

"We were not!" I protest. "And I don't even know what *canoodling* means."

They squint their eyes at me and then hold up a finger with two sparkling rings on it. "If you don't know what it means, then how do you know you weren't doing it?"

I don't have an answer for them so I just go to hang up their coat and grab the chairs I had kept folded and reserved for them. I make my way through the crowd and over to where Prescott is standing alone going over his notes. As soon as I am next to him he hands me his notebook.

"Here, I've underlined some of the most important information about the Yardley House," he says. "Most of it is in order and I think my notes are legible. You do the talking. I can help change the slides from my laptop. That way I'll still be a part of it."

"I don't know anything about the Yardley House or the Second Empire. The only empire I know is *The Empire Strikes Back*. You're the expert. You know more about that old stuff than anyone."

He looks around me to the crowd of people and I notice his leg starts jittering a bit and he bites his lip. "I know I said I could do it and that I would do it. It's just that there are a lot of people here. A lot more than I thought we would get on such short notice. I was thinking it would maybe be single digits."

When we first met, Prescott was mostly thunder and annoyance, but as we started to plan this event another side of him has emerged. I saw his reluctance when we met with Serilda and it made me soften toward him. I know the whole town thinks I have a crush on him but it's not like that. We're just working on this project and I care about saving that beautiful bank. If that means I have to help this guy, then so be it. I'm sure once the buildings are saved we will go back to being mortal enemies but right now we need to help each other. I try to think of something soothing to say. "Sure it's a lot of people but it's not like it's Yankee Stadium and you need to sing the national anthem in your underwear."

"Oh, no," he says and covers his eyes with his hands.

That was not the thing to say.

"Let me get you some water." They always do that on TV.

"No. No more water. I'll float away in the middle. I'm not good speaking in front of people like this. I'm awful at it. Maybe we should revisit the web page idea. I could go home now and work on it," he says, thinking he has found a way out.

"Prescott, come on. You'll be great. I know it."

"How do you *know* it?"

I look at him carefully. I've watched him in the shop talking to people and he's wonderful—captivating in fact. Sure it takes him a while to get going but once he does and he finds his groove he's charming. "Because I hear you in the shop all day. Like with that man who bought the telescope," I remind him.

"That was one time and you were interested because of the alien angle."

"True, I'm a sucker for aliens. But do you remember when we had that man in the shop the other day who wanted to know about that god-awful nautical gauge you had on the shelf?"

"You mean that piece from the USS *Philadelphia*. He bought it without even negotiating the price. Actually, that ship was in the First Barbary War. You know what's interesting about that war..."

I cut him off. "Nothing," I say. "Absolutely nothing is interesting about the Barbary Wars but I couldn't help overhearing you talk with him. Thomas Jefferson was not playing games when he took down those ships."

"How do you know that?" he asks, almost afraid to hear the answer.

"Because the way you spoke about it was so passionate and so engaged I couldn't help but listen and take in everything you said. You have this way of talking about the beautiful things you love that is, well, beautiful. All you have to do is focus on that. You think the Yardley House is beautiful. Don't you?"

"Yes, of course. It's exquisite. The railing on the window frames on the second floor alone is important enough to..."

"See, right there. That's all you have to do. Only you can take something as boring as window doodad and make it sound interesting. You've got this, okay?" I look at him squarely and make sure he understands how sincere I'm being. "Also we said we were doing this together. I can't do it without you. Not really."

"Okay," he says softly.

"Now I'm going to welcome everyone. Then explain a bit about the bank and why it inspires great feeling in me and then when I'm done I'll introduce you." Before I walk away he puts his hand on my arm and I feel his fingertips make a gentle squeeze through the thick wool of my sweater. "Danny, thank you," he says and my insides realize I have very little chance of pretending I'm not crushing hard on Prescott J. Henderson.

*Prescott*

"…and so as one of the finest examples of nineteenth-century architecture representing Eastern Pennsylvania in the Second Empire style, we have a responsibility to make our voices heard and save this building from destruction. Thank you for listening."

Everyone in the room applauds and it isn't the polite-sounding applause you hear at the symphony; it's rock star applause and I like it. They are riled up and excited about saving the Yardley House and while I'm always thrilled to see other people as enthused about the Second Empire as I am, it's more than that. I'm feeling like I'm a part of something right here and now. Not something that happened in that past. That's a new feeling. Perhaps even most importantly, I see Danny in the back of the room clapping long after everyone else has stopped. I could not have done this talk tonight without him. It was hard to admit my weaknesses, but Danny truly listened and encouraged me when he really didn't need to. He could have taken my notes and done the whole thing without me but he wanted *me* to do it. He wanted me to shine.

"That was an excellent talk," Serilda says, coming up to me as soon as I've finished. Arthur is right behind them. "These developers think they can come in here and just tear down part of our community. Isn't that right, Arthur?" they ask, tenderly grabbing Arthur's arm.

"Yes, Serilda," he says with a smile.

"The next step is to get the city council and the developer in a room to listen to reason."

"And what if they don't?" I ask. I've never been a part of something like this before and I'm glad people as experienced as Serilda and Danny are leading the way.

"If they don't, we take to the streets and protest. You can't tear down a building when the sidewalks are flooded with concerned citizens," Serilda says. "We have a good number of people here tonight but we'll need more. And we'll need banners and signs..."

"We could make them here at the store," I say.

"Totally, as soon as we close the shop this place can become poster central," Danny adds. It feels good to be thinking the same thing at the same time.

Serilda looks at me, then Danny. "The two of you make an excellent addition to our community. A fine couple," Serilda says as they move to the back of the room to get their coat with Arthur in tow.

All night people have been insinuating that Danny and I might be more than business partners, but it's always hard to tell. Tack used the word *date*, but I figured that was simply a miscommunication. What exactly does Serilda mean by couple? Maybe it's that weird gay thing when you use the term *partners* and the context is unclear. Danny and I are partners in the business sense of the word, but it could never be anything more than that. Could it?

I watch him as he helps each person with their coat and thanks them for coming. I'm too shy and awkward to do any of that so I go back to my laptop and pretend I'm looking through some notes from my talk, but the truth is I can't take my eyes off Danny. He's so warm and easy with each person he talks to. He doesn't see people as an obstacle the way I do. I think he sees each person as a potential friend. Usually that type of sentiment would make me uncomfortable but watching Danny I don't feel that way at all. It makes me want to be more like him in fact.

Vince and Tack are the last to leave. I decide to take inspiration from Danny and join the small talk as they are saying goodbye. Having Danny at my side makes chatting easier. I know I can count on him to fill any awkward silences.

"Thanks for coming," I say, hoping I don't sound like a complete fool. I figure a simple thank-you is innocent enough.

"Glad we came," Vince says. "I knew the area had a great deal of Queen Anne style from the latter part of the century but this is the only building in the area with such exceptional Second Empire details." Vince clearly knows what he's talking about and I appreciate his comment.

"Jules says that the bank looks like a drive-in burger joint in outer space. They love that building. We can't let those buildings be torn down," Tack adds.

I must have a confused look on my face about who Jules is exactly or maybe I missed something. I'm so bad at carrying on a simple friendly conversation. I think maybe I should ask who Jules is. This is exactly why I hate small talk with new people. Is Jules someone I should already know? Will anyone be offended if I ask? Should I ask? As if he is reading my mind, Danny steps in.

"Jules is Tack's adorable eight-year-old kid."

"Right," I say. Suddenly I remember hearing about Tack's kid and a Strawberry Dumpling doll or something. I can't believe I forgot. Glad I didn't ask. This is the kind of barbed wire that keeps me away from small talk.

"Don't let them hear you say that. They are eight and three quarters, almost nine in a few months," Tack says.

"Nine. That's a big one," Danny says. "Let me find something special in the store. There's a unicorn Beanie Baby with a glitter horn that I'm sure they would like."

"That's super sweet of you, Danny. We better let the two of you get back to whatever it is you do when you're in the store alone after hours," Tack says, with his signature grin pasted across his face. Vince sighs and puts his arm around Tack. You can almost feel their connection from where I'm standing. It's a sweet electricity and I wonder if it is contagious. Something stirs in me as I watch Danny smiling at them.

"I'm glad you came to New Hope, Prescott. I hope we'll be seeing more of you. Of both of you," Vince says and he shakes my hand. He and Tack step out of the shop into the cold night air.

We spend a few minutes restoring the shop to its previous

condition in silence. It's not the icy silence from moving in a few weeks ago. This silence is satisfying and comfortable. I think we both know tonight was a big success and that we have the support of the community behind us now. Now we can really make sure the city council and real estate developer listen to the community. We help each other move tables regardless of which side of the shop they are on, gather trash and put away folding chairs.

"Look! Look!" Danny says suddenly, pointing out the window. The lights that are still on make it hard to see through the reflection in the large panes of glass. Danny walks to the wall and hits the light switches so only the night lights are on and immediately the window glare disappears to reveal a moon so bright it illuminates the entire town. I can see down to the river and moonbeams almost dance across slippery waves like candlelight on glass.

"Hold on. I've got the perfect idea," Danny says and he grabs a black-and-red-plaid thermos and matching tote that he has for sale on his side and goes back to the pantry. A minute later he comes back holding the tote in one hand and his camera in the other. "It's a Snow Moon."

"A Snow Moon?"

"Yeah, the full moon that rises in February is called a Snow Moon. It's a Wolf Moon in January and you don't want to know what it is in March."

"I don't?" I ask playing along.

"In March it's called a Worm Moon." He shudders. "Isn't the very idea of that disgusting? But that's what they call it." He shrugs and it makes me laugh. He's always making me laugh. I used to think Danny's knowledge only revolved around toys and trinkets, but the truth is he knows a great deal about many things. Whereas my knowledge is so specific and focused, his is broad like an omnibus. "A moon like this when it's snowing will make the most extraordinary light. I put some of the leftover cocoa in a thermos and I've got my camera. Let's go take some pictures of the bank and Yardley House for social media. The moonlight reflecting off the snow will make that odd couple look stunning. What do you say?"

At first, I don't say anything. But then the feeling of exhilaration from being a part of something like this tonight overtakes me. I've spent so much time by myself in study carrels researching little-known facts about ephemera and I'm beginning to see what I've been missing. I usually would never accept an invitation like this, but tonight I just grab my blazer, square the brim on my Harris Tweed and say, "Let's go."

# Chapter Eleven

*Danny*

It's late enough that everything is closed and the sidewalks haven't been touched except for a few spots where prepared shop owners have salted the surface. It's not wide enough to walk next to Prescott so I let him go ahead of me.

My decision to let him lead is purely selfish. While I try to keep my mind on avoiding the slipperiest surfaces I'm actually staring at the nape of his neck. The space between where the tweed of his hat stops and where the collar of his coat begins is exposed. It's only a small patch of skin but it's so sexy. It's winter and his skin still retains a natural bronze tone. His slightly delicate earlobes stick out from under his hat and I wonder what he would say if I told him how much I want to nibble on them.

"Whoa," I say as my foot gives out from under me. Prescott turns around immediately and grabs my elbow to stop me from falling.

"You okay?" he asks. His blue eyes sharpening with sincere concern. He grabs my other elbow to steady me and now we are standing face-to-face, him holding my forearms. He looks at me and I look at him but before the moment becomes a moment I lose my footing again and begin to slip. I grab for a parking meter and use that to steady myself.

"Sorry. I hit a slippery patch. I'm not good at walking on snow. We didn't get much of it in Texas." The sidewalk widens and there is enough room to walk side by side.

"Is that where you grew up?" he asks.

"Yeah, mostly. I'm part Mexican and some of my extended family is in Mexico so I spent a lot of time there, but I went to school in Texas." I don't say I went to one of the most elite boarding schools in the state or that the library and art museum in our town were named after my family. "Texas doesn't really have seasons. Everything is sort of the same all year where I was. I love being up here, where every few months the world completely changes. It makes me feel like there are always possibilities for change." I'm dangerously close to having to say more about my background so I toss the focus back to him. "Where did you grow up?"

Prescott points across the river.

"You grew up in New Jersey?" I ask, unable to conceal the surprise in my voice.

Prescott laughs. "You don't have to worry. I'm used to that reaction."

"And I thought I was doing such a good job of covering up my surprise."

"Danny, you do not have a poker face in any way. Everything you think or feel is always shown in your eyes." He looks at me and shakes his head as if he has just said the most obvious thing in the world. "People look at me and think I'm very 'to the manor born' but that is *far* from the case." There is a hint of disdain in his voice that makes me wonder what he would think about my background. Would it bring this evening to a halt?

"What part of New Jersey?" I ask to keep the conversation moving.

"As we say in the Garden State, I grew up 'down the shore.'" He says the last part of the sentence in a pronounced Jersey accent that is too authentic not to be real. "And not in one of the idyllic retreats like Cape May. More like Atlantic City."

"Oooh, Atlantic City. I bet you strolled the boardwalk on summer days and ate saltwater taffy in the waves."

Prescott stops and looks at me. "Let me guess. You've never been to Atlantic City. It's nothing like that. At least not the part where I grew up. It's seedy and depressing and I hated it. The water smells and there's nothing for a kid to do. My dad was a blackjack dealer. Still is. I grew up in this cramped studio apartment on a street you'd recognize from Monopoly. It was hot in the summer and cold in the winter."

"Oh," I say, genuinely surprised by his revelation. "I had no idea."

"People see me surrounded by antiques and they hear my name and they assume a narrative for me. I was named after a character on a soap opera, if you're wondering, which is why I took such offense when you commented on my name when we met," he says without a hint of contempt.

"I'm sorry," I say. "Sometimes I just say whatever's in my head. I don't always have control over it. It just comes out."

"I can't imagine," Prescott says and then exhales and looks up at the sky. "Most of the stuff in my head just stays there." I get the feeling that he wants to let some of it out.

"I come from a big family. Everyone was always talking all the time so I just tried to keep up. The only time we weren't talking was when we were eating or sleeping. Oh, and even that's not true because one of my brothers talks in his sleep."

Prescott laughs and it's the exact reaction I'm looking for in the moment. I'm about to make another joke when I look at Prescott and realize I don't need to keep him laughing. I can maybe just ask him what I want to know and see where it takes us.

"Do you have any brothers and sisters?" I ask.

"No. I'm an only child and my mom passed when I was a kid. I spent a lot of time by myself."

My heart twitches a little hearing him say that. "I'm sorry," I say.

"Thank you." He takes a deep breath and stares straight ahead. I can tell he is uncomfortable sharing this much about himself, but I also see that he's trying to crack open just a bit. I feel him struggling and again quiet my own usual urge to make a joke or provoke him. I let him get where he needs to go with my silent support.

"Mostly growing up was lonely. When I was a kid I'd wait for hours on my own for my dad to finish his shift. Behind the glitzy casinos in A.C. are rows of pawn shops.

They had every kind of thing you could imagine. Tubas and skeletons and rare stamps and wedding dressings. There was this one shop where the lady knew me and my dad pretty well since he sold off almost anything we had that was worth anything. I'd go in there all the time. I got to know some of the merchandise well and every day Carol Ann would..." He stops midsentence and shakes his head like he's trying to change lanes.

I don't know what to do. Usually I would jump in and finish the sentence for him. Carol Ann would jump up and down like a deranged turkey? Eat a rack of ribs? What? What? I take a deep breath and quiet myself letting Prescott take the lead.

"I'm sorry," he says finally. "I've been talking too much."

"Not at all," I say realizing that he simply wants permission. "I want to hear more if you feel like telling me." I look right into his beautiful eyes so he knows I'm sincere.

Prescott looks back at me and starts talking again. "This woman, Carol Ann, she would teach me about all of the stuff right in the front of the store. She seemed to know everything about anything they had and her stories were fascinating."

"Is that how you first developed a love for antiques?" I ask searching his eyes to make sure I am not digging too deep.

"Exactly. She was an expert in coins and she taught me to tell the difference between a fake and the real thing. I had an eye for it and I got good at it. I loved hearing about the history of the coins." I love the thought of a tiny Prescott on his tiptoes looking over some case of ancient medallions. I wonder if he wore a tiny little tweed blazer but it also makes me sad to think of him there waiting for his dad.

"Are you close with your dad?" I ask.

"I guess. I mean he's very quiet and keeps to himself."

"Like you?" I say very gently as the moonlight illuminates our path. I'm not making a judgment. I'm trying to make an observation. Prescott is reserved and keeps everyone at a distance. I know it shouldn't, but seeing a crack in his exterior makes me want to rush in and open that crack more. But I'm careful. We walk a few yards in silence.

"I suppose I'm like him in that way." He wrinkles his nose just a bit as he says the words and it makes me think maybe he doesn't want to keep the world so far from him all the time.

"Sounds like Carol Ann is sweet. Are you still in touch with her?"

"No," he says sharply, and I wonder if I hit a sore point.

We get to a bench that overlooks the bank and the Yardley House. I use my hand to brush off some snow. Prescott sits next to me. Did I ask the wrong question?

"I'm not in touch with Carol Ann." He says the words slowly and deliberately. "One day," he starts very hesitantly and his willingness to share floods my heart. I make sure to listen carefully. "I walked over to the pawn shop excited about some new coin I had read about and there was Carol Ann, in handcuffs."

"What? That must have been devastating," I say and put my hand on his arm to comfort him. He looks down at it as if it is the license he needs to continue.

"It was. While I was in the front of the shop getting lessons from Carol Ann, the back of the shop had some nefarious criminal activity going on. The little boy at the counter was just a cover I guess. Or a distraction. I never found out."

"I'm sorry. I'm really sorry." I'm devastated to hear that anyone could manipulate a child like that either intentionally or unintentionally.

"Don't be," he says and shakes his head. "I learned a lot about history there and that's what I majored in at U Penn before getting my Master's in Decorative Arts there. I made sure I would never be able to get fooled by a fake again. I love spotting a forgery and exposing the guilty party." He folds his arms over his chest signaling a decision to change the subject. He's been incredibly open with me in ways that are clearly beyond his boundaries. "What about you and your dad or mom?" he asks clearly changing the focus of our chat. "Are you close?"

"Well everyone says I look exactly like my dad and he looked like his dad so we are definitely close in appearance. My dad was working all the time."

"Yours too? My dad would take any shift he could at the tables. Anything to pay the bills and make ends meet, right?"

"Yeah, something like that," I say hoping that isn't too much of a fib. I don't want the mood to change with some big reveal about how we never had to worry about money. He's just told me this devastating memory so I might not share too many details about the trust fund that has been a part of my life as long as my cowlick. Maybe for once I can keep my mouth shut.

I take out the mugs I snagged from the pantry and open the thermos. The steam from the hot cocoa rises up and I tilt the container toward him as he sits down next to me. "I put some marshmallows in so I'm sure they're nice and mushy now." I pour the milky brown liquid into a mug and hand him his before pouring one for myself. The snow has slowed down but there are still enough flakes that a few land on the surface of my cocoa and melt instantly. I hold my mug up in front on my face, letting the steam warm my skin.

"A toast," I say. "To saving the First Bank of Bucks *and* the Yardley House."

He smiles, holds up his mug and says, "To opposites." His grin warms me more than the mug in my hand. Honestly I don't know if he's toasting the buildings or us.

We clink and both take a sip of the hot beverage. The two buildings are such an odd couple. The bank on the left is all lines and windows while the one on the right is formal elegance. Something about the dusting of snow makes their differences merge in the moonlight. I should be taking some pictures for social media but the mood is too sweet and too gentle to start thinking about anything other than just being here in this moment.

"That's curious," Prescott says, taking a sip of his drink.

"It's cinnamon. I always put some in my hot chocolate. There is even a hint of nutmeg in there. It's a family thing." I don't tell him it's the recipe my grandfather built his whole food empire on. Amore Chocolate is the cornerstone of the empire but right now it's just cocoa in a thermos.

He chuckles softly and his breath makes brief clouds of moisture appear before his face. "Delicious but I mean I was just thinking... I've never told anyone about Carol Ann at the pawn shop before." He takes another sip and smiles.

"Why not? I mean I'm sorry it turned out so badly but

it's also nice to know that there was someone who helped you and encouraged you."

"I'm not good at talking about myself. I mean give me a piece of garniture and I can go on and on. But when people ask me about myself I always start with my time at U Penn. It's not like I'm embarrassed of how I was raised or where I grew up. But the deeper background is actually kind of messy."

"Well, I know how you feel about mess," I say raising my eyebrows.

"You're right. I don't like it. I like things organized and tidy. I like to study history because it is a series of events where one leads to another. Even though it's unpredictable it's something that can be contained because those are all events that have already happened."

"I get it," I say softly. I think I'm beginning to understand Prescott. He like things the way he does because he really struggles being in the moment. I noticed how much he hides from people when he isn't talking about antiques and I remember how quick he was to turn down that dinner invitation to Vince and Tack's. I don't think he was being a snob. I think he was scared. "Well maybe next time you tell the story of your life you should find a new beginning. I like to think of you as a young numismatic."

"Numismatic? Don't start going all stuffy on me," he says.

"Not a chance." I raise my mug again. "Another toast. To new beginnings."

Prescott raises his mug also and looks right in my eyes. I notice a few flakes have fallen on his thick lashes as he says, "To new beginnings." We clink mugs again but this time, our eyes never leave each other.

*Prescott*

My eyes are focused on his as the snow falls gently on both of us. A snowflake lands on his nose and melts. I think about brushing off the small droplet of water left behind. I've said more about myself tonight than I think I've ever shared with anyone before. He made it so easy. He made it so I wanted to do it and now I just want to be even closer to him.

I move my mouth closer to his. He tilts his head and that makes me stare at his lips. They're dry from the cold air and what I think they need more than anything is my lips on them. For a split second I think about fighting the urge to kiss him but I feel so close to him in the moment, so appreciative of the warmth of the evening despite the falling temperatures. I've worked so hard to keep myself in check to not show any cracks to anyone that when I finally do my entire being seems to want to emerge and right now it wants to share itself with Danny.

I close my eyes and slowly move toward his lips, hoping I'll find his easily. When I do, I'm suddenly aware of how connected I feel to this man who I thought I despised. When he invites me in, I accept the invitation warmly. My lips open gradually and my tongue begins to entwine with his. I can feel the snow landing on my cheeks, and the scent of hot chocolate and marshmallows wafts up from the mugs we have managed to somehow still hold on to. We are on a bench with snow falling all around us and the moon shining like a lantern in the sky. We are kissing.

I put my mug down on the bench and go to touch his face. The feel of his stubble against my hand is electric and the sensation goes straight from my finger to places deep inside me. A sharp wind races around us and I feel Danny shiver. I go to put my arms around him but he pulls back and shifts away from me.

"Brrr. That wind is cold," he says abruptly. "The snow's slowing down. We better get some good pics before it stops completely." He gets up from the bench like he's been ejected from it, grabs the camera and starts snapping away. I'm sitting by myself feeling like a balloon that has just been popped. What the hell is going on? How did we go from kissing so sweetly to a photo shoot in under five seconds?

"Danny," I say even though I'm not sure what will follow.

I put my hands to my lips. Am I that bad a kisser? Did I totally misread the signals? Was it all one-sided? I thought we were feeling something. I thought we were connecting. This is why I never open up to guys. It's not worth it. But that kiss...

I feel as unsure as I am confused. Only a few seconds ago we had our lips pressed against each other. Our tongues were just beginning to explore parts unknown. I felt him, not just physically. I felt his compassion, his understanding, his humor. How does he go from that to standing in the middle of a snow-covered road taking pictures of two buildings that are about to be torn down?

"Danny, what are you doing?" I ask calmly, hoping there is some explanation for this berserk behavior. I'm devastated. "I know we came here to take pictures but we were just..."

"About to miss this great shot. I agree," he says cutting me off swiftly. "I saw a few clouds approaching and the moonlight is so pretty right now that I didn't want them

to suddenly drift in front of the moon and ruin the pic."
He continues getting different angles. I don't see a single
cloud. In fact the flurries have stopped and the night air is
crisp and perfectly clear except for the giant Snow Moon
that hangs above us. I'm not a meteorologist but it doesn't
seem like there's even a chance of a cloud appearing.

I'm too humiliated by him bouncing away from me to
say anything and too hurt to participate in his pretend excuse for a photo shoot. I just sit on the bench, more uncomfortable with each passing second.

"You know I thought maybe you were a reasonable
person," I say breaking my steely silence. "But I see now
you must have laced the cocoa with something because I
think I temporarily lost my mind," I say unable to contain
myself any longer. I don't know what else to do. Danny
is ignoring me. He continues to take pictures like I'm not
even there with him. I'm beginning to feel invisible. How
can he neglect me like this after I shared more with him
tonight than I've shared with anyone in a long time? After
I just had my lips on his beautiful face and felt his scruff
against my cold cheek. He left me midkiss with my lips
puckered to cold air.

"Danny," I say quietly and the only sound in response
is the snow crunching under his feet as he works the shot.
"Danny!" I say again much louder but the silence from him
is just as loud. I can't take it anymore and shout, "Danny,
stop it! Why are you being such a jerk?"

He lets his camera drop to his waist and freezes. We
are staring at each other. I don't know what is happening
in this moment. Maybe he'll come back to the bench and

finish what we started or maybe he'll walk away and we'll never mention it again.

"I knew it," he says turning his face away from me. "I knew you would eventually say something insulting like that. We came out here to take pictures and all I'm doing is making sure I'm getting the best shots. That makes me a jerk?" A gust of cold air sweeps around us. "Here," he says walking over to me. As soon as he is within kissing distance again my entire body tenses. For a second I think maybe we are having a breakthrough but instead he hands me the camera. "It's a self-explanatory DSLR. Take as many pictures of your precious Yardley House as you want." He puts the camera in my hands and then goes to the bench and starts packing up the thermos and mugs.

"You're leaving?" I ask, my voice made dull by the patches of snow.

"I've got some work to do."

"It's almost midnight," I say.

"Just bring the camera in tomorrow. I'll download the images for social off the card." He grabs his stuff and disappears around the corner.

"Wait… Danny… Danny." I call after him but he's already gone around the corner. I go back to the bench we were sitting on and stare straight ahead. I can't believe what I did. Opening myself up like that and then not being able to see the difference between friendly chitchat and flirting. He kissed me back. I know he did. But then why did he jump up and try to pick some stupid fight with me? I'll take a pair of pewter candlesticks over a guy any day of the week. Pewter is easier to figure out.

# Chapter Twelve

*Danny*

I walk away from Prescott with my thermos and mugs but as soon as I'm around the corner and sure he can't see me, I run. The sidewalk is icy and there's a good chance I might fall and break both my arms, not to mention the two precious midcentury ladybug mugs I'm carrying in the tote, but I don't care. I need to get as far away from him as I can. I run all the way back to my apartment and up the stairs straight to Lizard's room. I open the door. The lights are off and she is clearly sound asleep. I sit down next to her snoring face.

"Lizard, are you awake?" I ask shoving her with my hand. She doesn't move. "Lizard," I say a little louder but my shove is more like a strong poke.

"Get your finger out of my belly button," she grumbles through clenched teeth, eyes still closed.

"Oh, good, you're awake," I say turning on the lamp next to her and crawling into her bed.

"Danny, what are you doing? I gotta work a double tomorrow." She puts her pillow over her head and turns the lamp off.

"He kissed me," I announce.

"Oh, crap," I hear from under the pillow.

"I know, right?" I say in agreement.

"Not you," she says, removing the pillow and sitting up like a jack-in-the-box that has just been released. She turns the lamp on. "Oh crap, me. I owe Vince twenty bucks. He had tonight. I had next Tuesday. It was the only square left by the time it got to me."

"Please don't tell me what I think you are telling me. There isn't a pool about me and Prescott kissing. Tell me there isn't."

"Okay, there isn't," she says in a tone that tells me there absolutely is. "But, can you lend me twenty bucks?"

"This is exactly what I didn't want to happen. I don't need this pressure. I don't want to be with anyone right now, you know that."

"Then why did you kiss him?"

"That's not exactly how it happened." I sigh, lying down next to her in bed and staring up at the ceiling. I thought maybe once I broke the spell of the moonlight I would be able to stop thinking about how his lips felt on mine, but it's all I can think of.

"How exactly did it happen?"

"He kissed me," I say. "*He* kissed *me*." It's so hard for me to believe that I have to say it out loud twice. "Can you believe it, Lizard?"

"What are you talking about? Of course I can believe it. It's so obvious he has a thing for you. I saw how he was looking at you at the meeting. At one point I thought Serilda was going to put on Luther Vandross, light some candles and make us all leave so the two of you could get it on."

"Oh, that's not true," I say waving her away.

I close my eyes. I have to struggle to push the image of Prescott's face so close to mine out my brain. I don't want to be the center of town gossip. "This is bad. So bad."

"Why? He kissed you. That's great. How was it?"

"Wonderful," I say immediately. The word races out of my mouth before my brain can stop it. The truth is it was wonderful. I felt connected to him, and the kiss was such a natural progression. "It couldn't have been more perfect except for the small fact that it never should have happened."

"Why? Because you work together? So what? It's not like you're his boss or he's yours."

Certainly working together is an issue. Not an issue of a power imbalance but still it's a bit of an issue. The bigger issue is more complicated.

I sit on the bed and hold my legs. Lizard does the same and grabs my hands. "Danny, what's going on? Just tell me."

I'm intentionally silent for a few moments.

"Is it Paul?"

My throat and the muscles in my back tighten.

"I'm sorry he hurt you that way," she says putting her hand on my chest and rubbing gently. "That guy is such a…"

"I know. He is. I mean, he was. I'm not hung up on Paul. I'm not. It's just that…" I can barely finish the sentence. Finding Paul in our bed with another man was so painful. My mind flashes to walking in on them naked and entwined. Waiting in the kitchen as the personal trainer that I paid for each week got dressed. Discovering he had maxed out three of my credit cards. I trusted him and thought he loved me. But I was so wrapped up in pleasing him that I couldn't see the truth. That's more painful than anything else. When Paul said he was stressed I immediately booked a trip to Costa Brava. When he was bored with his workout I hired an exclusive personal trainer for him. Not my greatest idea.

"Lizard," I say and swallow hard. "The problem is when I fall for a guy I completely lose myself and ruin the entire thing. Paul turned out to be a colossal jerk, but if I hadn't jumped in so hard and fast I would have seen the signs. I don't want to do that again. I want to focus on my business not someone else right now. I can't."

"I guess that makes sense," Lizard says brushing her hand on my arm for comfort. Her care makes me feel a bit more confident in my decision,

"Signing the lease for the shop wasn't just about starting a new business. It's about starting a new chapter in my life. Leaving my family's shadow to start something on my own, supporting myself with my own income. Standing on my own two feet. With Paul I was throwing money around to the point that I didn't even know who I was or why I was doing it. I do it all the time with guys and I don't want to do that again."

"Danny, if you really have feelings for this guy you won't act like you did with Paul. And you aren't the kind of person who can hold back their emotions. That isn't you. You always follow your heart even when it leads you down some rough roads."

"Well, not tonight. For the first time ever I found the emergency brake. I could feel things heating up and before it could go any further I jumped up and pushed him away."

"Huh? I don't get it. What did you do?" she asks yawning but engaged.

"Oh, Lizard, it was awful. I'm so embarrassed." I cringe thinking about how mean it was but it was a fight or flight moment and I chose both. "I started taking pictures, which was the pretense for being out there in the first place. I just got up midkiss… I was enjoying it too much. I knew deep down that if it went on even a second longer it would be too late. I knew I'd be hooked on him. But I'm not sure I got away in time."

"So now he thinks it was just a what? A lip slip?"

"Yes, that's it. A lip slip. One that will never happen again."

I smile at her, hoping she will believe me. Pulling away from Prescott was painful and immature. I know it. I felt like a kid who gets his tongue stuck to a frozen flagpole on a dare. I loved having our tongues entwined and waiting to see what would happen next but I had to stop it. I had to shut it down because the fact is I could very easily fall for Prescott and once I start falling I'm all in and start trusting guys I shouldn't and doing things I shouldn't. It's better to stop it before it gets out of control again, right?

"Hey, Lizard?" I ask softly. "Is it okay if I just sleep in here with you tonight?" I ask. Her bed is huge and we've done this before when one of us had a stressful day or disaster date. It just feels good to sleep and know that there is someone near you sometimes.

"Of course." She turns off the lamp and rolls over to the other side of the bed and starts snoring.

I stare up at the ceiling. The Snow Moon creates shadows so crisp that the branches from the tree outside the window appear like shadow puppets across the room. I notice one branch intertwined with another that creates a cluster of dark shapes that combine to create one continuous figure. It might as well be a silhouette of Prescott and me on the bench in the snow kissing. I close my eyes and try to sleep holding on to that beautiful image, but I know that once the sun rises, the shadows will have disappeared.

# Chapter Thirteen

*Prescott*

I keep replaying last night in my mind as I'm sitting at my desk alone in the shop staring out the window. I see us setting up for the event, Danny making me feel confident about giving my talk, seeing him beam at me during my lecture. Feeling so comfortable with him that I just opened up and told him things I don't really tell anyone. But it's not even what I said. It's how he made me feel.

I can't stop thinking about it all—the snow, the hot cocoa and the moon illuminating the whole town as we sat on the bench next to each other.

Finally, the kiss.

I bring my fingers to my lips. I can still feel how his

mouth felt on mine and how his scruffy beard rubbed against my cheeks. The snow from last night has settled and a sharp wind is making its way through the streets and alleys of New Hope. My mind was so preoccupied with going over the details from last night that I barely felt the cold as I walked across the bridge this morning to the store. Then a gust of wind attacked my exposed skin and *boom*, I remembered the humiliation of him jumping up, away from me.

I get up and head to the pantry when I notice that there are four blue creatures sitting on a shelf next to my garniture—an urn, matching candlesticks and elegant castor set in crystal. At first it makes me giggle to see the little creatures mixed with my pieces. They must have gotten mixed on my side when we were cleaning up last night. My smile grows until I remember how it felt when Danny ripped his lips away from mine and my smile vanishes. It's replaced by the attitude I usually show the world—reserved and in control.

I've worked very hard to make sure my displays are perfectly arranged; the last thing I want is some of Danny's toys mixed with my merchandise. I walk over to the shelf and pick one up. This particular blue elf is brushing his teeth, the toothbrush up to his mouth and a tube of toothpaste that he has squeezed hard enough for the paste to wriggle out of the top in his hand. I can't help but smile. It's so silly and overdone and childish. It looks ridiculous next to the sleek crystal bottle in the castor set which is also overdone but in a much more serious and somewhat maudlin way. Seeing the two together makes me think how Danny would appreciate this and that makes me laugh out loud.

"What's so funny?" I hear Danny ask as he walks in the store. Just seeing him again makes me want to run over and give that kiss a second try but my brain steps in and tells me that he's already rejected me once and that's more than enough. I won't humiliate myself again. "Nothing," I say sharply, putting the figure down.

"Hey, is that Toothy? What's he doing over there?" he asks, his big smile brightening the room in a way that I can't deny. He wants to pretend like last night didn't happen? Fine. I can do that as well.

"That's an excellent question," I say with a tone sharper than the spires of Notre Dame. "What is *your* merchandise doing on my side of the shop? We've made very clear rules about who is responsible for which displays. I kindly ask that you keep your toys on your side of the store. My customers do not want little blue men on their antiques."

He walks over and grabs each of them. "I've told you before. They're called Smurfs."

"I don't care what they're called. I don't want them over here," I say, trying not to look at him.

He walks back to his side and then stops. "I thought you said you ordered more wood for the potbelly." He looks at the small stack of remaining logs to the side of the stove.

I forgot to order wood but I'm not going to let him get the better of me. "We have enough to get through the end of the week. I'll order it later."

"It's supposed to snow more. You know the truck they use to deliver the firewood won't be able to get through the alley if it's covered in snow," he says taking one of the smaller logs and adding it to the fire I started when I walked in earlier.

"So what? We have a boiler and the tank has enough oil to get us through until summer if we need it."

"That's not the point. Why burn oil when we can use wood? It's less expensive to use wood and you shouldn't rely on fossil fuels. You should be thinking about that."

"Should I? Do you think I'm not aware of my carbon footprint? I know exactly what I'm doing so thank you very much," I snap at him. Just like that we are back to our old dynamic, whether we like it or not. It's like last night was deleted from the timeline. I watch him take off his coat and as he pulls off his sweater the front edge rises up over his furry midsection and I know that last night happened because I'm feeling the same feeling I felt then. Still, I have to shut it off. In my head I pick up my sabre and shout, "En garde!"

"You always think you know better, don't you," Danny says his voice already louder than it should be.

I match his volume. "When I'm right, then yes. I do know better. Of course, you make it easy when you spout such nonsense."

"Nonsense?" he shouts.

"You heard me," I shout back and then we just start screaming at each other until the bells on the door chime.

Arthur walks in.

"I'd like to think the two of you would be celebrating last night's success, but from the sound of things it seems like that's not the case."

Last night. A huge success followed by a devastating humiliation. I'm not sure if I can think of one without the other.

"What's going on here?" Arthur asks.

"Oh, no big deal," I say not wanting to let Arthur know that we have turned his sweet shop into a boxing ring.

"Actually," Danny says before I can add anything else, "we were having a disagreement about ordering supplies for the shop. It seems someone forgot to place an order for firewood."

I laugh through clenched teeth. "Oh, Danny. We've already gone over this. We don't need firewood until next week." My pleasant tone is as fake as the wax flowers he sells in old Coke bottles. "You need to keep your merchandise…"

"Stop it. The two of you can't even agree on what you're disagreeing about."

Danny and I both lower our heads like schoolboys caught fighting in front of the headmaster. "I thought last night was a tremendous success. I had breakfast with Serilda and they are already operating with all pistons. Serilda has a phone call in to the mayor's office." Arthur smiles each time he says the name Serilda.

"You've already had breakfast with them this morning?" Danny says with a sly tone revealing that he might have the same suspicions I've been having about them being a couple.

"With Serilda?" I ask with a sly smile. "Who was looking absolutely lovely last night I might add."

"Yes, they were in that cute little red parka with the trim." Danny picks up my lead and goes with it. Why is it that when we are on the same path we sort of have this unspoken way of working together? We start asking Arthur a series of questions that make the skin behind his translucent gray beard just pink enough to let us know we are hitting the target.

Arthur can't help but release a tight smile. "I did not come in here to be interrogated by the two of you. I came here to update you on the delivery van. There was a small problem with the suspension but the mechanic promises me that it's as good as new now. I have it parked in the spot around the corner in case you need it."

"That's perfect," I say. "I need it this weekend."

Danny walks over to me and says, "Ah, not so perfect and not so fast. I need the van this weekend too."

Far in the distance I swear I can hear the echoey whistles and reverberating brass of the theme song from some classic cowboy Western. I'm ready for a shootout.

*Danny*

"I've had this weekend on my calendar for months," I say. "I *need* the van. The St. Stanislaw Church Rummage Sale only comes once a year. I always get some major pieces and the elders make me a special order of pierogi, not to mention the pastries. I'm not missing it."

"A rummage sale? Are you kidding me?" Prescott asks. I'm growing to love watching his pupils flicker when he gets angry with me. I swear I get him going sometimes just to see the way it makes his eyes dance but I know making him angry is also a way of distancing us from any tender moment we may or may not have had last night. "This weekend is the McKinley estate sale at Brown Brothers. They're auctioning off some of the finest items to be found this season on the entire Eastern Seaboard. I need to be there. They have a piece of Cunningham pewter that will complete my set. It raises the importance of my collection considerably."

"Well, la di da," I say putting my finger to my nose to raise the tip. "God forbid you don't have a matched set." I knew it. This guy is so obsessed with aesthetic uniformity. There's no way we could ever make it as a couple. I don't know what I was thinking.

"Do you see the vulgarity I have to endure, Arthur?" Prescott sighs dramatically.

"Do you see the snobbishness I put up with?"

"If only the two of you could see what I see," Arthur mumbles as he rubs his face with his hands. "Wait, Danny, your rummage sale is in the morning, at St. Stanislaw?"

"Right," I say nodding, but wondering what he has up his sleeve.

"And Prescott, Brown Brothers is doing the auction. They don't usually start the smalls until after lunch if I recall," Arthur says, clearly cooking up something in his head.

"Smalls?" Danny asks.

"Smalls refers to anything smaller than a biscuit box in the antiques trade," Arthur explains.

"Oh, so my Smurfs would be smalls," I say.

"The thought that those pieces of plastic would be part of any serious auction house's collection is beyond ridiculous."

"Prescott, please, I'm trying to find a solution," Arthur says, stroking his beard.

"What scheme do you have in mind?" I ask.

"Well since the rummage sale is in the morning and the auction is in the afternoon you could simply share the van," Arthur says matter-of-factly.

"But our events are in opposite directions. If I had to drive all the way back to New Hope just to hand off the van..." I start to say.

"...then I would never make it to the auction in time," Prescott says completing my thought. The synchronism of the moment does not go unnoticed and it makes me melt a little inside. We are so often on the same path until one of us drives into a ditch.

Arthur takes off his gloves to warm his hands in front of the potbelly stove. He sighs, turns around to look at us both and says, "Precisely."

"Arthur, if this is some reenactment of the judgment of Solomon and you plan to cut the van in half, don't bother," Prescott says.

Arthur laughs. "No nothing quite so dramatic. Prescott, you join Danny in the morning and then Danny, you join Prescott for the second half of the day. That way you don't have to drive all the way back here. And as a bonus I will donate my time to watch the shop while you two are out picking."

The whole day with Prescott? Avoiding the way his sapphire eyes narrow as he examines an antique? Ignoring how cute he looks when his bangs fall in front of his face and he gathers them with one hand before pushing them back? Making sure that no matter what we don't have even an inch of physical contact? It's not a day out with the van.

It's a game of Operation with little chance of the patient's red-bulb nose not turning on.

"Absolutely not," Prescott says.

I join the protest. "No way."

Arthurs frowns and looks at us both. He puts his gloves back on and walks toward the door. "I guess you aren't interested in bidding on the pewter from the Cunningham Studio that I know would complete your set. And Danny, I'm sure you can wait another year to get your special order of pierogi."

I gasp. "Uncle Arthur, you're not playing fair. You know I look forward to those pierogi more than my birthday."

"I have wanted to get that piece of pewter in my collection for years." Prescott's voice goes up at the end and he looks at me and wriggles his nose.

"Then it's settled. You will share the van," Arthur declares although neither of us has exactly agreed to it.

Prescott shrugs and says, "Fine."

"Fine," I say knowing it's impossible to argue with a man as sweet as Uncle Arthur.

"See what happens when the two of you work together?" Arthurs says. His face beams like a child who has just been told she can have cake for breakfast. "I'm leaving the keys here." He puts them down on the table by the side of the door. "I hope you both find exactly what you need." He walks out the door and waves his hand backward at us as he goes.

I look at Prescott. He looks at me. I pretend I have no idea what Arthur is talking about.

# Chapter Fourteen

*Prescott*

It's so cold Saturday morning I think parts of my body might freeze and break off as I walk across the bridge toward New Hope in the dark. Danny insisted I meet him at the shop at the obscene hour of 6:30 a.m. Considering what a jerk he has been to me this week he's lucky I got out of bed early to be on time. I swear he is the most confusing, annoying, *sexiest* guy I've ever met. I stop in my tracks. Why does *sexiest* stay on that list? I resume my stride and ignore my last thought. I do not understand how you can go from kissing someone on a bench one night to fighting with them nonstop the next week. I suppose I could have approached the subject and found an adult way to talk to him but it was too humiliating. What am I supposed to do, ask, "Hey, Danny, why did you stop kissing me the other night? Do you find me grotesque or did my breath smell or both?" What's he supposed to say? It doesn't take a genius to figure out that you stop kissing someone because you do not want to be kissing them. At least he's being honest in his feelings.

When I arrive I see that Danny has already gotten the van warmed up and is in the driver's seat. "Good morning," I grumble as I open the passenger side door and pop on my sunglasses despite the complete lack of sun.

"Hello, hello, hello," he says as if he is about to burst into song. He's wearing a Fair Isle knit sweater in deep greens and blue. The semicircular pattern makes his already-broad shoulders look even more impressive. His body is so different than mine. I'm toned but thin. He's thick and strong. I'm in the van all of eight seconds and I'm already focused on his body. Today should be a breeze.

He hands me a travel mug. "This is a coconut latte to say thanks for getting up so early. I hope that's what you like. I thought I smelled coconut from your side of the shop the other day, and I remembered you had one when we met with Serilda." I take the lid off and the comforting scent of coconut warms my nose. Danny really does pay attention to detail. It's impressive.

"Thank you," I say taking a sip of the delicious drink, hoping it will wake me up. Why does he have to go and do something sweet when I'm still stinging from what he did the other night. Could he possible regret the way things turned out? I push the thought out of my mind as he drives out of the parking spot and we start up the road with the river on our right. The sun begins to peek through the gathering clouds and I'm reminded of the ungodly hour. "Did we have to leave so early?" I ask.

"The sale doesn't officially start until 8:00, but I like to get there at 7:00."

"Are you telling me I could have had an hour more of sleep?" I ask over my sunglasses.

"I'm telling you the ladies at this church make the best *paczki* you've ever tasted."

"I got up this early for a donut?"

"Oh, so I see you are no stranger to the fried deliciousness of the Polish people. So you know we have to get there early to get them fresh. There is a woman at the church named Kasia who makes them exactly like my mom made them growing up."

The sun begins to poke through streaks of gray and the barren trees look almost black in silhouette. It feels like we are the only car on the road.

"Is your mom Polish?" I ask. It's not like me to just blurt out a question like that. The thought sort of bubbled out on its own. I realize I know very little about his background except his father is a chef of some sort. I think.

"My mother's whole family is actually from Poznan in Poland but most of my Dad's is from Mexico. I actually grew up eating a combination of *paczki* and the *conchas* my aunt made sometimes. I suppose you're familiar with *conchas* as well," he says raising one eyebrow.

"As a matter of fact I am and I prefer the pink variety," I

say letting him know that I've eaten my share of the sweet soft dough.

"I'll make a note," he says and his eyebrow lowers.

"Did your mom work?" I hope it isn't too personal a question. Am I supposed to ask this differently? I never know.

"Oh, my mom did this and that," he says not really giving me an answer. I told him my dad was a blackjack dealer so I can't imagine his mom did something I would look down upon, but I guess I still give off a snobby impression sometimes.

Small clusters of ice move down the river in the opposite direction we are headed. The roads are clear but frozen mounds of icy plowed snow line the edges. I take a sip of the latte to abate the chill that threatens from the outside.

"This is delicious. Mona really outdid herself. I didn't know the Honeysuckle was open so early on a Saturday."

Danny grins and checks something in the rearview mirror but I think he might be catching a look at me so I turn my head just a bit making sure I'm showing off my best side.

"I made the latte myself," Danny says raising his eyebrows just a bit.

"You made this?" I ask, my voice rising at least half an octave.

"I'm not *just* a handsome burly shopkeep. I'm also an excellent at-home barista."

I take a sip and say, "Thank you. It's delicious." I don't tell him my surprise isn't in his ability, it's in his generosity. Although when I think about it, I shouldn't be surprised at all. I constantly watch Danny opening the door for people, taking extra care to wrap a package or giving a discount when someone is in a bind. Danny got up extra early to make something he knew I would enjoy. I take another sip of my latte and let the sweetness linger on my tongue. It makes me think of the sweetness of feeling his tongue against mine. Why can't I stop thinking about that kiss or the devastating way he ended it? If only I knew why? Of course I could come right out and ask him but that's way beyond my psychosocial abilities. I'm still treading the water with small talk. Still, I wish I had some insight about what's going on in that handsome head of his.

After driving for almost an hour past snow-covered forests and frozen ponds we start down a road that climbs to one of the highest hills in the area. The trees begin to thin and the land becomes open and unending with snowy whiteness creating soft blankets across the empty fields. An impressive brown and gray stone church with a bright red arched door sits at the top of the hill. As we get closer I notice a string of icicles have formed just above the front entrance. Danny parks in the back near the church hall entrance, and once he does I tell him I'll wait for him in the van. The less interaction I have with him, the better. I don't want my heart getting any more ahead of my brain.

"It's freezing, Prescott. They have a great little cafeteria. Just come inside," Danny says. Waiting in the van might cause hypothermia. Still, it's a tough call.

"Fine," I say and get out, but before I close the door I see Danny running over to a woman standing in front of the open tailgate of an ancient station wagon.

"Kasia, do not even think of lifting those heavy boxes.

I was hoping I would beat you here. Remember how you hurt your back last year?" He grabs a box out of her station wagon. "You just go inside. If you see Andrej you tell him he is *not* to try moving that speaker again. That's why I'm here. I can't have my favorite church elders in the ER."

I thought Danny would be making a beeline for donuts and ugly knick-knacks, but that isn't what's happening at all. We didn't get to the rummage sale early this morning so Danny could leap on the bargains or taste fresh donuts like he said. We got here so he could help a bunch of seniors who seem to adore him and rely on him.

*I'm on to you, Mr. Danny Roman.*

*Danny*

Prescott walks toward the church hall as I carry the sewing machine Kasia has brought for the rummage sale across sporadic spots of gravel and ice. She might as well be selling a Buick because it would weigh as much.

"Thank you Danielek. That one's a little heavy. You have certainly earned your pierogi this year. You still like extra cheese?"

I nod. Prescott calls to me, "Danny, do you want help with that?"

"No, no," I say grunting. "It's a one-man job. I'll see you inside." If he helps me there is a chance that our fingers could touch and I'm sure even in this cold air there would be a spark so intense a few pacemakers might go on the fritz.

Once Prescott is inside Kasia runs over to me. "Danny, Danny," she says excitedly. "Is that your new young man?"

"No," I say, trying not to drop the sewing machine.

"He's so handsome. What a face on that one. Like an angel. Are you sure?" She's talking to me like I'm sitting across from her at a table and not carrying the land mass of a small country between my arms.

"I'm sure," I say barely getting the words out and putting down the sewing machine. "He's only here because he works with me at the shop and we share a van. This is a business outing. That's all."

Kasia looks toward the door Prescott went in and then at me. "Look, it's been a while since my pilot light has made a pot of water boil and I may need cataract surgery according to my doctor but, *kohanie*, even I can see the way he looked at you when you were outside."

"How exactly did he look at me?"

"He looked at you the same way my Michelle looked at me. Danielek, my boy. He is definitely smitten." She nods slowly with a grin that's half mischief and half sweetness.

I pick up the sewing machine again and slip on the gravel. I almost fall to the ground but Kasia puts her arm on my back just in time for me to stay standing upright. It takes me a second to catch my breath. She opens the door to the church hall and I think about going to the rectory, lighting a candle and saying a few prayers to make her prediction wrong.

I help a few of the other parishioners with their tasks before the doors open. I've been going to this rummage sale for years and I've gotten to know a lot of the community even though I'm not part of the church officially. They are mostly older folks, many of them Polish, so I get to practice a few of the phrases my mom taught me as I help them move things around and do some of the other grunt work that might be too difficult.

This sale is one of the biggest in the region and I always come away with a big haul at a reasonable price. The church hall is filled with a well-organized inventory of things from lamps to linens.

Once the doors open to the public I start scouring the rooms for things that I might be able to sell in the shop. There's a Teenage Mutant Ninja Turtles Party Wagon that's only missing one wheel, an incomplete set of Holly Hobby mugs featuring those signature country braids, a huge mid-century long-pile rug with purple and magenta stylized flowers and an old-style toboggan with smooth weathered wood and enough room for two people. But the piece de resistance is a ginormous painting of a sad clown holding a drooping flower in one hand. I've put the small things in the van, but I decide, as much as I loathe to ask, I need Prescott's help with the painting. It's just too large.

I settle up at the cash box station and thank everyone for a great sale. I see Prescott in the church kitchen. I expect him to be studying one of his books or on his phone planning how we'll get to the estate sale but he isn't. He's in the kitchen with Kasia, behind the line, wearing a pink apron with ruffles down the side. He looks ridiculous and adorable.

I walk over to make sure what I see isn't some kind of hallucination.

"Your friend, he has such good hands for making

pierogi." Kasia grabs Prescott's hands and holds them out to me in front of the bowls of dough, cheese and mushrooms.

"Who knew?" he says and his smile beams across the kitchen at me so brightly I almost use my arm to block it. What has gotten into him? I guess Polish cuisine was an undiscovered passion.

"Danielek, you know how to make pierogi," she says to me and then turns to Prescott. "I've been teaching him the past few years."

"Yes, Kasia is an excellent teacher but I promised Prescott we would get to an important estate sale this afternoon." Kasia is as subtle as a kielbasa sandwich.

"Danielek, you're usually not so impatient," she says pooh-poohing me. "I just need one more dozen of these and he's doing very good. Almost as good as you." She puts her hand over his and teaches him how to press the dough together tightly but not too tightly. "See how I use a gentle pressure and just little bit cold water." Prescott is usually so well put together. It's funny to see his hands full of sticky dumpling dough, in an apron covered in flour. His usually perfect part is definitely not so perfect.

"Don't forget to buy your tickets for the fifty-fifty raffle. We will have our first drawing in ten minutes," someone announces from the floor of the cafeteria.

"Oh, fifty-fifty raffle. I forgot. I have to buy tickets," Kasia says suddenly. She wipes her hands on her apron and then walks over and pulls me next to Prescott. She grabs my hands and places them over his. "Here, Danielek. You know how to do. You show him. Best way to learn is through hands," she says and takes off her apron.

As soon as there is skin to skin contact I feel my heart run like a dog to its owner up my throat. I immediately lift my hands off Prescott's. Kasia looks back and sees the disconnect. "Tsk, tsk. Danielek," she says with an overexaggerated frown. "You know you must get the pressure exactly right. Please, *kohanie*, I don't want them to explode when they cook." She looks sternly at my hands and then at Prescott's hands. It's a standoff and I don't have much choice in the matter. I sigh to signal my surrender and put my hands back on Prescott's, who is most likely oblivious to what is going on. As soon as she sees my hands on his she smiles broadly and leaves the kitchen.

I take a second to just feel Prescott's hands under mine. They are strong but also smooth and elegant. My hands are thick with hair even above and below the knuckle. I can feel the heat from his hands radiate across my palms and I try to keep the rest of my body as far away from him as possible. The only way to get through this is to focus on the pierogi.

"After you have the seam wet you just need to press along the edge like this," I say like a surgeon narrating a complicated procedure. I swallow hard trying not to think of how close his body is to mine; how close our lips are again. I should just walk away. I know what Kasia is up to and the world won't stop if a dozen pierogi explode but the truth is I'm enjoying feeling his fingers underneath mine. The pretense of making the dumplings is silly but I'm willing to go with it if it means an opportunity to be close to Prescott without concern of it going any further.

He presses the next dumpling closed and I feel his hand

respond to the pressure from mine. The rummage sale and last call for the fifty-fifty raffle are going on outside the kitchen but we work in silence. He spoons the last bit of filling onto the final pierogi and now his hand is under mine. I'm just along for the ride and enjoying every second of it. He has the technique down perfectly which isn't surprising. Everything he touches seems to yield to his perfection.

"That's the last one," he says without looking up from the flour-covered counter. I see the corners of his mouth rise up in a satisfied smile.

I take my hands off his and step away from him like he just announced he was radioactive. The pretense is gone so any lingering touching of body parts is a bad idea. I'm trying to keep my distance from him and was doing an average job at it until this impromptu adventure into Polish cuisine.

"What's wrong?" he asks softly.

"Oh, nothing," I say. "I know you want to get to your estate sale and I don't want you to miss that pewter thing. I've loaded most of my things in the van and don't worry, there's plenty of room."

"I'm not worried," he says with a crooked smile that makes me think he knows something I don't. We wash our hands next to each other in the sink and by the time we are rinsing he is still smiling. I enjoy making pierogi, but I've never come close to enjoying it as much as he seems to have.

"Are you okay?" I ask wondering what has gotten into him.

He keeps rinsing, but then turns off the water in his sink

and dries his hands. He looks at me and says, "Who me? I'm fine. Actually, never been better." A strange smile is still on his face. "But I wanted to ask you..."

His eyes look the same way they did in the moonlight. I feel like I'm about to go under his spell again so I quickly interrupt. "Wait, before you finish that thought," I interject. "I wanted to ask you to help me move something into the van."

"Sure," he says with more enthusiasm than I expect. "But then can we..."

"Yeah, yeah, yeah," I say quickly cutting him off so I don't really have to commit to anything. I walk to the door where I left the painting and drag it inside the kitchen and say, "Isn't this going to look amazing in the shop?" I know the sad clown is exactly the kind of kitsch that makes Prescott nauseated. He'll turn blue when he sees the painting and start yelling about how he's not going to have his fine antiques next to something as hideous as this clown painting, how black velvet is not an appropriate canvas, yadda, yadda.

"What? In the world? Is that thing?" he asks, his eyes widening like I just revealed a killer python in my hands.

"That thing, as you call it, is art. Look how the brush stroke reveals the texture of the velvet and the expression on the clown is so meaningful. You see, he's sad but he's also a clown." I do a Celine and gently pound my chest with my fist. "Oh, the irony of it all. I can't decide if this should go in the window or maybe next to the door so it is the very first thing people see when they walk in."

He walks over and stands between me and the painting.

I look to make sure he hasn't grabbed a knife to shred the velvet canvas, and when I'm sure he hasn't I just stand there smiling. I know this will make him absolutely explode. He breathes in through his nose like a bull about to charge a matador and then says rigidly through clenched teeth. "You want to put that on display in our shop?"

I nod my head and smile brightly. "Uh-huh."

He looks at the painting and I know I'm about to see cartoon steam coming out of his ears. I hunker down, ready for one of our brawls, ready to put him in his place with his snobby attitude and bring to light how different we are. *Bring it, Prescott.*

He looks at the painting again and then at me. He moves even closer to me and I can feel what I think is his building anger. He looks me in the eyes and says, "Great. It's lovely. I'm sure it will look very nice wherever you put it. Let me help you carry it."

"What?" I feel like a rocket that has just failed to launch.

"I said that I think it will look very nice in the shop. But we should wrap it with some of the materials I have in the van. I don't want it to get damaged. I'll be right back."

Prescott walks out the door to the parking lot and I'm left in the kitchen wondering exactly what kind of mushrooms are in those pierogi.

# Chapter Fifteen

*Prescott*

This time I'm in the driver's seat and I'm quite enjoying it. Danny isn't sure where we are or what's going on and I'm kind of enjoying seeing him so flustered. "I think we missed a turn back at the dairy farm up the hill," he says.

"Relax," I say shifting gears. "I know exactly where we're going." I keep my eye on the road but make sure the most devilish smile I can conjure appears across my face. Danny thinks he can just pull the plug on what we started last week. After what Kasia told me in the kitchen privately, I'm not going to keep pretending he doesn't make me smile from ear to ear or cover my laughter at his silly jokes with a fake cough or quick sip of coffee. When he finally went to scour for bargains, I went into the kitchen, where Kasia cornered me alone and—unsolicited—helped me put everything into context.

"So, you have feelings for Danielek?" she asked as soon as the door swung closed behind her.

"What? Who? Me?" I stammered. "Feelings? For Danny?"

Without missing a beat she grabbed a woman spoon, held it near my face and said, "Feelings. You. Danny. You have, yes?" I kept walking backward until she had me pressed against the industrial-sized oven.

"I don't know," I said hoping it was close enough to the truth to throw her off the scent.

"You be very careful," she said backing away from me and starting to prep the kitchen for her pierogi making. She pulled ingredients from the refrigerator. "Danielek is a good boy. Very sweet. Very nice." She pulled down the large bowls from the shelves.

"He is very sweet and very nice," I agreed. *He's also super sexy and I can't stop thinking about him naked,* I wanted to add but didn't.

"Ah-ha," she said turning to me and holding her wooden spoon out again. "Just as I say. You do like him." She started adding things from the fridge into the bowls and turned her attention to her cooking. She knew she had me baited just enough. There was no hiding from her. She saw through me like I was covered in the industrial plastic wrap she had on the counter.

"And," I said cautiously, "what if I do like him?" The words fumbled out of my mouth like a new pair of dentures that don't fit.

"Danny is very special boy. Has been coming here for

years, not just for the sale but for helping anytime anybody need something. Last week Andrej need ride to doctor. Boom. Danny is here. Everyone here love him." I wondered if that's where he went last week when he said he had an errand to run.

"I'm not surprised. He's very kind and funny," I said thinking about him and the kiss and how he always makes me laugh all the time with stupid jokes.

"You be careful. I know he is always with the ha-ha and jokes. Making fun of himself even. I tell him stop, but he does that because he is very scared."

"Of what?" I asked. He seems like the most confident guy on the planet. He has no fear in talking to anyone about anything. What could he be scared of?

"Not important," she said brushing me off. "What is important is that you don't hurt him. He has been hurt by guys like you before. He seems strong and tough but he's very fragile. Hurt easy."

"Guys like me?" I asked. Am I a type? I didn't think so.

"Take advantage. Of his big heart."

"Ma'am," I said, mustering as much sincerity as I could from deep in my heart, "I would never do that."

She looked me up and down and squinted her eyes. I knew I was being inspected and I held my breath hoping to pass. After a few seconds her scowl switched to a big bright smile.

"You good man too," she said. "Danielek is more complicated than seems at first. Promise you not hurt him."

"I promise," I said knowing there would be consequences if I wasn't sincere. "I would like to get to know him better but..."

"But what?"

"I'm not sure he's interested," I confessed and as soon as the words came out of my mouth she started laughing.

"*Czujesz do niego miete,*" she said after wiping a few tears. "I knew it!"

"What does that mean?"

"In Polish when someone has, what you say a crush, on someone or if you like them, we say you smell mint on them. I knew you smelled mint on Danielek and I know he smells it on you too. I'm sure of it." She clapped her hands together with a big smile. "Good. Now you are in for special treat. I show you how to make best pierogi."

Then I spent the rest of the morning doing what she said until Danny came in and I decided to stop pretending what happened didn't happen.

Kasia helped me understand. He's nervous but so am I. He's been baiting me, pushing me to walk away from whatever we're feeling for each other because he's scared. Seeing the look on his face when I suggested we hang his ugly clown painting in the window was priceless. He thinks it's easier for us to keep fighting rather than deal with whatever is lurking underneath all that arguing. I get that. I'm unsure as well, but that doesn't mean what I'm feeling will just go away. One of us has to take the wheel and after my secret talk with Kasia, I feel like I can drive us where we need to go. I put my foot on the gas pedal, glance over at Danny and accelerate toward our destination.

While the church rummage sale was a charming collection of odd leftovers, Brown Brothers is more austere and intimidating—a large pristine warehouse with a loading dock and ample parking. It's a transactional location where deals are made and personal estates are sold and resold. Most of the heirlooms come from multimillionaires many times over who have either not established an advanced directive or have left their estate to heirs who want to simply cash out.

I'm sure Danny thinks this place is snob central. I want to be sure he feels comfortable. "I know Browns can feel intimidating but they really have some great things. Why don't you browse with me?"

"That's okay. I was going to play Candy Crush on my phone," he says. "I'm almost at Marshmallow Meadows."

"Come on. I'll even let you make fun of the antique doorknobs," I say.

"Really?" His eyes light up just a bit. "Okay then."

At the rummage sale everyone was dressed casually but neat. At the auction house, more formal attire is common with some people in suits. I'm wearing my usual blazer and slacks. At first I was worried about Danny feeling underdressed but of course that was me projecting how I would feel. Danny feels at home wherever he is.

As we walk past the room where the bidding is taking place a heated auction is escalating. The auctioneer is furiously taking bids as the price for a piece of Bavarian china climbs higher and higher. "Isn't it exciting?" I whisper to Danny, moving my mouth a bit closer to his ear than I may actually need to.

"Ugh," he says. "No, I don't find it exciting at all. It makes me anxious. All this competing. The stress of it. No thanks. I'd much rather be sifting through a dusty bin of old Barbies any day."

"You know, your dusty bin and my rapid bidding aren't as far apart as you might think."

The auctioneer slams his gavel and announces the sold price. "Are you kidding? Did you just hear that? The price for that dish is twenty times more than the entire contents of the St. Stanislaw rummage sale."

"That's true but that's not what I mean," I say pleasantly. "Both are really about the thrill of the hunt, aren't they? We have that in common and maybe more," I say making sure my tone is as flirty as possible.

Danny looks at me with a quizzical expression on his face and then takes out his cell phone.

"Hang on a second. I want to call St. Stanislaw and see if they accidentally did some Polish exorcism on you. You were super nice on the drive here and now you're being even nicer. Not to mention I think you should see an optometrist because you treated my clown painting like it was a Degas."

I chuckle on the inside knowing that not reacting to his painting would throw him for a loop. I want him to see that I can be magnanimous under the right conditions. For a second I think about telling him about what Kasia said right then and there, but I think I may just wait on that.

"Put your phone down," I say laughing. "There's nothing wrong with me. Let me register and then we can go to the smalls in the West Room. I want to show you why we're here." I give him a big smile then gently touch him on the arm. I make sure my hand lingers on him just long enough before heading over to registration.

I've never acted so outré in my entire life, but Kasia has given me a boost of confidence and helped me realize I'm willing to come out of my shell if it means Danny might be there waiting for me.

*Danny*

"I don't know why you made me get a paddle," I tell Prescott. "I have no intention of bidding on anything here. I should go back to the van."

What has gotten into this guy and how can I make it stop? It's one thing to argue and bicker with him and pretend that I'm not attracted to him, but it's another entirely to have to stop myself from jumping on his lips when he's being so sweet—dangerously flirtatious, even. I'm trying to stay focused on keeping it professional and resist him but he's making it impossible which is making me mad which is making me horny which puts me right back to wanting to jump on his lips. This is not going well.

"Something might catch your eye and you can't bid without a paddle." He holds his up to me and for a split second I think about taking him back to the van with our paddles. Instead, after we register we go to find the piece he has come in search for. I walk through the doorway and survey the old, dusty antiques. It's like a snooze fest on display tables. "This is like some museum for the boring."

"Well, yes the quality of *objets* here is museum standard but they're anything but boring. Oh, look, there it is." He points to a table a few yards away. "Let me show you." He pulls out a retractable pointer that I have seen him use in the store to point out detail in some of his more delicate objects. Watching him grab the pointer and fully extending it should not be part of my erotic fantasy but I can't help myself. I shake my head and cover my eyes with my hand.

"Is everything okay?" he asks not knowing the gymnastics happening in my brain.

"Yes, fine," I say fanning myself with my paddle.

"Don't do that in the auction. You'll bid on something without knowing and be stuck buying it," he says. A look of horror washes over me at the thought of having any of this stuff in my possession.

"There it is. Isn't it magnificent?" He uses his pointer to identify the ugliest metal mug I've ever seen. It's actually not ugly. Ugly would be an improvement. It is a few inches high and made of gray, dank metal. There is a dark patina covering the entire thing.

"Prescott, if I saw this mug on the street I would put it in the garbage. No, wait. I'd see if it was recyclable metal and then I'd drop it in the recycle bin."

"I'll have you know this mug is one of the rarest examples of nineteenth-century pewter ever made. At the time this design was unique, innovative even. Most of the mugs were straight cylinders but this mug was made in the Cunningham Studio just outside of Philadelphia. It was one of the first mugs to use a more bulbous form. They call this the pear shape or belly."

Despite my outward protest I love hearing him talk about the things in his collection. The way he makes things that are part of the past part of the present is both intriguing and attractive.

"If I can add this mug to the collection of Cunningham that I already have it will increase the value tenfold. I might even get the collection featured in *Art & Antiques*."

"I bet if you really polish it up you might even get the centerfold," I tell him. He laughs but then his mood shifts abruptly.

"Oh, no," he says and a dark cloud has descended.

"What?" I ask. Without thinking I put my hand on his arm to comfort him. My hand should bounce off him but in this moment it stays there and it doesn't seem like I want to move it.

"This isn't good. They raised the estimated value. This might be out of my price range."

"Let me see," I say moving toward the identification tag. "What?" I shout so loud a few people stop and stare. "For that mug?" I'm about to go into how overinflated all of this stuff is but instead I change my tune. He's been so nice today and I might as well reward his effort with being nice back. "Well if that is what you think it's worth..." I start to say when I am cut off.

"Daniel Roman? Is that you?" A distinguished gentleman in a three-piece suit walks over to me.

My heart drops into my stomach when I see who is approaching me. "Mr. Cassiday. Hello, how nice to see you," I say smiling. How am I going to explain knowing one of the richest collectors in the world? I've been leading Prescott to believe I come from good working-class stock so this might blow my cover. I think I can use some smoke and mirrors as long as he doesn't mention my father.

"I was just speaking with your father on the phone last week." Crap. Well, how am I going to explain that? "He told me you had a little shop in New Hope."

"I do," I say. "Well, we do. We share the floor. Prescott Henderson, I'd like to introduce you to..."

"Christopher Cassiday," Prescott says extending his hand. "It's an honor to meet you in person. I've been a long admirer of your collection. In fact, I studied it extensively in graduate school. Your salt glaze collection was transformational for me."

"Well, thank you, young man," Mr. Cassiday says. "Daniel, please give your best to your father if I don't speak to him first. A piece I'm interested in is just about up. Prescott, so nice to meet you," Christopher says as he leaves.

Once he is out of earshot Prescott turns to me with his mouth wide open. "You *know* Christopher Cassiday?"

"No, not really," I say. "I mean my father does."

"You father actually *knows* Christopher Cassiday?" he asks with the same level of shock and excitement.

"Just a little tiny bit I guess," I say as nonchalantly as possible, pretending I have no idea who the man is even though I've known him since I was a kid. He bought my sister a pony for her birthday last year. Well actually it was a racehorse but same idea.

"He's one of the most important collectors in the country. No, wait. Scratch that. He's one of the most important collectors in the world. How does your father know him?"

"I can't remember. I think my dad worked on one of his cars or something…" I say the first thing that comes to mind that's as close to the truth as I want to get in the moment. My dad and Cassiday share a love for vintage automobiles and they each have a private garage full of them. I do remember my dad helped him with something on his Duesenberg.

"Is your dad a mechanic? I thought you said he was a chef," Prescott says, more confused than suspicious.

"He knows his way around an engine so he does a lot of odd jobs," I say trying to be as vague as possible but remain technically accurate. The truth is my father sold Cassiday an entire chain of automotive parts stores that he acquired as part of some larger deal. The transaction was in the multimillions. Of course, now that I've led Prescott to believe that my dad was a part-time mechanic, I can't go telling him the truth. What would be the point? "Hey, shouldn't we get a seat so you can go bid on your whatever that boring thing is?"

"Moving on to lot 871. Armoires and desks," I hear coming from the main auction room.

"Didn't you also have your eye on a few of the small furniture pieces?"

"Yes, but don't change the subject..."

"We drove the van all the way here. If we just go back with your little mug you could have ridden here on a bicycle. Now grab your paddle and let's see how much fun we can have," I say and then I pause. "Oh, that's weird," I say putting my hand to my mouth.

"What?"

"I never thought one gay man would say that to another outside of a leather bar on Folsom Street but there you go."

Prescott laughs and I definitely notice it's his real laugh, not his fake one. Which I probably don't deserve, seeing as how I've just almost-but-maybe-not-quite lied to him. Suddenly the name of the racehorse Mr. Cassiday bought my sister comes to mind—"Moment of Truth"—and the knot in my stomach tightens.

# Chapter Sixteen

*Prescott*

How in the world does Danny know Christopher Cassiday and why was he cagey about all of it? I mean, Danny knows every single person within a ten-mile radius of New Hope so I suppose I shouldn't be surprised, but Cassiday lives in New York City and Paris and Rome. The story he gave me about his father doing work on one of his cars doesn't completely add up, but I can't figure out which number is in the wrong column.

"Moving on to the nine-hundreds lot. Silver, pewter and metalwork," the auctioneer says. As much as I want to find out the answer to what's going on with Danny, I need to focus on the auction. I go over what I've spent so far on furniture. I'm at the absolute limit of my budget, but I should have enough for the tankard if the bidding doesn't go wild. It's hard to know what the crowd's appetite for metal will be. We get a few pieces in and it seems like things are hot. A set of Victorian serving utensils goes for way more than it's worth, but still utensils and tankards often circulate in different markets.

Danny gently taps me on my knee with his paddle. "Good luck," he says and it gives me confidence. I want to linger on the feeling but I need to concentrate on the bidding.

The auctioneer moves to the next item up for bid. "Here we have an exceptional and rare pear-shaped pewter mug forged at the Cunningham Studio outside of Philadelphia."

"The pear shape is quite rare, I'm told," Danny says with encouragement.

"So it is," I say, staying focused on the auctioneer.

"I will open the bidding at…"

As soon as the amount comes out of his mouth I move my paddle up. This is finally my chance to complete my Cunningham set and make my pewter collection one of the most outstanding in the region. Danny smiles at me with pride and although I haven't really done anything impressive it makes me feel good. At first there are no other bids. For a second I think I might get this for the opener but auctions are always unpredictable. They can trick you into a false sense of comfort. One second you think you're in control and the next you're in over your head.

"Do I have any more bids—going once…" My heart races quickly thinking I might be getting the deal of the century. Then suddenly a murmur spreads around the room like the simmer in a pot of boiling water.

"Mr. Cassiday meets the bid with paddle 456." The auctioneer himself looks impressed.

"Why is everyone freaking out?" Danny asks.

"If Mr. Cassiday bids it creates a sort of uncontrollable wildfire. He has one of the most important eyes in the industry. Some people will bid just because they see he's bidding since it means it must be undervalued. This is not good."

The bidding heats up and I do my best to stay in the game. Cassiday bids again and then some others and then back to me. I am over my budget for sure but I can't help bidding. I want that piece. The bidding gets even hotter and even though I am in over my head I can't help but stay in. Cassiday drops out but another bidder makes a huge increase and I put my paddle on my lap.

"What are you doing?" Danny asks.

"I can't stay in. It's way over my budget. I can't afford it."

The bidding keeps escalating even with Cassiday out of the competition.

"Do I hear any more bids?" the auctioneer asks.

"Let's just get out of here," I say.

"Going once, going twice, all in or all out…"

The auctioneer raises his gavel and is about to close the deal when suddenly I hear Danny say, "Me! Yes. I want. Please accept my bid." He uses his paddle like a fan waving at the auctioneer despite the fact that one only need raise it without emotion. That's Danny. He leads with his enthusiasm. But what in the world is he doing?

"I've got a new bid from the very excited young man in the *Star Wars* T-shirt," the auctioneer says with a snarl.

"It's *Star Trek*, you heathen," Danny shouts back and there is a roar of laughter. Only Danny could take a room of overstuffed collectors and make them snort sounds of laughter.

"Danny have you lost your mind?" I ask him. Does he have any idea what he's doing?

"Yes," he says surveying the room almost daring anyone to bid against him. "I'm absolutely crazy for that cup."

"It's a tankard," I say. "That's an absurd amount of money."

"Do I hear any more bids?" the auctioneer announces.

"Then I'm absolutely crazy for that tankard. I want it in our shop," he says raising his paddle again.

"Sir, you have the high bid at the moment. Unless you wish to pay more I suggest you put your paddle down," the auctioneer says from the stage, smiling at Danny and obviously taken in by his charm.

"Thank you," Danny says.

"Sold!" the auctioneer shouts and there is a polite smattering of applause.

"I'm going to put that tankard right next to my new clown painting," Danny says turning to me and looking in my eyes. I can't believe what he has done. The price for the pewter piece went through the roof. There is no way I could afford it and I don't see how Danny could. Even Cassiday knew when to bow out. You need deep pockets to be so aggressive at an auction like that.

"Now we go check out. Is that how it works?" he asks

standing up from his seat. He suddenly seems a bit nervous and I wonder if the gravity of what he has done is sinking in.

"Yes, I guess so," I say. But I have so many questions. I'm not sure what's going on. He knows how badly I wanted that piece and it was an incredibly kind thing to do. But that was an obscene amount of money for something that wasn't even for himself. How in the world could he afford to make a bid like that?

*Danny*

"I'll meet you at the cashier. I have to run to the restroom," I say and scurry away as fast as I can, avoiding Prescott and the catalog of questions he must have.

"Danny, wait what…" I hear him say as I break out in a near jog.

Once I'm safe inside a private bathroom the reality of what I just did hits me. I just bought a *two-thousand-dollar* mug. Two thousand dollars. On a mug. Correction, a tankard.

I look at myself in the mirror and grab the edges of the sink. I turn on the taps so I can splash some water on my face, hoping that it will bring me to my senses. Where is Cher when I need her to give me a good slap and tell me to snap out of it?

I've completely destroyed any pretense that I'm not interested in Prescott. It was impulsive and reckless but what could I do? I looked over at him during the auction. Seeing him place that first bid was thrilling, a major turn-on. His eyes were dancing like children bouncing off the walls the night before Christmas. I've seen him intense and even passionate about things but that childlike joy was a first. I couldn't stop watching him.

But then it looked like he wasn't going to get the high bid and everything just sort of collapsed inside him. I know how much he wanted to complete that set. I could see the happiness evaporate from his eyes and it did something inside me. I felt his disappointment. I felt it with him. Then I just wanted to stop him from feeling anything bad. I wanted to protect him, but I also wanted to see that joy return to his eyes.

My arm was like, "Hey, buddy, I have an idea," and without any approval from my brain, just rose up and stuck my paddle in the air.

I bought a two-thousand-dollar mug. I promised myself I would support myself only from the shop's income, but this means I'll need to transfer money from my trust fund to stay in business. It won't make a dent in the account but it does damage my credibility in being able to support myself on my own financially. Then there's the big stink bomb that I have led, or rather misled Prescott to believe that I am, shall I say, not the child of a gabillionaire. How does someone who is working tirelessly to make the store a success just drop 2K on a hunk of metal? How am I going to explain this to him?

Maybe I should take this opportunity to come clean. But then I think about how nice he's been today and I don't want to ruin that. He thinks I'm just a regular hardworking guy and I am except for the fact that I'm also not.

I splash my face with water one more time, hoping it

will give me an epiphany about how to either explain what I've done or just avoid talking about it altogether. The latter seems like the only realistic option though it will take some maneuvering. We'll get in the van, drive straight back to New Hope and this confusing, exciting, excruciating, partly wonderful day will come to an end.

I feel the cool water tighten my skin. I take a towel from the stack and pat my face dry, stalling as much as I can. I open the door and head to the cashier to meet Prescott.

We wind up in different lines, him ahead of me, and he leaves to move the van to the delivery area and load up the larger items. I'm able to carry my purchase out the door in a small box. One thing I'll say is that when you drop enough money on a small object they really don't skimp on the bubble wrap.

"All loaded up?" I ask jumping into the driver's seat, still not sure what to say. It started snowing while we were in the auction. It's not enough to make the roads too dangerous but there is a fresh, lovely blanket of white over the fields surrounding the auction house.

"Yes," Prescott says buckling his seat belt. I begin the drive back home.

We are barely out of the parking lot when he says, "I don't totally understand what happened but I want to thank you. Sincerely. That was very nice of you and I would like to find a way to buy it from you for what you paid, plus interest, of course. It will take me a little while but I know you don't really want that mug."

"Are you kidding? I love pewter. Haven't you heard? Pewter is the new black."

Prescott laughs and it makes me smile. "Let me at least help you. Maybe I could make a down payment with what I have and cover the balance..."

"Sure, but let's not talk about any of that right now. We'll figure it out eventually."

"I know but I just have a lot of questions, like..."

"The roads are getting slushy. I think I should focus on that. You know, for safety." The roads are a bit slick and I'm grateful the van is so weighted down with our haul because it makes the tires grip the surface that much more. Rolling hills are quickly changing from earth browns to opaque white as snow begins to stick to the ground. Suddenly a thick squall appears, making visibility a bit of an issue.

"Do you think we should take a break?" Prescott asks.

"I'm sure it will pass," I say with hesitation. I want to get us home as quickly as possible to avoid having to deal with the mess I've created, but I still want us to be in one piece.

Prescott takes out his phone and examines the screen. "According to the weather radar it looks like this is moving in quickly. Is there any place for us to pull over? Hey, what's that up ahead on the right? Should we stop there?"

The most romantic spot in all of Bucks County appears before us. Oh, great. Exactly what I don't need. In winter, The Langford Lavender Farm transforms into Peppermint Twist—a weekend sledding destination with a charming snack hut. My options are drive a rickety van over icy roads with little visibility or grab a hot chocolate with the sexy guy who has been so nice to me today that I think my insides have melted like a bag of candy left in the sun too long.

"I think we should keep going," I say gripping the wheel with determination. I've been redirecting my feelings for Prescott all day but I'm not sure I can keep this up much longer.

"The sign says they serve hot chocolate and I think it's safer to take a break," Prescott says. "Let's stop and I'll buy you a treat to thank you for your bid. And you can explain more about Christopher Cassiday."

The snow is not letting up at all and the snack hut does have incredible hot chocolate so I say, "Fine, on one condition."

"Name it."

"No more talk about the tankard or that Cassiday guy."

"But you spent two thousand dollars…" he starts.

"Ah, ah, ah. Nope. Not another word and that's my final bid," I say firmly.

"Sure," Prescott says. "My word of honor."

I start thinking about the menu at the snack hut and quickly add without thinking. "I'll also need a Peppermint Kiss." As soon as the word *kiss* comes out of my mouth I regret it. The last thing I want either of us thinking about is kissing. This is a safety break.

"One Peppermint Kiss. If that's what you want, you got it," Prescott says and I do my best to ignore his flirty tone. I hope the weather is going to clear soon but when I look up at the sky all I see are delicate flakes of white precipitation telling my willpower to take a snow day.

# Chapter Seventeen

*Prescott*

We pull in to park and the farm is buzzing with people ready to take advantage of the recent snows. One side of the hill has rows of lavender bushes all wrapped up in burlap like butterflies waiting to break out of their chrysalises. The other side is full of families racing down the hill or making the climb back up to dash down again. Bursts of laughter and shouts of excitement punctuate the snow-filled air.

A small building that looks like an ornately decorated gingerbread house that has come to life sits at the top of the hill. Majestic pine trees tower over it and their branches create a protected nook with benches and tables. Hanging fairy lights are just beginning to twinkle against the evening sky. I couldn't ask for a more perfectly charming setting.

Danny is wearing his sherpa-lined jacket and the flaps on his fake-fur-lined trapper hat flutter in the wind as he walks away from the van after parking. At the auction it was almost entertaining to watch him fight the urge to let happen whatever needs to happen between us happen. Of course, we were there for the bidding so I had to keep part of my attention on work. But with the snow falling and evening beginning to create a soft glow over everything, work is over. It's time to play.

We walk over to the window of the snack shack to order and a teenager with bright blue hair asks, "What can I get you?" They are wearing a red-and-white-striped leotard under a chunky red sweater vest with a They, Them, Theirs pin.

"We'll have two hot chocolates—" I look up at the hand-painted menu that hangs above the hut "—and two Peppermint Kisses," I say and then turn to Danny. "Kisses?" I ask. "That is what you said you wanted? A kiss, right?"

"Yes," Danny says and I can see my relentless flirting is breaking him down. I never thought this could be so much fun.

I pay and grab us a table as Danny waits for the order. The cold air is making his round cheeks ruddy and giving his whole face this glow that makes me want to run over there and kiss him so badly I can barely contain myself. I've never acted like this before in my life. I can't even say I've ever really flirted let alone leaned into it with the weight of the spruces that tower over us. I can't help it. I watch him chatting at the counter. He says something that makes the teenager laugh and they both smile. Danny makes every single person he meets feel important. It's an uncanny talent with which I am becoming deeply enamored.

He brings over a tray with our order and we sit next to each other watching the sledders as we sip our hot chocolate. "I guess you didn't go sledding growing up in Texas," I say. I want to know so much more about him, but I don't want to rush things. This is a good place to linger.

"No, but I used to love the Chilly Willy cartoons. He was this sassy little penguin who slid around on ice roller coasters and made everyone laugh. I have a Chilly Willy cookie jar but I keep it at home. I love it too much to sell." Danny's smile is radiant like the stars that are beginning to twinkle in the lavender sky.

"You really love the things you collect, don't you? I mean, more than love. They make you happy." I think about when he's straightening up his collection of matchbox cars. He goes over each one so carefully. I'm careful with my things too but it comes out of reverence more than joy.

"Of course. I only collect the pieces that make me happy and I know a lot of them are throwaway things like fast food stuff and cartoon cereal characters but my dad worked a lot. My mom had other kids to take care of. A lot of my happy memories are focused around TV shows and junk food. That stuff made me feel normal. I guess when I see those things they bring me joy. Maybe they aren't traditionally valuable but they make me happy, so they are to me."

It's time for me to put some steam on the situation. I look him in the eyes as intensely as I can and say softly, "That's really a wonderful way to look at it. The things that make us happy can be beautiful. Very beautiful." I wonder if I am pushing it too far. I stay focused on his eyes and Danny returns my gaze. His eyes are not just looking at mine, they're connecting with mine. But it becomes too much for him and he breaks the spell.

"Did you go sledding in New Jersey? You got snow there even though it was by the ocean, right?"

"Sometimes," I say releasing my intense gaze and allowing the evening to have peaks and valleys. "But it was really flat. There weren't hills like this one. Look at that kid in the green." I point to a boy flying down the hill with only a wooden sled between his belly and the slick surface.

"It looks like a lot of fun," Danny says.

"I was just about to say that it looks terrifying," I say laughing. We have such different ways of seeing the world. I'm learning to appreciate seeing with his eyes. The fact that they are always twinkling topaz and filled with a positive energy doesn't hurt. He takes a sip of his hot chocolate and I take a sip of mine.

"Are you ready for your Kiss?" I ask knowing exactly what I'm doing.

He is startled for a second and then looks at the cookie I have in my hand. He doesn't say anything. He tilts his head up and I feel like maybe something inside him is changing. He takes a sip of his hot chocolate and he gets a hot chocolate mustache over his regular scruff. Without thinking I go to wipe it away and brush my fingers just above his lips. It's a bold move but I'm ready to give this a try.

"Let's do it," he says and I sense a shift. I think the moment has finally arrived. I'm expecting him to close his eyes and put his lips on mine but instead he grabs the tray and brings it back to the person who served us and then heads back to the van.

Too much? I should never have touched him on his face in such an intimate way. I scared him off again. Why did I do something so bold? It's not like me. I trail behind him and start my apology, "Danny, I'm sorry…" But he has gotten too far ahead of me to hear. He's already back at the van and ready, I assume, to go home. But instead of getting in the front of the van he opens the back door and starts rearranging what we have inside. It looks like he's trying to pull something out.

"What are you doing?" I ask.

His thick arms reach into the van and struggle with the stuck object but it quickly gives to his strength. "I'm getting this," he says and pulls out the long vintage toboggan that he purchased earlier at the rummage sale. "You wanna?"

I have to admit I'm totally confused. I can't predict anything this guy is about to do. I guess that's part of what makes him so attractive to me. I'm a Swiss clock and he's a slot machine.

"We aren't kids," I say defaulting to my usual guarded attitude. Why do I always do that? Why do I always shut down any experience that might force me to engage? At least when I do it around Danny I'm aware of it.

"So what? That doesn't mean we can't act like kids. Sometimes."

He's got a point, but I can't stop my mind from generating excuses. "I'm wearing a blazer!" I say unable to imagine tumbling down the hill on a thin piece of wood.

"So what? I'm assuming you sleep in that blazer," he says those dark gold and brown eyes in hypersparkle mode.

"Wouldn't you like to know?" I tease back. Why not?

"I just might," he says and that makes me smile. I knew something shifted and that confirms it. He's ready.

"Fine," I say showing him that sometimes I can be crazy and impulsive like him. "Let's try this out."

*Danny*

"I call back seat," I say and Prescott grabs the toboggan and starts running with it to over where the sledders are gathered. I watch him bouncing along toward the hill. I don't know what I was thinking. He's gorgeous and attentive and engaged with me on a level that penetrates through my entire being. Resisting him is completely futile. Even a Naboo starfighter's deflection shield deteriorates at the deepest levels of hyperspace.

We find a spot to launch where the flatness ends and the decline begins. Prescott takes a seat, grabbing the curved wooden front. "How do I steer this thing?"

"I have no idea."

I look down and realize that this ride means I'm going to have to wrap my arms and legs around Prescott. I've gone this far. I might as well take the next step.

He looks back at me. "Hop on."

I sit down and tentatively put my legs over his. Then he cups his hands under my ankles and even though the snow is making every extremity on my body feel a chill, being connected to Prescott in this way gives me a warmth deeper than any sweater could provide. I put my arms around his waist, as is custom in sledding from what I've seen. He turns his head back to me and I see a smile on his face. He's holding my legs and I'm holding his waist. It feels so right and so perfect. I look down at the hill that looks much steeper than it did from the benches and have second thoughts about going down. I just want to stay holding him like this. I think about going in for my kiss but before I can he says, "Hold on."

"Prescott maybe we should think this through," I say wondering if two grown men should be sledding down an icy hill.

"Look who's the cautious one now? Not a chance, Danny. On the count of three."

"Are you sure?" I ask. The winter sun has set. A pink-lavender glow from the west shares the sky with stars in the east. I don't want this perfect moment to end.

"One, two…" And before getting to three he lets go of my ankles and uses his hands to push us off the lip of the hill so the toboggan tips down and the weight of our bodies forces us speeding toward the bottom. I hold on to Prescott by squeezing my arms more tightly around his waist. He moves his hands to my arms and I feel a sudden rush that is as intense as the wind, ice and snow that swoosh past us. The hill is a tangled racecourse of kids and families but at this moment it feels like we are the only two people in the world.

"Watch out!" I scream when I see we're heading toward a massive pine tree just up ahead on the left.

"I can't steer," Prescott yells trying to twist the lip of the toboggan like it's the wheel of a ship.

"Lean right," I yell and then grab him even tighter and push both of us to the right. But he is lighter than I expect and I am heavier than I think so I pull us both so hard that we tumble off together but the toboggan continues down the hill passengerless.

We don't let go of each other. We roll toward the side of the hill away from everyone and watch the toboggan run smack into the tree. We both laugh so hard that we lean back and lie on the snow. I'm still holding Prescott and he turns so that we are facing each other. His warm breath makes a small cloud in front of mine. His cheeks are red from the cold and even though his slightly chapped but extremely beautiful lips are still closed his eyes continue to laugh. There is a calm silence between us. He smiles and puts his hand on my cheek so softly that for a second I think the snow has started falling again.

I know this might be a mistake. I know he might break my heart and I might not be ready for it. I know this is complicated. But in the moment it feels simple, hopeful and right.

Faster than our sled careened down the hill I move my lips to his. I can't think in the moment or I know I will stop myself. Once I meet the deep warmth and delicious wetness of his lips all thinking stops. It's just his lips, my lips and our bodies pressed against each other on the cold snow, which I imagine is a puddle underneath us considering how hot the kiss is. Last time we only just began letting our tongues journey wherever they wanted. This time there is no passport control. We both surrender in the same moment and take each other in through our mouths. I turn my head and he turns his and we move without hesitation from kissing to making out. Luckily we have rolled far enough away from the hill that we are in a secluded-enough spot to enjoy the make out session. My hands move from his waist to just inside his jacket. There are still too many layers of clothes between my fingers and his chest but for the moment it will have to do.

"Are you okay with this?" Prescott asks me without pausing. The words come out sort of distorted since he breathes them into my open mouth and tongue but I understand what he's saying.

"Yes, yes," I say, assuming the panting is showing him how turned on I am right now. "I'm sure this time. I am." I wonder if he's thinking I might run away again, but this time I'm staying right where I am. "I'm sorry about the other night. Very sorry. I wasn't ready. I was…"

"Shh," Prescott says putting his finger to my lips. "I understand." He removes his finger and replaces it with his lips and our smooches grow hotter and deeper.

I love feeling connected to him like this, lying next to him and feeling the snow fall and melt on us as we kiss. He nuzzles his nose against my neck and then looks up at me revealing a big smile with a small secret lurking beneath it.

"What?" I ask.

"You smell good, Danielek. I smell mint on you, a lot of mint right now."

Mint? I'm not sure what he's talking about. I'm assuming it's the peppermint cookie when…

Boom!

For a second I'm seeing stars. Not from the passion but from the sled that has just careened into us.

"Dad, I told you we were gonna crash. That was amazing. Let's do it again," Jules, Tack's kid, says as they grab their sled ready for another run. Tack and Vince get up from the ground and brush snow off their pants.

"Well, look who we ran into. Literally," Tack says with his usual devilish grin.

"Sorry about that, guys," Vince says sincerely. "Tack, I told you to lean the other way," he says, knowing that his fiancé loves to stir the pot.

"Oh, did you?" he asks with mock innocence.

"Dad, come on," Jules says tugging at his hand.

"Nice to see you. Dinner next Monday night? The inn is closed so just upstairs at our place. Please join us?" Vince asks calmly and politely.

"Unless you two are at the intimate candlelight dinner for two stage still?" Tack grabs the sled from Jules and runs up the hill effortlessly. Vince grabs Jules and puts them on his back and follows Tack up the hill with Jules piggyback.

We are alone again in the snow and lying on our backs. All traces of the sun are gone now and a purple-blue ocean appears above us.

Prescott pops up. "That's it," he says with an unfamiliar enthusiasm in his voice.

"What's it?" I ask sitting up mostly because I want to see his beautiful face.

"The candlelight dinner stage. We don't want to gloss over that. I mean we have to follow the rules," he says. I love this playful side of him. I know how reserved he is usually so seeing him act sort of silly like this makes me think I am getting to see a side of him that he doesn't share with everybody and it makes me feel special.

"Yes, I don't want the romance police to show up and charge us with skipping a step," I say just as playfully as him.

"Then it's settled. Tomorrow night. Candlelight dinner at my place. I'll file all the paperwork with the authorities," he says and then lies back down staring up at the sky.

"Sounds like a plan," I say and lie down also.

The storm has passed and there isn't a cloud above us. The stars seem brighter and the sky darker. The crowds on the hill have thinned and a deep but wonderful quiet has fallen over the hill. I can hear Prescott breathing and when I move my eyes to the side I see a small cloud of air just above his mouth. I also see that his eyes are not looking straight up but out to the side at me. As soon as he sees that I caught him looking at me he moves his eyes back to the stars. I move mine back as well but I take my hand and inch it toward his. I get closer and closer until I sense his hand is next to mine, then I put my hand over his upward-facing palm. As soon as I do he moves his fingers to clasp mine and just like that we are on the side of a snow-covered hill under a star-filled cloudless sky holding hands. I don't want to let go of him until spring. I rest my head on his chest and for a second I think I smell it too. Mint.

# Chapter Eighteen

*Prescott*

I'm not a great cook. Most of the meals I prepare involve a rather pedestrian frozen dinner. Still, I've managed to make a simple fettuccini dish with truffle cream sauce using tinned ingredients from the Italian grocery in the Ferry Market.

My small studio in Lambertville is above the local pharmacy. There's room for a cafe table between the couch and the bed and a small fireplace makes the entire apartment more cozy than cramped. A neon light with the word *Prescriptions* buzzes just outside the window facing the street. Usually at night I shut the blinds but tonight the red glow that floods the apartment helps create the romantic mood I want to achieve.

I want to kiss every part of Danny's body and find out about him on this whole different level. But I'm also worried about things going too quickly. A lot of guys expect things to move faster than I can manage. It makes me uncomfortable, but it's hard to imagine Danny being that way.

I check the gilt-brass carriage clock that sits on the shelf next to the door and unfortunately I have a few minutes still to ponder my insecurities. I know I'm okay looking and that I have a certain broad appeal. I'm not ready to walk the runway, but I'm a visual person so I'm able to be objective and say that many people consider me good-looking. I'm not overly confident but I'm also not pretending to be something I'm not. In this moment I'm not worried about what most people think of me. I'm worried about what Danny thinks of me.

I walk over to the ornately carved acanthus mirror hanging next to the bathroom door and try to see myself as Danny might. I'm wearing black pants and a crisply pressed black shirt. I've combed my hair back and added some product so it looks a bit darker blond than usual. For a second I think I look nice, then I think I look like I'm auditioning to be a pall bearer at some very chic funeral. The buzzer rings and it's too late to think about changing. I let him in and hear footsteps bouncing up the stairs. I can't believe how nervous I am to see a guy I've been sitting just yards away from for the past few weeks.

"Hello," I say smiling at what I see in front of me. He's wearing his usual sherpa-lined denim jacket. The fluffy lining makes him look like a real-life teddy bear that anyone would just want to hold on to and squeeze. He has his *Star Wars* knit cap on that he told me looks like an android named R2-D2 and I make a mental note to not confuse *Star Wars* and *Star Trek* although until recently I thought they were the exact same things. He's holding a bouquet of plum-speckled Stargazer lilies and box from the Honeysuckle Bakery. His eyes smile as much as his mouth and his round cheeks are pink from the cold.

"These are for you," he says, holding out the flowers and greeting me with a kiss on the cheek. The scent of his cherry lip balm passes by my nose and it's a promise of things to come later in the evening.

"Thank you," I say gesturing for him to come in. "I have the perfect vase for these. You can put your coat on any of the hooks by the door."

I run some water for the flowers but steal a look at him as he's taking off his coat, a habit I've acquired each morning in the shop since he usually stretches his arms back in a way that makes his shirt rise up enough for me to see the furry patch that covers his tight tummy.

"I was going to put them in this pretty vintage Maxwell House coffee can I have but I figured you'd want something more…"

Before he finishes I jump in. "These are lovely and I would have appreciated them no matter the vessel," I say realizing I'm being a bit too grandiose in my speech. I'm nervous. I tell myself to relax. I've been looking forward to this all day but now that the moment is here my excitement has turned into nerves.

"It smells fantastic in here. What are you making?" His voice cracks just a bit as he speaks which makes me a pinch more relaxed. Maybe he's nervous too.

*Danny*

It took me a good five minutes to summon the courage to ring the buzzer and now that I'm actually standing in Prescott's apartment I'm even more nervous. I'm sure he could hear it when my voice cracked. That hasn't happened since I was a teenager—which isn't entirely inappropriate because that was the last time I felt this way. No one who has met me would ever say I'm shy but tonight I feel a strange mixture of eagerness and mystery.

"Just some pasta," he says busying himself in the kitchen.

I take a deep breath and notice a fancy mirror near what must be the door to the bathroom. Since he's turned toward the sink I grab a quick look at myself. Why did I wear this shirt? It's my favorite vintage Hawaiian print, surfers and waves and flowers, but it's as loud as a parade down Christopher Street in June. I think about tucking it into my slacks but there isn't enough time. I quickly pass my hand over my cheek. I should have shaved more closely. Then I get a quick whiff of the cologne I put on. It's way too much.

I'm with this guy every day in the shop and most days I want to strangle him, so why am I so freaked out about being with him now? A dozen new second guesses fill my head but I hear him turning off the faucet. As I turn away from the mirror I see him, really see him, for the first time this evening.

He has got to be the sexiest preppy-boy I've ever seen. He always looks like he belongs in one of those clothing ads where people are sailing on yachts or picnicking at a vineyard. He's impeccably groomed as usual. His hair is slicked back and perfect and there isn't a wrinkle to be found on him. He's head to toe in black which is something I haven't seen him wear before. It makes him cross the line from daytime cutie-patootie to nighttime hottie.

"Do you want some wine?" he asks. "The man at the liquor store said this goes well with truffle-flavored things. I'm afraid I don't really know wine that well."

"I'm sorry," I say quickly realizing my mistake. "I should have told you that I don't drink. Fine if you want to have some. It's not an issue for me—I just never had a taste for alcohol." Usually I go on and on when I have to decline a drink. It feels good to be able to say things plainly with him. But he starts laughing and I wonder if I have made a mistake.

"I shouldn't be laughing, but I am because… I don't drink either. That's why I had to ask the guy at the liquor store about the wine." He opens a cabinet next to the stove, displaying a small assortment of those little glass-and-a-half bottles that they serve on airplanes. "I even bought all of these in case you wanted something stronger than wine."

There is a short silence and then we both start laughing. "Well, it looks like we have been making a lot of assumptions about each other that turn out to be incorrect so let me pour us some sparkling mineral water and toast to that."

He grabs the green bottle of San Pellegrino and pours some into a glass filled with ice and a lime. He hands it to me and I wait for him to pour one for himself. I raise my glass and say, "To no more assumptions about each other."

He nods and raises his glass to mine. "No more assumptions." Our glasses clink and our eyes lock on each other as we take a sip. Suddenly, all of my nervousness is gone.

We chitchat as he prepares the final parts of the meal. I watch him in the shop a lot—probably more than I care to admit—but seeing him in his home is different. He's more relaxed and less uptight. I wonder if the difference is seeing him in this setting or the fact that the way I see him has changed.

We talk about our plans to meet with the city council about the demolition planned for the buildings as he finishes preparing dinner. Of course he waxes poetically about the Yardley House, but he's begun to include the First Bank of Bucks in his rhapsody and it's a tune I love to hear. We sit down to eat and he puts a perfectly presented plate of pasta with a taupe cream sauce on it before me. I'm about to compliment him on the dish when he jumps up from his chair.

"Oh, I almost forgot." He walks over to the shelf and grabs two candlesticks that a few weeks ago I would have thought seemed overly ornate and dreadful. Tonight their gleaming brass seems solid and trustworthy. "We can't have our candlelight dinner stage without candlelight." He takes a match from the kitchen and sparks a flame, lighting both of the white taper candles and putting them on the table.

The yellow glow from the flames dances across his face, interrupting the red glow that must be coming from the sign of the pharmacy downstairs. His eyes, which usually sparkle like blue spheres, display just a touch of violet in the show of light that tickles across them.

"Well, now everything is perfect," I say smiling.

"No, not just yet," he says. An exaggerated frown flashes across Prescott's face. He puts his hands on the edge of the small table and rises up from his chair. He moves his head toward me and puts his lips on mine for a short but very sweet kiss. Then he sits back down. He gives me a smile so seductive I consider using my arm to clear the plates in one swoop and lying down on the table. He says, "Now everything is perfect."

He dives into his food and I grab my fork and decide to show the same enthusiasm. The truth is I hate truffles. They taste like armpit. But I'm so touched that he cooked for me that I'm sure I'll be able to smile after every bite.

After dinner, I help him clear the table and he sets out two perfectly formed panna cotta with ruby-red berry coulis from the Honeysuckle. "Those look so pretty," I say.

"Mona has outdone herself," he says.

"I'm going to miss her this spring. She's traveling and her brother is going to run the place."

"Well, I hope he gets all the recipes. We don't want an interruption to the scone supply chain." He grins at me and I know he is thinking about our argument at the Honeysuckle that first week. I never thought a night like this would come after an introduction like that.

"Look. It's snowing again." I turn to the window and see big fluffy flakes gently moving through space. Prescott puts the dessert on a tray and carries it to the coffee table in front of the couch. "Let's watch the snow fall as we enjoy these."

I take a seat on the couch. He puts the tray down and sits next to me. Immediately I'm aware of the proximity of our bodies. We haven't been this close since the sledding moment. I'm hyperaware of how good it feels to be this close to him. The snow falls silently as we eat our dessert. Sitting on the couch quietly next to each other, gazing out the window feels so right. I take some time to just enjoy it and let the feeling ripple through me and settle.

Prescott adjusts a bit and I do the same. The brush of his arm against my waist makes my entire body respond with a focused attention that penetrates the quiet calm of the moment. An uncontrollable sensation ricochets around me covering every inch. I wonder if his body also suddenly feels like a pinball machine that has malfunctioned and released all the steel marbles at once. I catch a blurry reflection of him in the window and I am able to see that his face is flushed. Mine is as well. I think about slowly moving in to finish that kiss he started earlier, but before I can the arcade game inside me goes into hyper mode and I turn toward him just as he's turning toward me and we both are thinking the same exact thing. Our mouths reach for each other and we kiss so deeply and passionately that it feels like we're about to make high score.

His hands reach for my chest and I hold his wrists to show him exactly how hard I like it. I guide his hands over my nips as our mouths continue to be entangled. I teach him to squeeze them hard.

"I don't want to hurt you," he says through a deep moan of pleasure.

"You won't," I say showing him how to press even harder. He hits the exact right level of pressure that shoots immediately down to my groin and I release a heavy breath.

He pulls back just a bit. I can tell he's examining the look of pure pleasure that must be pulsing through my face. "It certainly doesn't look like I'm hurting you," he says, smiling and looking right into my eyes.

I move my hands to his chest and give him another deep searching kiss. "What about yours?" I ask. "Hardwired?"

He looks at me shyly. "I honestly don't know."

"Okay to find out?" I ask. He nods and I pull out his shirt from his pants. My hands dive under his undershirt and up his completely smooth torso until they find what they want. I don't move in for another kiss. Instead I keep my eyes on his face to enjoy the effect my hands are having on him. I start very gently, like butterflies landing on a daisy. He is smiling but not giving me that look that says he is in ecstasy. I lock my eyes on his. Nothing will dislodge us during this race down Pleasure Mountain. I increase the pressure but it's still not enough to get where I need to go. Prescott is full of surprises and the fact that he might like it rougher than I am expecting is one that I am very much enjoying. I make another increase—not as hard as he was on my little bullets but harder than most guys can handle. There. It. Is. His eyes widen.

"Yes, yes," he says like the words are forming somewhere deep in his body and being released by the pleasure. "Yes. Like that. Please don't stop."

Now that I have my manifest I'm able to move my mouth toward his again while my hands stay occupied on his chest. He takes off his shirt and I'm able to really take in his body. He's smooth like one of the small marble sculptures he has in the shop. His muscles are long and in elegant proportions. His hands go back under my shirt and resume their earlier perfect dance of pressure and release. I keep hearing him moan deeply. I had no idea he would enjoy what I enjoy so much and from the sounds he is making he might even enjoy it more.

I move one of my hands down from his chest to my pants. I am rock hard right now and when I glance down I see he is too. I'm about to go further when Prescott says, "Danny, wait. Stop."

# Chapter Nineteen

*Prescott*

I put my mouth back on Danny's and give him the sweetest most sincere kiss I can before I continue. "I want to go slow. Is that okay?" I ask, searching his eyes. I've never been able to say this to a guy before. Not ever. I'm usually too scared and let the guy go a bit further than I'm comfortable with and then make up some excuse. But not this time. I want to share myself with Danny and that means telling him how I feel as much as anything else.

He doesn't answer at first and it makes me nervous. Then he kisses with a deep sweetness and sincerity and says, "Absolutely. I want to go slow too. I only want to do what's comfortable for both of us."

I kiss him back in a way that shows him I'm both grateful

and turned on by his response. Going slow doesn't mean we have to stop doing what we are doing and I don't want him to think I'm going at this speed because I'm not attracted to him. I am, and not just his hairy, thick body. It's his kindness, his humor and his attention that are causing my pants to bulge. "But I think it's okay if we…" I trail off, rubbing myself over my pants. He sees what I'm doing and does the same exact thing.

Danny smiles and says, "I mean, if it's okay with you. It's a long, cold walk home and I'm so hard right now I'm not sure part of my anatomy wouldn't break off like an icicle as I walk over the bridge."

I laugh softly. Only Danny could make me laugh and feel sexy both at the same time. "Maybe I could help you out?" I ask.

"Only if you let me return the favor."

"Absolutely," I say and we immediately resume our make out session but this time it feels like our hands are free to explore more uncharted territory. I feel the muscles in his back and even squeeze his strong thighs. He focuses on my biceps with his hands and a few sweet kisses. I get up from the couch and grab his hand. "I think we'll be more comfortable on the bed. What do you think?"

He nods and I hold his hand as we walk to the bed and lie down facing each other. Once we are horizontal we spend a few moments just looking at each other. He runs his hands through my hair and it makes me feel vulnerable but cared for. I touch my fingers to his lips and try to show him with my eyes just how happy I am we are together. We lie like this for some time but the sweet, gentle connection can't maintain the simmering that is building to a loud boil below. The fact that we were able to both agree to go slowly makes it so much easier for me to enjoy this experience. I want to come but I don't want to be worried about being pushed too far or having to perform in ways I'm not ready for. I just want to focus on the pleasure I can give him and the pleasure he can give me. We don't need a full menu of options. Not right now. I want to focus on our connection and that's enough. It's more than enough and Danny seems to totally get it.

I look down and put my hands on his belt. I undo it slowly, looking at his face to make sure we are still on the same page. He nods and that's all I need to rip off that belt, unbutton his jeans and push down his boxers. I give a few strokes, which make his head thrust back as he releases a moan of joy.

"You like it?" I ask and his head comes back up to nod an enthusiastic yes. I keep stroking him until he moves my hands so that he can get closer to the zipper on my pants.

Danny says, "I have an idea you might like." He puts one hand on my dick and the other on my nipple and starts stroking and squeezing with a rhythm that is syncopated and unexpected. The combination of these two erogenous points being worked in unison by a man who is so incredibly sexy and so deeply attuned to how I'm feeling pushes me over the edge. I want to hold out. I want to last longer. I put my hand over his and stop it from the next stroke. I put my mouth on his for a long sustained kiss and then pull back to look at him.

His face tells me everything I need to know—or else

he is doing his best impersonation of the *Ecstasy of Saint Theresa*. I go back to stroking and tweaking his nip with the other hand and he goes back to mine. Within a few beats we are there. It's not just the rhythm we've found; it's more than that. We feel totally in sync. We don't need to be physically inside each other in this moment. At least, not yet. Right now we are inside each other in all the important ways that matter.

The very thought of our synchronicity pushes me over the edge and I look down and see the head of his dick quiver also. Without saying a word we both come within seconds of each other. The release is so intense my entire body shakes and when I look at Danny I see that he looks as satisfied as I feel.

"That was…" I start to say.

"Amazing, mind-blowing…"

"Yeah, both those words come to mind."

"But it wasn't just the orgasm," Danny says as if he is reading my mind.

"I know, it felt like more to me too."

Danny turns toward me and I can't help but move my fingers to his furry chest and feel the hair move around my fingers. He gently brushes my face with the back of his hand and even though it tickles I make sure I don't flinch. I want him to know how much I love his touch.

"I wonder where we are?" Danny asks plainly.

"Uhm, in my apartment in Lambertville. Wow, maybe that orgasm popped a blood vessel," I say teasing him gently.

"I mean we can check the romantic candlelight dinner phase box," he says slyly.

"Yes, we can. In fact, I would give it a check plus."

"Good idea. So what phase are we in now?" he asks. This time his tone is less playful and more serious. It's a fair question. We just moved from playful flirting and kissing to dinner and orgasms. We can't really pretend nothing is going on, can we? Obviously I have feelings for him and it seems like he has feelings for me.

Danny is a great guy, a good guy, a sexy guy, in fact, a very sexy guy. He's not like anyone I've ever been with before and I thought that was something to overcome, but sitting across from him I realize that it's the opposite. It's not something to overcome at all. It's something that makes the situation even more compelling.

"I'd have to do the research," I say with a mock professional tone. "But I would say if we have successfully completed the RCD phase..."

At first a puzzled look appears across Danny's face. "Oh, the Romantic Candlelight Dinner Phase."

"Exactly. Then I guess we show up to Vince and Tack's place as a couple. Or at least we try this out." My playful tone is replaced by a more tentative nervous quiver in my voice. I'm being pretty bold and I'm not sure how Danny will react. I'm about to say something to backtrack, but before I can figure out what to say he kisses me again and I realize there isn't anything I need to say at all.

# Chapter Twenty

*Danny*

Why do they call it The Walk of Shame? Sure, I'm wearing the same coat, shirt and pants I wore on my walk over to Prescott's last night, but shame is the last thing I feel and, in fact, I don't even feel like walking. I feel like dancing across the bridge and singing a melody of show tunes that would bring any audience in any piano bar across the globe to its feet with wild applause. The early morning air looks almost frozen over the river and some hunks of ice sail under the bridge but I don't feel cold at all.

Last night was beyond my expectations. Prescott was charming and caring. He made dinner for me. No one has ever done that before. That alone made me feel all weak inside. Actually that might have been the truffles. One day I'll have to tell him that I don't actually like truffles. I feel like I won't be able to erase the smile that's on my face until the truth about truffles reminds me that I have a much bigger truth I need to tell him.

I'm almost halfway over the bridge. The sky is a robin's egg blue, but I expect a sudden surge of black clouds considering how quickly my joy has turned to worry. I think about turning around, walking back to Prescott's apartment, swinging open the door and saying, "I'm the heir to a fortune. I'm sorry I didn't tell you but can we please get naked again?" I'll make it quick and painless but with a surprise twist at the end.

I hate misleading him this way, but this is all still so new to me—the relationship, the independence from the baggage of my family, feeling like I'm participating in the relationship as an equal—all of it. Usually guys just know about my background on their own or I've telegraphed it in some way right from the start. I've never had to come out of the closet this way and I'm not sure how to do it. Maybe once we move forward I'll find a way, but then I realize we can't really move forward until I come clean. "Arrrghhh!" I yell across the river and my voice reverberates against the struts and decking of the bridge.

I should call him right now and tell him the truth, but then I realize that's what I always do. I put everything out there all at once and maybe this time I shouldn't do that. Let me get to know him better, and then when I find the right time, I'll find the right way. I don't know if this is good logic or excellent procrastination, but right now I just want to linger in the feelings I'm having for him.

I touch my bottom lip with my fingers and I can still feel his goodbye kiss on it as I stood at the door. My lips are chapped from the cold morning air and my fingers are almost frozen but remembering his mouth on mine makes me feel warm from the inside out and I can't risk letting go of the feeling. I'll find a time to tell him when the time is right.

When I get near the other side of the bridge I see the sun appear low in the horizon, turning the entire sky a pinky orange that cuts through small gathering clouds. The colors are a mix of dark and light, pastel and more saturated hues. It's a strange combination full of unexpected contrast that somehow all mixes together beautifully.

# Chapter Twenty-One

*Prescott*

A week ago the thought of attending a small dinner party voluntarily seemed as impossible as sprouting wings and flying over the Delaware River. The idea that I might look forward to it was alternate universe material. But here I am, putting on a blazer, straightening my tie and getting ready to meet Danny so we can join Vince and Tack and a few of their other friends for dinner.

I'm usually on the edges of experiences watching from a safe distance, but there is no such thing as a safe distance with Danny. Most people see my wall and leave it at that but not him. He sees all my walls and is determined to take them down. But he also respects my boundaries which makes me all the more willing to move beyond where I am. I've been with guys who either push me too hard or worse, lie to me and tell me what they think I want to hear and keep the truth from me. Danny is letting me go at my own pace and it makes me want to share myself with him more—both emotionally and physically.

He's like a sexy wrestling coach but it's not just his incredibly hot physical appearance, it's the fact that he's so open about who he is and what he likes and what he wants. I wonder if he knows how sexy honesty is to me.

I take one last look in the mirror and use a comb to make sure my part is perfectly straight. I head out of my apartment and walk over the bridge to meet Danny. Cars gently rumble across the transom and I look out across the river. Stars coruscate through the silky darkness of the night sky sending their energy across the light years. In the distance I see The Hideaway Inn bathed in moonlight.

There is no way I could maneuver a night like tonight without Danny at my side. I'm not worried that I'll say the wrong thing. He'll coax me through an awkward silence or make me feel like it's fine to not say anything. He's a talker; he can talk about anything. I listened for twenty minutes yesterday to a story about those silly Smurfs and I loved every second of it. The fact that part of the time my eyes were searching for the places where Danny's thick muscles stretched the fabric of his shirt and pants probably did something to keep my attention but that was only part of the reason.

When I get to the entrance for The Hideaway Danny is wearing a newsboy hat that makes his cherub features even more adorable. "Hey, babe," I say trying out the term of endearment. As soon as the word comes out of my mouth my entire face, no, my entire body smiles. I have never in my life ever used a term like *babe* with someone before and, if I'm being honest, I always thought it was strange when other people didn't use proper names. With Danny, though, I want to call him something sweet and let him know what he means to me.

"Hey, babe," he says back but he doesn't smile. Instead he goes right for a kiss. It's not a sweet, greeting kiss. It's a dirty, *I want to be naked with you in the snow* kiss and I couldn't be enjoying it more. I think we might just get down to business on the sidewalk when Danny gently and tentatively pulls away.

"I've been wanting to do that since…well…since the last time I did that. Are you ready for this?" he asks grabbing my hand. The warmth of his palm presses against mine and we generate a new heat through our skin. "I know you don't like this type of small party thing. We could make up an excuse and curl up by the fire and…"

I put my finger to his lips. "Stop that thought right there. If you go any further I'm liable to take you up on it. But you're right. This type of thing usually makes me nervous as hell but not tonight. I'm looking forward to being with you and your friends."

He puts his arm around me and we walk toward The Hideaway together. Having him hold me makes me feel safer than I've ever felt before.

*Danny*

I follow Prescott up the stairs to the owner's suite above The Hideaway that Vince and Tack share. His blazer is just short enough to show off his butt as he climbs. With each step it bounces like a soccer ball someone is dribbling. I can't wait to get his clothes off later. We've been taking things slowly both on the physical and the relationship sides and I'm really glad about that because it feels like we are building something together. Maybe we really have a future. I shake my head to stay in the moment and join Prescott—babe—on the landing.

"Welcome, gentlemen," Vince says, his deep voice booming down the stairwell. I pop up the stairs and join Prescott as we enter. Tack is in the small kitchen focused on the meal. They pushed some of the furniture to the walls so that there is a large dining room table set up in the main room. Arthur and Serilda are seated on the couch and we both go over to greet them. "I'm afraid Toula and Anita couldn't join us tonight. You know, because of the big news."

"What big news?" I ask. "There's big news and I don't know. How is that possible?"

"I guess you're losing your touch, Danny-boy," Tack says from the kitchen.

"They're in the process of becoming foster parents and they had an appointment with the agency tonight," Vince says.

"That's wonderful," Prescott says.

"Wow. They'll be amazing parents," I say. I'm truly overjoyed for them and I impulsively grab Prescott's hand and his fingers gently caress mine. Could there be a baby in our future? I wipe the thought from my head like a wet cloth on a dry-erase board. Too soon. Too soon. But… maybe?

"So are we still pretending that the two of you aren't the most adorable couple in town?" Serilda asks.

I think Prescott might bristle at Serilda's comment but instead he leans into it. Hard. He puts his arm around me and gives me a kiss on the cheek.

"Hey, I heard that! What happened to me and Vince? Did we lose most adorable?" Tack says from the kitchen.

Serilda responds to him from the couch, "You just keep your focus on my sweet potato pie recipe and stop worrying about how adorable you may or may not be."

"Ay, ay," Tack says and gives Serilda an improvised salute. "Hey, Danny, would you pass the starter around?" he asks holding out a piece of pottery with a design I recognize from a local art shop.

"Sure, no problem," I say and walk over to the kitchen area.

"These are truffled goat cheese stuffed mushrooms," he says as he sprinkles some kind of fresh herb on them. Then he adds, "And don't worry. The ones on the edge I made *without* truffles just for you. I know you hate them."

I quickly turn my head to see if Prescott is paying attention. Luckily he is deep in conversation with Serilda and Arthur. My heart skips a beat with the reminder I'm keeping something much bigger than a distaste for truffles from Prescott. I know I'm being immature but I'm not ready to face the music and dance. Well, I'm always up for an impromptu dance party but not the other stuff. Every time I feel like I'm almost there he looks at me a certain way or brings me a treat and frankly, I don't want it to end. I don't want him to think of me differently. I take my worry and concern and lock it inside a little box in my brain and then I lock that box in a bigger box and throw it all in the river. At least for tonight.

"Now listen, you two," Serilda says to me and Prescott. "I spoke to each member of the city council. They are willing to listen to our reasons for saving both buildings. But we really have to put pressure on the developer."

"I've searched the corporate website and left a message for every number listed but there aren't any actual names of human beings on it so I've made a bunch of calls but I haven't actually spoken to a real person," Prescott says, his voice displaying a mix of anger and frustration. I love seeing how worked up he gets over saving the buildings. When I first met him it was hard to imagine him getting worked up over anything that would matter to me, but sharing this purpose together has brought us closer.

"A lot of these real estate holding companies can be pretty shady when they want to be," Vince says.

"Well, you should know," Serilda says, throwing the jab at him like a dart aimed for a bull's-eye.

"That's true. I speak from experience. Have you checked to see if there is an LLC filing?" Vince asks.

"I haven't," Prescott says. "I'm afraid this is terra incognita for me."

"Why don't you let me poke around and see what I can find out?"

"Thank you. That would be very helpful. We're getting to the bottom of this and finding out who is responsible," Prescott says and his passion rises to the surface just enough to make me melt a bit inside.

★ ★ ★

The meal is absolutely delicious; rich hearty flavors that have made The Hideaway one of the most popular places in the area. There is a creamy mash of carrots and leeks topped with buttery crumbs that I'm immediately obsessed with. But my attention is on Prescott. I want to make sure he isn't feeling nervous or stuck in a conversation he doesn't want to be in. But he seems relaxed and comfortable. He's chatting with everyone and laughing and he doesn't seem a bit anxious. I get up to help Tack with the sweet potato pie and he pulls me aside. "Serilda's right," he says.

"They almost always are. But about what exactly?" I ask.

"You two *are* adorable and Prescott seems to care for you very much."

"Do you really think so?" My track record is so bad, and I think my ability to tell the difference between a guy who is really into me and a guy who just wants a quick fling is completely broken. I'm beginning to trust Prescott. It's my own judgment I question.

"Totally," Tack assures me. "He's a keeper."

We pass out the plates of Serilda's famous pie and I take my seat next to Prescott. As soon as I sit down he takes my hand and holds it in his. We've been connected like this all night and it feels like a dream. Usually I like to attack Serilda's pie with both hands but tonight I couldn't be happier leaving one hand on my lap with Prescott's soft skin gently rubbing against mine.

# Chapter Twenty-Two

*Prescott*

The shop has had an entirely different vibe the past two weeks. It's gone from a war zone to a love nest. We're entirely professional, especially when customers are browsing, but when we're alone and Danny sees me going through my spreadsheets he'll come over to my desk and give me a gentle shoulder rub to help relieve the stress. One afternoon I turned the open sign to Closed and led him to the pantry and we made out until the mail carrier knocked on the door. It's all so bold, but with Danny I'm not worried he'll make me feel foolish or needy.

As I walk back to the shop holding two steaming lattes from the Honeysuckle, I realize I'm not just feeling more comfortable in the shop but also in town and with the town. When I moved here from Philadelphia, I thought it was just going to a place to live. I wanted an apartment close enough to the shop to have a walkable commute and that was about the height of my expectation. I thought I'd make the business a success and look for an opportunity at one of the big auction houses back in Philadelphia or maybe New York. This wasn't supposed to be a destination, it was just a pit stop. Being with Danny is amazing but it's more than that. Meeting the people here and becoming part of the community effort to save the historic landmarks has made New Hope feel like more than a place to live. It's beginning to feel like a home.

Danny was having an involved conversation with some customers about some apparently very complicated Cabbage Patch doll so I took the opportunity to run down to the corner and grab us some refreshment. We have a coffee maker in the pantry for emergencies, but whenever we have a caffeine urge we try to run to the Honeysuckle to support the local community. Even an incidental purchase can help a small business and we are both aware of that.

When I arrive back at the shop I see he is still talking with the couple he was with when I left, but instead of showing off his collection, he's standing in front of one of the most expensive items in my collection: a Queen Anne letter opener with an enamel handle. How did they go from talking about a baby-face doll to one of the rarest forms of metallurgy?

I stand outside and watch through the shop window as Danny talks to them. His hands move around with his fingers pointing out different parts of the antique. He smiles and then says something very quickly and I see the couple laugh and nod their heads. He's so good with people. I've shared some deep knowledge about my collection but I don't think I've ever made anyone laugh in the shop. For weeks I've been trying to identify what it is that Danny has and I think I've finally figured it out. He has charisma. People just like *liking* him. They can't help liking him.

I feel the same way now. I can't help liking him, in fact, I think I might not be able to help falling in love with him.

The thought of being in love with Danny Roman makes me very aware of the cold wind on my knuckles and the warm cups in my palms. There is a sharp contrast between the two sensations but together they become something that is more than the sum of its parts. I use my foot to open the door. Danny sees me and runs to help me.

"Prescott, I'm glad you're back. This couple is looking for a present for their uncle's seventieth birthday. When they mentioned he still loves sending handwritten letters, I thought your letter opener might be a good match but I told them you were the expert. Could you tell them more about it?" he asks passing off the sale and grabbing the lattes from me.

I walk over to the couple and introduce myself before giving a brief but salient history of how the opener was forged. They seem impressed.

I look over the woman's shoulder at Danny and he smiles at me and shrugs like it was a coincidence that he directed the woman to one of my pieces. If I wasn't about to make a sale I would turn that sign to Closed and have him in the pantry so fast he wouldn't know what's going on. Instead I ring up the sale and wrap up the item.

Once the couple has left the shop I log the sale and notice that I've made a sizeable profit. "I'll be able to pay off the balance on the pewter very soon," I say to him as he's going over some receipts in his hot chocolate tin at his desk. I know he doesn't like to talk about the debt. Growing up without a lot of money made conversations about financial arrangements difficult. Still, I want to make sure he understands I have every intention of paying him back.

"I'm not worried," he says. "I know where you live." He lifts his head up and gives me that warm smile that makes me want to hold him in my arms and squeeze him like a soft teddy bear.

When Serilda walks in with Vince to collect us for the city council meeting, Danny immediately walks over to give them a hug. I wish, for the hundredth time, I could be more like him and just embrace people—embrace life for that matter.

"We got him," Serilda says.

"Got who?" I ask as we begin preparing the shop for the close of day.

"The real estate developer who plans to tear down the buildings. It took some sleuthing but I was able to get a name attached to the project," Vince says.

"Turns out he's a local investor from Philadelphia so I invited him to an upcoming city council meeting. He declined the offer. Humph! He has no idea who he's dealing with. His name is Mr. Jefferson Worthington."

I steady myself on my desk. "What did you say his name was?"

"Jefferson Worthington. He goes by the nickname…"

I don't let them finish the sentence. "Worth," I say and the name in my throat feels like I just swallowed the letter opener I sold.

*Danny*

"Not that awful guy who was in here before we opened for Winter Festival?" I ask, closing the hot chocolate tin and putting it away.

"How many Jefferson Worthingtons can there be in the greater Philadelphia area? I mean I'm hoping there is another one but it seems unlikely." The stiffness Prescott showed when we first met is back.

Worth. The guy who came on to Prescott so hard I thought he was going to spontaneously combust in front of me. Expensive camel hair coat, fancy cashmere sweater, deep tan from recent visit to a five-star resort. He was like an animal stalking his prey with Prescott. I remember the guy, and the thought of him being anywhere near Prescott after we have gotten so close makes me scratch the back of my knuckles nervously.

"Who does he think he is, refusing to come to town and meet us face-to-face? I'm ready to give the city council a piece of my mind tonight and make them order him to attend a meeting so we can make this person aware of how much those buildings mean to this town. You two hurry up and close up shop. We don't want to be late. I need you both."

When Serilda gives you an order there isn't room for delay. I finish with my receipts and start putting the dust covers over the displays as Prescott closes the windows and turns off the lights. This week we started combining our efforts for shutting down, whereas before he did his side and I did mine. It's nice to share it this way and work in tandem with him. I smile as I quickly finish my tasks but then remember that Worth is involved in this whole thing and my smile dims just a bit. We leave the shop and the sidewalk has iced over enough to make walking difficult. I'm worried about Serilda making it all the way to the municipal office in their heels but Arthur appears as soon as we are on the street.

"I was hoping we could walk over together," he says. I notice that Serilda's eyes light up when Arthur arrives.

"Always a lifesaver, Arthur," Serilda says taking his arm and Prescott extends his for me.

"If I slip I'll just drag you down to the cement. You're safer on your own," I tell him. I weigh a lot more than he does. I'm sure a guy like Worth would be easy to keep vertical. The two of them probably weigh the same exact amount within a few ounces.

"I don't want to be safer on my own. I want to be in the grips of danger. With you!" Prescott puts his arm around me and suddenly I don't want to be on my own at all.

We walk behind Arthur and Serilda and I get the courage to ask Prescott what I need to know. "How exactly do you know Worth?" I ask quietly.

"We dated a while back," he says matter-of-factly, as if he just said they met at the gas station or on jury duty.

"You dated?" My shock comes through more clearly than I want. I can't believe Prescott would ever be with someone as snobby and pretentious as Worth. Is that the kind of guy he usually goes for? I can't imagine someone more my opposite than that guy—unless, of course, it's Prescott.

"It was a long time ago," he says rubbing my arm.

"How long?" I ask. I can feel my suspicion rise as my self-esteem plummets.

"Just before I left Philadelphia."

"That's actually not very long ago," I say.

"Maybe not, but it feels like a million years ago. It was nothing serious. I'm with you now. I'm exactly where I want to be."

I squeeze his arm tightly, satisfied with his answer, at least for now.

# Chapter Twenty-Three

*Prescott*

Our charming antique shop turns into protest central in the evenings. Serilda is still trying to persuade the city council to demand Worth attend the next meeting, but even if by some miracle he does we all know he might not listen to reason so we want to be prepared. At the end of the workday Danny and I move the display tables to the edges of the shop. I put away anything fragile and he lays out poster board, paints and markers. The first night also included various pots of glitter but when I started finding pieces of pink sparkle in the tiniest crevices of my finest porcelain we made a compromise. All glitter work now takes place in the alley behind the shop. Last night after everyone left Danny glitter bombed a poster out back and came back in with green and purple sparkles stuck to his scruff and the hair that peeks out from his chest. It made me laugh because he looked like a big sexy Christmas ornament. I started picking it off him and before I knew it we were kissing gently with the glow of the streetlamps illuminating the store.

Tonight we might not have a chance for a make out session. The shop is full of people. I have a jar with extra markers and pencils and I'm walking around taking in all the wonderful work that is happening. There are families, couples and groups of friends all mingling and mixing, drawing on poster board or coloring in letters. Whenever anyone needs a supply I bring it over and chat for a few seconds about what they're making. I'm not unaware that my ability and desire to make nonantique-related small talk has greatly expanded recently.

Tack's child, Jules, raises their hand and asks for a green magic marker. They are working on a poster that says Buildings are People TOO! I walk over with an assortment of colors. "Hi Jules. I'm Prescott. We met at the sledding hill."

Two women are with them. The one with short blond hair says, "So you're the Prescott everyone is talking about. I'm Evie, Jules's mom, and this is my partner, Ines."

"Nice to meet you both," I say. I'm a little embarrassed by her comment but not in the way I would have been a few weeks ago when the very thought of people I don't know talking about me would have made me run away. Right now I don't mind it. I'm not sure if it's the fact that I have finally found a community that feels like home or that being identified as a couple with Danny makes me melt a bit. I'm surprised by how good it makes me feel. I thought keeping to myself was protecting me but I'm beginning to see how much I've been missing out on. There might be more to the world than nineteenth-century antiques. The very idea!

"What happened to all the glitter?" Jules asks.

"Danny is doing special glitter sessions in the alley. No more glitter in the store, I'm afraid," I say with a frown.

"That sounds like a more than reasonable request. In fact, I think maybe we should consider that rule at home." Evie turns to me, "Do you have any idea what glitter does to a vacuum?"

"Can I go out to the alley with Danny?" Jules asks. Their mom agrees and Jules runs off with their poster in hand.

"Jules really loves Danny," Evie says with a bit of mischief in her voice. "You know, he would make a fantastic dad."

"Oh, absolutely," her partner says putting her arm around Evie.

"Yes, I'm sure he would," I say smiling, acknowledging the massive hint they are sending. It seems like everyone in this town not only wants us to be together but start a family right away. Surprisingly, it doesn't feel intrusive. It makes me feel like people are watching out for me, for us. And they're right, of course. Danny would be a wonderful father, even though we're nowhere near having that on the horizon. I never thought having a kid would be part of my future but now... Who knows?

I walk around and chat with a few more people and then see Danny taking a break from his glitter duties and showing his latest creation off to Evan and Kevin. Danny introduced them to me the other day when they came into the shop. They own a farm down the road that makes unbelievable goat cheese and other organic agricultural products.

Danny is smiling that carefree smile that shines like the mother-of-pearl inlay on the letter opener I sold last week.

"I don't get it," Evan says.

"Oh, don't listen to him, Danny. I think it's perfect," Kevin says.

Danny holds up a poster board with the phrase New Betta Hope! on it. "It's like RuPaul says, 'You betta work.'" Danny and Kevin both emphasize the phrase with a finger that wiggles in the air.

"I get it," I say immediately recognizing the reference. I may not be RuPaul's biggest fan but I haven't been living in an Edith Wharton novel my whole life. Danny looks at me with a combination of shock and joy. Then he spontaneously kisses me on the cheek. I'm sure I blush deeper than the reddest magic marker in my jar.

"Do you see why I'm so into this guy? He's always surprising me."

An impulse overcomes me and I kiss Danny back on the cheek right there in front of Evan and Kevin and everyone else in the shop. I grab Danny's hand and hold it tightly, enjoying the moment without giving a single thought to the shade of my cheeks.

*Danny*

Serilda walks in with Arthur and catches Prescott kissing me. "I certainly hope the two of you can save all that kissy stuff for *after* we have saved these buildings." Their content is scolding but the delivery is all honey. They smile at us and Arthur gives an approving nod. "I have some good news," Serilda says.

"Great. As you can see we have a small factory pumping out materials," Prescott says. I'm so proud of the way we've worked together on this. I always thought relationships were a you-do-your-thing-and-I-do-mine experience. I'm beginning to see the joy that comes from working together on a project. Being with Prescott doesn't feel like he is the star pitcher and I'm in the stands giving him batting signals or ordering him a stunning new uniform. It feels like being on the same team and that makes me think I'm not losing myself for once. It makes me appreciate being seen for who I am and not just for what I offer.

"What's the news?" I ask.

"We got Jefferson Worthington to come here and meet with us at the next city council meeting."

"You got Worth to come here?" Prescott says releasing my hand from his. "I thought you said he kept refusing to meet?"

"He did, but pressure from the council forced him to change his mind. He wasn't happy about it," Serilda says.

I'm feeling an unpleasant ambiguity. I want to confront the person who plans to tear down our historic core but I do not in any way, shape or form want that person to be Worth. I look at Prescott and he is biting his lower lip—something I noticed he does when he is deep in thought. I want to know what he's thinking.

"I plan to let this Worth know that just because you have money doesn't mean you can come into our community and pave over our historic landmarks. I hope he'll see reason but if he doesn't we will take to the streets and block his way. We're going to need every single poster you have here for the biggest protest this town has ever seen," Serilda says. Everyone in the shop nods and murmurs in agreement. Jules runs over to Serilda and shows them their Buildings are People TOO! poster.

"What about this one?" they ask. The poster is almost as big as they are. Serilda looks at it carefully.

"Oh, yes," Serilda says bending down a bit to address Jules. "We will need that one front and center right on Main Street. It's wonderful." Jules smiles at Serilda and Arthur.

"I'd be delighted to treat all of you to a hot chocolate after-party at the Honeysuckle. Let's help Prescott and Danny clean up and head over," Arthur says. He's always so sweet thinking about what people need and when they need it.

"You all just head on out. Prescott and I can take care of all this," I say.

"Yes, you each deserve a hot chocolate and without the glitter, tidying this up is a breeze," Prescott adds.

Everyone grabs their coats and bags from the pantry area and we say our temporary goodbyes as they head out. Once we are alone we start gathering materials and throwing out trash. I look over at Prescott and I can tell he is still preoccupied. "Are you okay?" I ask gently.

"Yeah, that was a great turnout and I think the community is really behind this effort. It's just that…" he trails off and his voice has a slight quiver.

"What?" I walk over to him and put my hand on his arm.

"I've seen how these things play out with people like Worth. I'm worried that a public event might make him dig his heels in more. He gets off throwing his money and power around so everyone can see." Prescott's voice is growing quieter as he speaks. "It's wonderful the way everyone has come together but I'm worried this is going to backfire. I was thinking maybe a private meeting would work better," he says.

"When he was in the store that time he seemed pretty obnoxious." I think back to the five minutes I spent with him and how he insulted me and talked to me like I was beneath him. "Do you really think we should…"

"Not we," he says, swallowing hard. "I'm not sure the both of us approaching him is a good idea. There was definitely friction when you met. That was obvious. I was thinking I could talk to him." He takes a pause, as if to make sure he wants to say what he is going to say. And then the word comes out. "Alone." He looks down.

"Just the two of you?" I can't hide my discomfort about the idea. I'm willing to do whatever it takes to save the buildings, and if I thought the two of them having a meeting would work then I would support it, but we already have a plan in place, a good one. I think we should stick to it and not go rogue. Of course there's also the fact that the very thought of Prescott and that jerk being alone together makes me more than a little uncomfortable. "I don't think it's a good idea. I know you have your heart in the right place but it smells too much like a backroom deal," I say keeping my reasons purely professional although I'm aware they are tinged with personal jealousy.

I know Prescott said Worth was in his past but still they shared something. I get a flash of walking in on my ex and how painful that was. But Prescott isn't like that. I never fully trusted Paul and everything with Prescott feels different.

"The whole point is to bring the community together, not shut people out. I really think we should stick with the plan we have. You heard Serilda. If Worth doesn't see reason we'll be ready to meet those bulldozers on the street, all of us, together," I say praying he'll agree with me. We've been on the same wavelength recently but maybe my signals have been crossed. Is he going to fly solo or is he going to be on the same team with me?

"It was a bad idea," Prescott says quickly. "You're right. We have a plan in place. Let's stick to that." He puts the last stack of poster boards in the pantry and comes back out with both our coats. "Let's go over to the Honeysuckle, meet up with everyone and fight over who gets the bigger marshmallow."

I smile and kiss him on the cheek. He grabs my hand and we walk out the door together. I'm hoping it's Team Us all the way but I'm wondering if the home court advantage is enough to guarantee a win.

# Chapter Twenty-Four

*Danny*

The night of the city council meeting with Worth is one of the coldest I can remember. The air is clear but so frigid it feels almost hard. Prescott and I have started holding hands while walking more often than not, but tonight is so ridiculously bleak that we just walk side by side with our hands in our pockets. I was planning to chatter away in case there were any last-minute nerves but both our faces are covered in scarves so we walk in silence.

We get to the room in the municipal building where the meeting is scheduled and there are a few members from the planning commission, a good group of people from the shop with their handmade signs, and the very man himself.

Jefferson "Worth" Worthington is already seated, looking like a filtered Instagram post come to life.

"Press, it's so good to see you again. I wish it were under better circumstances," Worth says, extending his arm. They shake hands which is more physical contact than I want them to have but certainly a safe-enough interaction. I suppose Prescott has to be friendly to the opposition; it's good sportsmanship.

The meeting begins, everyone takes their seats and Serilda explains our position. Then I make a short but passionate speech about the bank. I emphasize the almost-intergalactic design and explain how many of the small shops in town got their first loans at that branch. My talk is a mix of ethnography, tribute and stand-up comedy. When it's Prescott's turn to talk about the historic significance of the Yardley House he is clearly in his element. He's able to make details that a few weeks ago would have seemed duller than an NPR membership drive *Raiders of the Lost Ark*–exciting. I'm absolutely swelling with pride when he speaks and it makes me even more determined to rip his clothes off when we get out of here.

We end our presentation and the room is silent. Surely after hearing how important these buildings are Worth will at the very least reconsider or commit to finding a compromise. I look at Worth, who is looking at Prescott… who is looking at me. It's a tense moment. Worth breaks his focus on Prescott and says, "A most interesting presentation. Thank you very much. I came here to listen and listen I did. Well done." He's praising us but I can tell it's a sucker punch. "But from a financial point of view, it makes more sense to tear them down. I'm looking out for the best interests of the investment. The parking facility will be very tasteful and as for all that nostalgia about the bank... well, you'll make new memories. Parking in this town is a nightmare. More places to park means more shoppers to shop. I'm doing you all a favor."

"A favor!" Serilda's voice has bite. Their tone is sharp and dangerous.

"Look, I'm not some heartless villain," Worth continues. "I love architecturally significant buildings as much as any-one, but let's face it, despite Dan's passionate speech about the bank that place is a dump and since the buildings share a support my hands are tied. But I have to be honest. I love the energy in this room tonight. I really, really do." He is so condescending you could play a clip of his statement on YouTube for those seeking a definition of the word. "Unfortunately the bulldozers will be on site as planned." Worth gets up and everyone starts talking at once, yelling at him to reconsider. Everyone except Prescott, who sits quietly without so much as a single peep of protest.

Serilda is almost shouting at Worth when he turns and says, "I'm sorry, but there is nothing more you can do." His words send a chill over the room and he's almost out the door but then zooms in on Prescott and says, "It was nice seeing you, Press. I do hope we can do it again. Soon." The words come out of his mouth like slime through a soft-serve machine. He walks out and I immediately to turn to Prescott, who still hasn't said a word.

"Why didn't you say something?" I ask.

"What could I say? There's nothing we can do."

I'm so disappointed right now. I expected Prescott to be as incensed as I am. His silence feels painfully loud.

"He thinks there's nothing we can do," Serilda says. "But he doesn't know our community. Those bulldozers are scheduled to be here next week and we'll be waiting for them. It's time for an old-fashioned protest. We'll need as many people as we can get. Can one of you contact the supporters who weren't here tonight and let them know the protest is on? Ask them to spread the word. We are taking over the street."

"Yes," Prescott says. "I can do that." He looks so utterly defeated that I can't help shutting down whatever frustration or disappointment I'm feeling in order to make him feel better.

"That's great," I say grabbing his hand, hoping to pump a bit more enthusiasm into him. I bring him in for a hug and although he squeezes me as tightly as ever, something feels off. We release the embrace and he won't meet my eyes. Instead he looks down and he bites his lower lip. His mind is somewhere else and I can't help wondering where that might be.

# Chapter Twenty-Five

*Prescott*

I've been quieter than usual around the store the past few days. The city council meeting threw me for a loop. Danny was brilliant, of course. He had everyone eating out of the palm of his hand. I even saw Worth crack a smile at one point. That's Danny. He can charm anyone, even a bore like Worth.

My talk was stodgy and uninspiring. Maybe it was unlikely that Worth was ever going to come away from that meeting changing his mind, but my presentation didn't do us any favors. I feel like I disappointed everyone and most importantly, I feel I disappointed Danny.

I've never felt a part of something like this and I don't want to see it fail. So when Worth texted me saying he wanted to meet with me privately because he had "big news" and that I was the *only one* who had a chance at helping "the cause" I agreed. I've been nauseated about it ever since.

Danny keeps trying to pull me out of my shell, but knowing I have this secret between us makes it impossible for me to relax. I'm just hoping Worth has something real to discuss. My stomach roils once again. To calm myself down I have to imagine the look in Danny's eyes when he finds out I was able to save these historic landmarks. I realize for the first time I'm actually more concerned about the First Bank of Bucks than I am about the Yardley House. I respect the Yardley House and appreciate it for its unique contribution to architectural design, but lately I've been walking by the bank and appreciating it just as much. The bank really is a memory of a better future, as Danny is always reminding everyone. I'm not sure if I'm expanding my aesthetic taste or if my feelings about it are simply entwined with my feelings for Danny and my own hopes for the future.

Danny always leaves early on Wednesdays to help at St. Stanislaw so I've arranged for Worth to meet me at the store. I'd rather be meeting him in another town or a different state altogether but with Danny taking the van to the church my only option is the store since at least I can lock the door. I stare at the hands on my Cartier clock and I'm almost shaking with nerves as they tick closer to three o'clock. For a brief moment I think about telling Danny everything. I want to be open with him about it but I'm finding the thought of having the conversation just too impossible. I need to find out what Worth has to say. If he's leading me on, I'll kick him out. If he has information that's useful we'll be able to reach our goal. Still, I wonder if that victory would be sweeter if we did it together. The clock creeps ahead and my stomach gets tighter. There's no turning back now.

"Look at the time," I say as naturally as a robot that hasn't been oiled. "You don't want to be late. Isn't Kasia expecting you soon?" Danny is rearranging some of his merchandise on a shelf.

"I didn't realize how late it is. I better get going. Are we still on for pizza tonight? I've been in the mood for a slice of Gaspo's pie since I went to bed last night."

"Absolutely. Now hurry up. You don't want to keep Kasia waiting. Didn't they need you to move a piano or something?" I say hoping to get him out the door so there is no chance of him running into Worth.

"Meet you at the pizzeria after you close up the shop?"

"Great," I say, my stomach in a potent twist of knots and butterflies. Danny grabs his coat and hat from the hooks in the pantry and heads to the door. He puts his hand on the doorknob but stops and turns back to me.

"What?" I ask trying to hide nervous frustration.

"I forgot this." He walks over and kisses me on the lips softly and heads out.

I collapse at my desk and hang my head in my hands. My plan has got to work. I take a second to gather my thoughts and then look out the windows to make sure Danny is gone.

With Danny out of the shop and Worth not yet here I'm

able to complete another task I've been needing to do in private. I walk over to Danny's desk and get a closer look at the tin where he keeps his receipts.

Luckily he has left it out of the drawer so I don't feel like I'm invading his privacy too much. The tin displays the words *Amore Chocolate* in swirly brown and red script. On the front of the beat-up tin there is a drawing that I have not looked at closely before. A man in a fedora drinks from a cup with a big hearty smile. I take a closer look before I snap a picture so I can go online later and see if I can find a hoodie with the image. He loves his hoodies, and I've been wanting to get him something special.

As I swipe my phone screen closed, I realize the man in the hat bears a striking resemblance to Danny—same big smile. I wonder if that is why this box is so precious to him. Maybe someone recognized the resemblance and gave it to him as a gift.

My heart drops when I hear someone at the door. I know exactly who it is. I quickly put my phone in my pocket and get ready to invite the vampire in.

Worth glides into the shop. His smugness surrounds him like a cloud of gray smoke. The sudden realization that Worth is alone with me in the shop hits hard. This is exactly the scenario Danny did not want and I've allowed it to happen. I should shove Worth right out the door but before I can make that decision he walks toward me.

"Press, I have to say that country life agrees with you. You look more dashing than ever."

"Worth, this isn't a social call. You said you had information that will help. So what is it?"

Worth ignores me. He starts casually walking around the shop browsing the merchandise. He picks up a Samuel Alcock porcelain vase with burgundy trim and an exquisitely painted pastoral scene on it. He admires it closely. Then he puts it down and sneers at Danny's side of the shop.

"For the life of me I'll never understand how something as impeccable as this vase can be in the same room with all this trash. The two just do not belong together."

I will not have Worth come in here and insult Danny or his collectibles. "Worth, if you just came here to start trouble…"

"Not at all," he says taking off his coat and sitting next to my desk. "In fact, I came here to ask you something. Please sit down," he says with a petulant sigh. Reluctantly I take a seat at my desk but I move the chair as far away from him as possible.

"So what did you come here to ask?" My voice is colder than the icicles that cling to the shop's awning. He stares right at me, his eyes slowly taking in the features of my face in a way that makes me deeply uncomfortable.

"What facial moisturizer are you currently using? Your skin is flawless and all the dry heat this winter has simply made my skin rougher than the roads out here."

"Worth, if that is what you came here to ask you can just leave."

"Well, excuse me for being distracted but it's hard to focus when your skin is so…" He reaches his hand toward my cheek and then moves his face even closer to mine. His hand is perhaps about to brush my cheek when I grab it and hold it a few inches from my face. I don't want him to touch me.

"Worth, this is your last chance to…"

"Fine," he says with a pout. "I was thinking about your talk the other night…"

"Yes?" I prod. Is it possible that Worth has finally accepted how important these two buildings are?

"Well, mother is hosting a huge event in Philadelphia at the club. Very Main Line. Super posh. And suddenly I had this brilliant idea. Why don't I ask my old friend Press to give one of his little lectures? I remember how stunning you look in a tux. I'd consider it a personal favor."

I laugh right in his face. "You would, would you? Worth, why in the world would I do a favor for you?"

His eyes widen in mock surprise. "Oh, did I forget to mention my news? See I was so distracted by your flawless appearance that I forgot myself completely. You know how these things work, one hand washes the other as they say. I thought you would do me this favor if I saved the building."

"Are you serious?" I ask.

"Sure." He shrugs as if he couldn't care less either way.

"Really?" I ask my eyes wide. "Thank you, Worth," I say wondering if I should be waiting for the other shoe to drop. But my enthusiasm gets the better of me and I go to shake his hand. He takes the opportunity to lean in and go for a kiss on my cheek. I don't want him anywhere near me in that way. My hand reaches for my cheek instinctively and wipes the spot where his lips touched. I get up and stand behind my chair like a shield.

"I can't wait to let everyone know. They'll be thrilled."

Of course I'm most excited to let Danny know the bank will be saved. "I'm glad there won't be bulldozers in the street," I say in a business-like tone.

He laughs and stands up. "Oh, I didn't say that. Maybe you didn't hear me. I said we can save the build-ING. As in singular. One."

"I thought that they were dependent on each other structurally. They said that if one goes down then the other goes down too."

"I guess some things just don't belong together," he says wrinkling his nose and glancing around the shop. "The engineers may or may not have found a way around that. We don't really need all that space with both lots so we can save your Yardley House. It's the whole reason you got involved with this hippie-dippie group. Isn't that what you want?"

"No," I say immediately. I could never sacrifice the bank. When I first saw those buildings together I never thought I'd see them as equals. They seemed incompatible. But Danny has showed me that the bank is just as beautiful as the Yardley House. He's taught me that staying open to new experiences can have greater reward than risk.

I look over at Danny's side of the shop and his hot chocolate tin catches my gaze. The man in the graphic reminds me so much of Danny and I think of him greeting people as they walk in the store like they've come to tell him he won the lottery and offering them a cinnamon snap from his Snoopy cookie jar. Or how he gets me to open up about myself and let down my walls. I don't want to be alone in a beautifully gilded cage. Danny treats every day like the circus has come to town and for the first time in my life I want to be inside that tent. With him.

I could never agree to let Worth destroy something Danny has worked so hard to fight for. It would destroy our relationship. It's all or nothing. "Get out!" I say trying not to let the anger I'm feeling take over my whole body.

I should never have done this. I should never have met with Worth alone. For somebody as educated as I am this was a pretty dumb thing to do. If I can get him to leave immediately I can just pretend this never happened.

"What? I just offered you exactly what you wanted." Worth looks at me with genuine surprise.

"Get out!" I repeat. "You have no idea what I want," I say hoping my words slice through his egotistical posturing.

He scans me up and down. "Well, it can't be these little toys," he walks over to the display of Smurfs and picks one up carelessly.

"Do not touch those! They are priceless Smurfs," I yell sharply.

He laughs and tosses the blue guy to the floor. "Did you just say *priceless Smurfs*? What has happened to you?" Worth sighs heavily. "You obviously aren't thinking clearly. I'll give you some time to get back in a proper frame of mind but you better do it quickly or you'll be walking over rubble on your way to work." He walks out the door.

I'm absolutely shaking with anger, frustration and fear. Worth has only ever seen me as an object to be put on display like garniture on the shelf. Danny doesn't make me feel that way at all. He makes me feel seen and that makes me feel confident.

I need to correct the mistake I made. I was stupid for thinking I could make everything right all by myself. I've been a solo act for so long that I'm not sure how to play a duet, but I should at least know that it means honesty and openness. I need to tell Danny everything about agreeing to meet with Worth. I just hope he'll forgive me for being so stupid. He's only been honest and open with me and deserves the same in return. I don't want to play by myself anymore. I want us to make music together as part of an ensemble.

I look over at Toothy lying on the floor where Worth tossed him, grinning his bright smile before he takes the toothbrush to his mouth. I pick him up and put him back in the village with all the other busy blue members of the community. Now he is exactly where he belongs.

# Chapter Twenty-Six

*Danny*

I'm a few miles away from the shop when I realize I forgot the vintage thimble I've been meaning to give Kasia for her collection. I hate having to backtrack but smile at the fact that it means I'll be able to give Prescott a second goodbye kiss.

As I approach the shop I notice that someone is inside talking to Prescott but I can't see who it is since the windows are frosted over. Something in my gut tells me to hang back a bit. Maybe I shouldn't spy on him like this but then I begin to make out exactly who is in there with him.

It's Worth.

I can see his face in one of the mirrors that Prescott has

on display and I wish I couldn't. What is he doing here and why are they sitting so close to each other? Prescott and I discussed meeting with him privately and decided it was a bad idea. Then I remember Prescott ushering me out the door to my appointment. Could he have planned this meeting in secret when he knew I would be away from town?

I'm about to step out of the shadow and enter when I see the only thing that could stop me.

A kiss.

As soon as I see their faces next to each other I turn away. They are definitely not a safe distance apart and certainly not far enough apart for an ex-boyfriend when your current boyfriend is about to come back. Everything is blurry through the window but I don't want to see any more. I walk a few yards past the window. How could he do this to me? How could he kiss Worth right in the shop?

Maybe there's an explanation. I think about going back to the store and demanding to know what's going on. But where would that get me? I saw what I saw. Ever since Worth's name was mentioned I thought I felt him pulling away. It was just a bit at first and then this past week after Worth's performance at the community meeting Prescott has seemed quieter than he has been recently, more shut down. Not to mention his silence after his presentation at the city council.

He assured me that Worth was nothing to him anymore and, gullible heartsick fool that I am, I believed him. I always do this. I jump in when I should tread. I thought we were going slowly. I though the whole point of going at this speed was to prevent the deep cut opening in my heart at this moment. I really thought we were on the same page about building this relationship but apparently not. Does he have any idea what he's throwing away?

How could he even think about being with the guy who is planning to tear down his beloved Yardley House? I'm sure he couldn't care less about the bank, but I believed him when he talked with such eloquence and passion about that special roof and the augmented doorways and hand-blown windows. How could he do this to me?

I can't face him or anyone. I'll go to Kasia's next week. I'm too angry and too hurt. I'll make up some excuse later. I can't get over the fact that he was with him right there in the middle of the afternoon in the shop where we both work. He's smarter than that. Then I think maybe that's exactly what he wanted. He wanted me to see. He wanted a scene where he could claim I was being dramatic and he could dump me without having any blood on his hands and then rush off with Worth to become a matching set of candlesticks. Were we just too different to make this work?

I march up Ferry Street back to the apartment with no intention of giving Prescott the big scene he wants. I open the door and Lizard is on the couch.

"It's the middle of the afternoon. What are you doing home? Are you sick? Oh, no. Did you eat the Pad Thai I had in the fridge because that wasn't Pad Thai."

"I'm not sick," I say and collapse on the couch next to her. "And what do you mean that wasn't Pad Thai?"

"That's not important—or at least not important right now. What's going on?"

"I saw Prescott kissing someone in the shop."

"He was what!" she shouts, jumping up from the couch. "Are you kidding me? In the middle of the day he is just making out with some rando in the store?"

"I wouldn't say making out and it wasn't some rando. His ex, that horrible guy Worth."

"Ugh. With the fancy car and million-dollar haircut who's tearing down the buildings?"

"Yeah, that guy."

I tell her the whole story about how I was on my way to Kasia and when I came back I found them locking lips.

"Well, what did he say when you walked in?"

"Walked in? I didn't step foot in the place. I don't even think he saw me. At least I hope he didn't. As soon as I saw Worth on him, I left."

*Prescott*

Where are you? You okay? I text to Danny. I've been sitting at the pizzeria waiting for him, wondering if I misunderstood the plans for dinner. I'm getting worried. I stare at my phone and nervously smooth out the red-and-white tablecloth under my hand. We've been coming to Gaspo's a lot since we got together. It's quickly becoming "our place" and I'm glad we decided to meet here. Kicking Worth out felt good. I'm nervous about telling Danny that I met with Worth privately but I'm glad I can tell him how I kicked him out. I hope he'll understand. He's got to.

Finally the bubbles indicating he is texting me back appear. I immediately feel relief. Maybe he ran into a friend, started chatting and lost track of time. He does know everyone. Maybe he and Kasia stopped for a cup of coffee somewhere. There are lots of reasons he might be late, I tell myself.

Ate some bad Pad Thai. Not feeling well. Went home. Poor guy. I hate the thought of him in any pain. I look at my phone and it takes me a second to realize why the text seems odd. There isn't a single emoji. Danny usually creates the strangest combination of tacos, smiley faces and flags in even the shortest response. He must be feeling really crappy.

I'm so sorry. Let me bring you some soup, I text back. Maybe something with a salty broth will make him feel better. I can fix a tray for him and tell him all about my afternoon. Come clean. Clear the air.

This time it barely takes him a second to respond. No, is all he says. I wait to see if he follows up with anything else but he doesn't. When I'm sick I just want to crawl into a spot and be alone. Although before I met Danny everything made me want to crawl into a spot and be alone. I want that a lot less currently, and I definitely want to crawl into a spot with him now—but still I need to give him the space he needs to feel better.

Okay. Just text me if you need anything at all. I stare at the text before sending it. First I think about including an emoji but that's really not my style. Then it hits me. What I want to say is: "Love you." I enter the text carefully and stare at it for a second. I'm shocked I wrote it but the fact is I do. I love him. I love his openness and honesty. I love how he makes me laugh and I love how he makes me feel when we are together. The cursor at the end of the message blinks like a siren forcing me to make a decision. *How do you feel, Prescott? How do you feel?* The answer comes to me quickly. I love him. I do.

But a text is not the way to express it. I delete it and just leave the part that offers my help if he needs it.

When I get home I mostly spend the time online searching for Danny's Amore hoodie. I pay extra for the overnight shipping and plan to give it to him the next day in the shop. I might even tell him exactly how I feel.

# Chapter Twenty-Seven

*Prescott*

When I get to the shop the next morning Danny isn't there. Normally I'd think that was odd because he's such an early bird. He usually has the potbelly stove roaring before I've started across the bridge. He must still be really sick. I checked my phone all night in case I needed to run over to his place with anything, but I didn't get any messages so I figured he was sleeping off whatever bug he might have gotten. The fact that he isn't in the shop this morning prompts me to check on him again.

How are you feeling? Do need anything? I can run up with a latte or breakfast if you're up for it.

No. Don't, he texts back immediately. Won't be in today. Maybe tomorrow.

I go to type a heart but I realize I'm not even sure how to use the emojis. There are dozens of hearts, all different colors in different styles. I have no idea what each one means and I'm worried I'll send the wrong one so I just type Feel better and wish it was easier for me to express my feelings even in text.

If yesterday afternoon dragged then this morning is going backward. I spend most of my time staring at Danny's desk and even walking over to his side and playing with some of the things he has on display. It's late afternoon when I'm in the middle of a hypnotic session with a Slinky Dog when the delivery I'm waiting for arrives. I sign for it and thank the woman before tearing the box open. It's Danny's hoodie, bright blue with the Amore Chocolate logo featuring that man who looks so much like Danny. I decide to close the shop and hand deliver the present to Danny hoping it will cheer him up. I won't stay long, just a drive-by to let him know I'm thinking about him. I can wait to make my confession until he feels better.

I knock on the door to the apartment and Lizard answers. She always makes me nervous but in this moment she has a scowl on her face that makes her usual scowl look like a Girl Scout salute.

"What do you want?" she asks.

"Uhm...hello... I was wondering if, please, Danny is feeling better. Is he home?" I ask. Her confrontation has me rattled. I expect her to open the door widely and let me pass but instead she steps outside and closes the door completely.

"You want to know how he's doing?" It sounds like she is revving up to lay into me but then she suddenly slams the brakes. She takes a breath and says, "He's fine."

I'm not sure if I believe her. "Could I step in and see him? I brought him a gift." I hold up the hoodie which I didn't even take time to wrap since I wanted to get here so quickly.

Lizard looks at the garment and laughs out loud. It's not a giggle. She's mocking me but I'm not sure why. Did I get the wrong size? The wrong color? Does he actually hate Amore Chocolate?

"What do you think Danny is going to do with a sweatshirt with a picture of his grandfather on it, you jackass?"

I can admit the guy does look like Danny but what is she talking about? "I don't understand. Grandfather?"

"You think Danny is some guy you toy with while you're on vacation from your rich friends? You don't know anything about him. The man on that sweatshirt is actually Danny's grandfather. He started the company a few generations ago. Danny's the heir to a fortune."

"What are you talking about? I thought he said his father works at a restaurant or on cars or something." I know Danny told me that. He never said anything about them being rich. He certainly didn't say anything to make me believe otherwise.

"Uhm, yeah, his dad loves cars," she says, the sarcasm dripping off her lips like ice cream down a cone. "He has a garage full. A Lamborghini, a vintage Porsche, a Bentley. Why don't you just get lost?"

She walks back inside and slams the door.

I walk off the front porch and stand on the sidewalk with my phone out doing some very simple digging. I just need to add his name to the search term *Amore Foods Inc.* and the hits just pour down my screen. Amore Chocolate is part of Amore Food Incoporated which is part of Amore Industries. The parent company is worth millions—no, actually billions.

I find an empty bench down the block and sit down so I can find out more. There are corporate headquarters made out of steel and glass in various cities around the world, headlines about growing revenue and corporate mergers and pictures of the man who must be Danny's father with celebrities and world leaders. In one image his father is at Buckingham Palace with an assortment of members of the royal family. Hit after hit about his family's massive wealth scrolls down my screen. Images of mansions, yachts and parties. How could he keep something like this from me? How could he lead me to believe something else? I specifically remember having a conversation about growing up and having our dads work so they could make ends meet. It doesn't make any sense but there it all is scrolling down my phone like rain ruining a picnic.

I shove my phone in my pocket. I can't look anymore. His father was off with Prince Whoever and my dad was dealing cards at a casino. Is that why he felt he couldn't tell me? This whole time I was opening up to him about my background, sharing with him who I really am, and he was feeding me a lie. I can't believe I told him about Carol Ann. *Tricked again, Prescott.*

This is what happens when you open up to people. They lie to you. I've spent my whole career developing an astute eye so I can always spot a fake. The problem is, I should never have let my heart enter the equation.

*Danny*

"Did you get rid of him?" I ask Lizard, unable to get up from my hiding spot on the couch.

"Oh, yeah. He won't be coming back here anytime soon," she says. I can still feel the apartment vibrating from the door slam.

"I have to work with him. I told you to just tell him I wasn't feeling well. What did you say?" I ask not really wanting to know. Lizard and I have always been fiercely protective of each other.

"You hated him for weeks. Now you can just go back to that. It'll be fine."

I'm not sure I ever really hated Prescott. From the moment I laid eyes on him I thought he was the handsomest guy I ever met and, sure, we clashed. We both shared a love for old things. They just happen to be different old things.

"I'm so stupid," I tell Lizard. "I really thought this time would be different. I really thought we were taking things slowly so we could trust each other. I thought I just needed to meet a guy who liked me for me. The truth is this is actually worse." I grab a throw pillow from the couch and hold it tightly for comfort. "At least before I could say that the guys cheated on me because they realized I'm not anybody's meal ticket. I could tell myself it had nothing to do with me as a person."

"It didn't," Lizard says firmly.

"He doesn't know my family is loaded. In fact," I pause, hesitating to reveal my omission out loud. "I led him to believe we were not very well-off." Lizard's eyes dart down and her head follows. "I planned to tell him. I thought that once we got past the protest I would be able to. We've been so busy and then Worth came to town and it never seemed the right time. Now who cares? It's not like the two of us were on the same page at all."

"I'm glad to hear you say that because I sort of let it slip," Lizard says peeking through her hands as they shield her eyes.

"You did?" I ask. The thought of him finding out from Lizard makes my entire body tense. That's *not* how I wanted it to go down. I was picturing a warm fireplace after skating on a quiet pond not the doorway to my apartment and by my best friend and her rather sharp tongue. Still, it's not her fault. It's mine. "It's okay," I say feeling myself sink deeper into my sadness.

"What did he say?" I ask knowing I shouldn't want to know the answer to that question as much as I do.

"I don't know. I slammed the door."

"This is all such a mess. I should have been honest from the start but I wasn't because…"

"Because you thought he would take advantage of you."

"No," I say. "I mean I'm always on guard about that and guys have in the past but Prescott isn't like that." I stare straight ahead and try to gather my thoughts so I can put them into words. "I think I didn't tell him because I was enjoying being seen without my family looming over me. It's more about how it made me feel like I could be myself all by myself and he seemed to like me for just me. I should have just told him the truth. I don't know how I thought we could build something when I wasn't honest."

"But Danny, he wasn't honest with you either. You told me he said he wouldn't go behind everyone's back and meet with Worth but he did. He must have known how much that would hurt you. And clearly from what you saw it was more than business. He's a shallow, self-important snob." She plops down in the chair next to me and puts her feet on the coffee table.

"He isn't any of those things, not really. I mean I thought that at first too but he's not that way at all." I think back to the past few weeks and how much I've enjoyed getting to know him. Maybe there's an explanation for what I saw through the shop window. Maybe there's something I'm missing. "You know, I didn't really give him a chance to explain."

"Explain what? You saw him alone with that jerk in the store. Kissing."

"Well, it wasn't like they were making out in Smurf Village. Maybe I overreacted?"

"I'm not saying you don't have a reputation for overreacting or that you don't have a history of blowing things out of proportion or being over-the-top dramatic…"

"Could you skip ahead to the part that makes me feel better?" I say, knowing Lizard only speaks honestly and isn't always aware of the impact of her words. It's why I trust her so much.

She leans in toward me changing her tone from flippant to concerned. "I know you think there is more to this guy than meets the eye but I have to tell you, I'm not so sure."

Lizard may be right but this is still hard to accept. I keep picturing him just on the other side of the closed apartment door talking to Lizard wearing one of his tight blazers, his nose just a bit rosy from the cold air and his beautiful eyes wondering where I am. I keep thinking about the kiss at the bottom of the hill after falling off the sled. I keep thinking about the way it felt to believe we were beginning to really build a relationship together of trust and respect. It felt like we were at the beginning of something really important and exciting. Was what we had just fragile and temporary? I lie down on the couch, close my eyes and prepare to take another nap but I know my dreams will only be about Prescott.

# *Chapter Twenty-Eight*

*Prescott*

The sun has set and the streets are cold and lonely. Freezing temperatures have either kept the tourists home or inside near a source of heat. I should button my blazer but I don't care. Let the bitter cold bite my skin and chap my face. At least the outside will match how I feel on the inside. I walk home with my head down.

I was really falling for Danny. He made me feel comfortable in my skin. It *all* felt different with him but I can't be with a guy who thinks so little of me that he keeps hidden such a big part of who he is. It feels like an imbalance—a seesaw on the side of a cliff and I'm on the low end about to slide off. In so many ways it's the small things that were more meaningful to me. Like when I had an idea for something to do in the store or what I thought about a meal we just ate. Danny made me feel like he wanted to hear whatever I had to say no matter how unimportant I thought it might be. He had this way of making the moment itself more meaningful than the content and that made me feel like anything I said was okay as long as it was real.

But none of that makes sense now. There I was, being all real and he was just lying his ass off to me the whole time.

I walk past the bank and the Yardley House and all I can do is think about that night under the Snow Moon and the kiss that started everything. It was so easy to talk with him that night, to share myself with him. I see the bench where I kissed him and if it weren't bolted down I'd throw it into the river. I don't open myself up to people like that. But Danny made me feel brave and confident. He made me feel like he really saw who I am and that made me feel like I could do anything.

I realize I'm standing on the very spot where we are supposed to be holding signs and protesting just two days from now. Together.

Then I think about the Cunningham tankard and Danny snapping it up like that without explanation. Throwing down money like I'm a charity case. Now, of course, the Christopher Cassiday relationship makes sense. I never really pushed it because I thought Danny had been so honest about everything. I could not have been more wrong.

I march away from the site of the future protest and head home. My hurt and disappointment grow with each step. I should have kept my distance. I should have stayed away. I've always been careful with people but a guy like Danny is like an unavoidable force of nature. Once I was in his orbit there wasn't much of a choice.

I run up the stairs and throw off my coat and collapse on the couch. The red glow of the light from the pharmacy sign washes over me like a hypnotic trance. I think about just going to bed and hoping I can sleep without dreaming of Danny but instead I do the opposite.

I grab my laptop and decide to throw just a bit more salt in my open wound of a heart. I open my browser and search for the picture I can't stop thinking about. Even though it will hurt I want to see it again.

I have to click through dozens of links and each one makes me ache more. Danny's family may be loaded but they certainly know how to spend down their wealth. For every fancy party I find I also see contributions to international social justice causes, and not just vanity donations. They majorly fund some of the most important causes that serve BIPOC, queer and disabled people among many others. It's easy to see that Danny inherited not only his family's wealth but also their compassion and kindness. Seeing all their incredible work makes me more confused and sad knowing he hid this all from me but my next click brings me about as low as I can go.

I saw the link earlier and couldn't get the picture out of my head. I click and hold my breath knowing seeing the image might push me over the edge. Danny is at some fancy party a few years ago with longer hair and a thicker beard. He looks so handsome in his suit but you can tell he isn't that comfortable in it. He is smiling but it's not his usual unapologetic grin that shoots a thousand bolts of sunlight across the room. It's more a smirk and even that makes me laugh. I can't help but focus on his light brown eyes and how they twinkle even in an old photo. I'm about to dive deep inside them but I immediately stop myself before any tears are able to form. I shut my laptop and push it away from me.

I should have kept my head down and stayed within my comfort zone. I feel like a failure. I couldn't get Danny to be honest with me and I couldn't save the buildings.

My phone rings and I'm so excited that it might be Danny that I leap up and answer it without looking at who the caller is. "Hello," I say almost breathless.

"Well, hello to you." Worth's snake-like smoothness crawls out of the phone. "You sound out of breath. I hope you weren't doing something naughty. Wait, strike that. Maybe I hope you were."

"Worth, what do you want?" He's the last person I want to speak to but I don't even have the energy to hang up.

"I hate how we ended things in your little shop. I wanted to remind you of my offer. The olive branch is still on the tree if you wish to reconsider? I'd hate to see that building go down if it doesn't have to and Mother would be so tickled to show you off."

"You're underestimating the power of the people of this community. You don't know them. I do." I think about all the people I've gotten to know since I've been here. I think about Serilda's strong voice and Arthur's sweet nature. I remember running into Vince, Tack and Jules on the sledding hill and mornings at the Honeysuckle when I thought I would catch up on work but wound up chatting casually with people. This town has changed me and if it can do that I have faith that it has a good shot at stopping Worth.

That said, he is a formidable opponent. And a sleazy one.

"They'll never get enough people to stop a snowball from rolling downhill, let alone a few bulldozers."

I'm bereaved at the thought of so much destruction in town. Then I remember what he said in the shop.

"Wait, you said you were able to save one of the buildings?" I ask to make sure I heard what I thought I heard.

"Changing your mind?" he asks slyly.

"Yes, I think I am. I do want to save one of the buildings."

"I knew you would come to your senses. There's just one teeny tiny little thing you need to do to sweeten the deal," he says and I brace myself.

"What's that, Worth?"

"Have one tiny drink with me tomorrow tonight. I'm still near town staying at my mother's estate. We can discuss the benefit. I can't really enjoy an aperitif on my own. It will be so much more fun if you're there."

"No," I say sharply. The thought of spending another second with this jackass makes my stomach turn.

"Look, I promise just a friendly drink to discuss the event, that's all. Nothing else. It seems a small price to pay," he says like a cat playing with its prey.

I don't trust Worth to be telling the truth but on the other hand, I trusted that Danny was honest and look where that got me. I can deal with a fake as long as I know what I'm getting.

"What time?" I ask and I can feel the walls around my heart returning like they never left.

# Chapter Twenty-Nine

*Danny*

Lizard makes me burnt pancakes for breakfast to try to lift my spirits. Her blackened discs aren't an accident. She likes the taste of char and syrup and thinks everyone else should too.

"I'm not hungry." I push the plate away. It's not that they aren't disgusting, they are. It's that I wouldn't eat a bowl of Fruity Pebbles with chocolate milk right now and that's my favorite breakfast in the world. I'm too depressed to eat.

"Looks like the roads are getting plowed," Lizard says looking out the kitchen window. "Are you going to the store?"

"It's Monday. We're closed. Maybe I'll walk around town

later this evening to see how pretty everything looks. Get out of the house a bit. Just check on the store."

"I don't see Mr. Fancy Pants braving the aftermath of a blizzard very well."

I want Lizard to stop bad-mouthing Prescott. She should have seen him on the sled with my arms around him and the adrenaline rush we shared. That's who he is underneath those tight-fitting blazers. At least that's who I thought he was. Now I have no idea who he is or what he wants. I just know he doesn't want me. At least not in the way I want him. Wanted him? I push my plate away and stand up to look out the window. The newly fallen snow creates a blanket of freshness that temporarily covers up all the dirt. It's like a new start for a few hours but the plows already reveal the black gravel that has been lying underneath. You can only cover up the truth for so long. The snow always melts.

After spending most of the day depressed and in my pajamas I finally get dressed and head out of the apartment just before dinner. As I step onto the sidewalk I exhale and my breath turns to thick clouds. I start walking to the store out of habit. I tell myself I'm going to just check on things and make sure that he's not there but the closer I get the more my heart starts to race and I realize I'm hoping he *is* there. I just want to see him without him seeing me. I want to remember how sweet and soft his smile is. I want to watch him push his reading glasses up his nose. I want to see him tap the side of his forehead with his silly mechanical pencil. My heart starts racing and then I realize all of those details are memories that I have to shed immediately. We aren't building a relationship. It was just a silly, casual fling and I have to stop believing he wanted anything more. I take a turn away from the store.

The sidewalk is slick and as I turn I stumble a bit but an arm comes from behind to help me.

"Careful there," Arthur says. "I'm the senior citizen."

"Uncle Arthur, what are you doing out? The sidewalk is too dangerous."

"I assume you're speaking from experience. Don't worry about me. I've got my trusty cane. I have the balance of a yogi master. Too bad the shop is closed today. I used to love to just sit inside and watch the snow fall. Are you and Prescott opening tonight anyway?"

"I don't know," I say. My tone is full of anger and disappointment and Arthur doesn't let it go unnoticed.

"Everything alright with you boys? I understand you were getting, shall we say, much closer."

"We were and then we weren't and now I don't know."

"What happened?"

"Let's just say we want different things. I want to start something real and he wants to keep his options open."

"Oh," Arthur says raising his eyebrows.

"I did something I maybe should not have but he did something that he really should not have and that's what's really the problem and when I think about it I think he's got to be the worst person I've ever met and I thought I ruined everything but really he ruined everything." The words just tumble together and I don't even know if anything I'm saying makes any sense.

"Danny, perhaps you're being just a tad overdramatic."

"You wouldn't say that if you saw what I saw, or what I think I saw through the window."

Arthur is too polite to ask for details but he's also very wise.

"So you think he's the worst person in the world because of something you *think* you saw? What did he say when you asked him about it?"

I'm silent.

"Danny?"

"It's just that I can't talk to him. If what I saw happened then it's too humiliating. It means…" I trail off and then summon the courage to share my fear with Arthur. "Uncle Arthur, the truth is I never told Prescott about the money or my family."

"Oh."

"I was vague. He had no idea and I wanted it that way because I thought we were really building something solid," I say staring at the ground.

"It looked like that from where I've been sitting. What if there's an explanation?"

I swallow hard, ready to say out loud what I've been dreading. "What if the explanation is that I'm not enough. I've been working so hard to get the business going on my own and not rely on my family's money in any way and it's felt great. For once I've had this independence and I wasn't losing myself in the relationship. I was finding myself, my true self. In the past I could always say that my family's money got in the way. But this time that's not possible, so what if the explanation is just that Prescott doesn't want me? What if I'm not enough? Do you see why I can't ask him for an explanation? I couldn't bear to hear it."

"Danny, I don't believe for a second that Prescott would be like that. You have a big heart and it's easy for you to be vulnerable. You need to be with someone who won't take advantage of that. Someone who will love you for who you are, all of who you are. Why do you think I put him in the shop with you?"

"Excuse me?" I ask trying not to have my jaw drop into the frozen slush at my feet.

"Your heart is always open but it needs to be received by someone good who you can finally trust completely. Prescott is a good, trustworthy fellow but he needs someone to help him open his heart."

"Uncle Arthur!" I say, shocked at his matchmaking confession.

"Opposite charges of a magnet are attracted to each other not because they are the same but rather, precisely, because they are different. It's the difference that creates an irresistible force."

I start thinking about Prescott and myself as a couple and that's exactly what we are, two opposites that when they come together make something more. Maybe Arthur is right. Maybe I do need to at least talk to Prescott and find out if he really does want to build something with me. The thought of seeing him makes a silly smile grow across my lips.

"Oh, dear," Arthur says. "Looks like you've got it bad." He takes his walking stick and continues on.

"Got what?" I ask as he keeps walking.

Arthur pauses and turns back to me. *"L'amour. L'amour. Toujours l'amour."* I know it's a line from one of his favorite movies but for the life of me I can't remember if it has a happy ending.

*Prescott*

I'm walking on Main Street but I take a turn on Ferry to avoid having to go by the shop. I don't want to see how sweet everything looks with the mounds of snow reflecting in the windows. The streets are finally clear but there are very few people out since the wind has made it bitterly cold and created an obstacle course of snowdrifts.

I walk with determination toward my meeting with Worth. I just want to get it over with. At least with Worth what you see is what you get. He may put on airs but at least I can count on him to not take them off, like Danny. My mind is still reeling over how hard Danny must have worked to keep the truth from me. It's not like his family is simply well-off, they are wealthy beyond what anyone could imagine.

I'm not sure how I'll ever be able to face him in the store. I think about splitting days with him so we don't have to see each other, then I think maybe I should leave New Hope altogether. I thought I could have a life here but every time I imagine it I'm here with Danny. I don't think I could ever do it alone. As much as it hurts to think about leaving, it would hurt more to stay.

I'm a few doors away from the restaurant where I'm meeting Worth when down the street coming toward me I see Danny. My heart immediately leaps to my throat and

I take a quick step to run toward him but then my mind catches up to the rest of my body and shuts down whatever impulse I'm having. This guy lied to me and led me on for weeks. A sharp and overwhelming pain stabs me in the gut thinking about the future we are never going to have.

I keep walking straight ahead and decide it's better not to let him see me run. There is also the small fact that something is drawing me toward him still. Making me want to snuggle my arms between his shirt and his sweater and feel the warmth of his strong body against mine. But instead of giving in to that temptation I put on my thickest armor and steel myself inside as best I can until we are standing in front of La Petite Fête and facing each other. I can see the sincerity in his deep brown eyes. How could those eyes lie to me?

"Looks like you're feeling better," I say colder than the night air that swirls around us.

"Yeah," he says. Is it possible he, for once, is out of words? Usually sentences just flow out of his mouth but now he's quiet. I wonder if he knows I found out he lied to me. "To tell you the truth I wasn't really sick. I was avoiding you because…"

"You're going to start telling me the truth. Now?"

"What's that supposed to mean?" he asks sheepishly. I stare at him, knowing he can see the hurt in my eyes because his face suddenly drops. His usual bubble and spark evaporate.

"Uhm, I guess you are referring to…" The words get stuck in his mouth like marbles caught in a funnel.

"I'm referring to the fact that your family owns a billion-dollar corporation and you led me to believe that you came from a working-class family like I did."

"I never lied to you," he says and then he looks down at the ground. "At least not directly."

"You led me to believe you struggled to make ends meet. You told me your dad worked with food, not that he owns a global food empire. There's a difference."

"I know," he says looking down.

"You told me he works on cars."

"That's true. He does. He loves cars. Always has. I swear it. He has a garage full of European sports ca—" Danny stops short.

"You seemed to have left out that last part when you told me about it." I can feel my face twisting in anger.

"You're right. I did leave that part out. And I know it was intentional. I wanted you to make the assumptions you made." Danny can barely look at me.

"So you admit it? You intentionally lied to me." I snap my head toward the street so I don't have to look at him.

"No, it wasn't like that, at least not exactly."

"What are you talking about?" I ask. I'm hoping there is some explanation that can make all this *Sturm und Drang* go away.

"Guys find out my family is loaded and they start treating me differently." Danny looks at the ground and I can tell it's hard for him to get the words out.

"Is that what you thought I would do?" I ask, completely hurt that he might think that of me.

"No, not after I got to know you. Not at all," he says.

His eyes are pleading with me and it makes me want to believe him.

"So why not tell me?"

Danny takes a deep breath and then looks up at the sky. I want to put my arm around him to comfort him but I'm too hurt by his deception to do it with sincerity. "In past relationships," he starts, "I used to throw the money around and use it to make the guy happy or solve the guy's problems. I once bought this guy I was seeing a boat." He shrinks a bit from what I imagine is embarrassment.

"You bought someone a boat?"

"Not a big one but yes. It wasn't that I wanted him to be impressed by the money. I mean he was. It was a freakin' boat but that's not why I did it. I couldn't stop myself from being this needy people pleaser so the relationships were always lopsided and doomed."

"That's not how you acted around me. We never felt lopsided like that," I say still confused about everything.

"I know and I liked it. You never made me feel like I was losing myself that way and it was wonderful. I got to show you myself without the money and it felt like a relief. I got to show you who I really am." He slowly raises his head to finally make eye contact like a small animal outside the nest for the first time.

"But did you?" I ask. "You showed a part of who you are and kept another part hidden. That's not what I wanted." I'm looking him square in the eyes. "I wanted all of you. I hate being lied to but it's worse to think that you felt you had to hide something from me. I thought trust only worked if both sides participated. Why would you keep so much a secret from me?"

"I—I…" Danny is stuck on the words again.

I'm aching over the fact that this was an intentional lie. Was he trying to trick me into liking him? Anger rises in me and I can't stop it. "I'll tell you why. You did it because you didn't trust me enough. I was opening myself up to you every day and you were just lying to me. I never lied to you—not once."

*Danny*

"Then why did I see you and Worth in the store the other day?" I ask. I know I should have been more honest about my background but Prescott's the real reason we've fallen apart. His actions caused this whole thing to avalanche like an out of control boulder down Main Street.

"I was just meeting with him to help save the buildings." Now Prescott is the one looking uncomfortable. He bites his lower lip and I imagine he is wondering how he can do damage control.

"How? By kissing him?" My words are like little darts. "I came back to get something and through the window I saw the two of you in a rather intimate position. That's why I left and why I've been avoiding you. That's why I haven't been coming into the shop. I saw you there with him when you knew I would be out of the store. If there is anyone who has been misleading, it's you."

"I'm sorry you saw that," he says, and his voice comes out weak but sincere.

"I'm sure you are," I say with a nasty tone to cover up how hurt I am.

"If you had just asked me about it I would have told you I want nothing to do with him."

I shake my head and look away. "Telling me and showing me are two different things. I see how you arrange things in the shop. You love a perfect set. Matching ugly candlesticks, matching boring china sets, matching dull-as-mud doorknobs. Match. Match. Match. That's what you want. You want things that go together in a tasteful combination. You don't think it would ever work between us."

"That's ridiculous."

"Is it? You think things that belong together are from the same studio, the same artists, the same style, the same century and I don't think that. Look at what you collect. You're always looking for a match. Like that dumb mug. You had to have it to complete your set."

"*You* bought it," he says, a tremble of disappointment in his voice.

"You're right. I did. But you can have it. I don't want it. You and Worth can drink out of it together."

"Danny! I do not want Worth. I want you. Can't you see that? Please. I made a mistake meeting him and that kiss was him invading my personal space. I never want to see him again."

I look at Prescott carefully. He isn't just explaining what happened. He's pleading with me.

I have no ability to make good decisions about men but maybe Prescott has changed that. Maybe he is one of the good ones. Arthur seems to think so and if I can't trust my own instincts maybe I should be able to trust someone who might know better.

"I guess I should have given you a chance to explain," I say feeling a potential thaw in my attitude. Maybe he really does want to build something special with me and saying that he never wants to see Worth again makes me think he wants to focus on us. "Do you mean it? Do you really want to start something serious here?"

"Yes," he says and I can sense the relief in his voice. "Yes. Worth means nothing to me. Worth is... Worth!"

He says the name a second time with a sudden jolt of surprise and he stares beyond my left shoulder. I turn around and there in front of me is Hot Lips in camel hair.

"Why hello, Press. Sorry, I'm late for our drink. Would you believe the heated driveway at my mother's chose now to break? We had to call the handyman to shovel us out. He's sixty-eight and it took him forever. What a bother." Worth suddenly sees me, which is surprising because I think I might be invisible to him. "The two of you are almost joined at the hip. Well, I won't interrupt the shoptalk. Literally, shoptalk." He laughs at his own joke like Narcissus staring at his reflection in the water. "Take your time, Press. I'll get us a booth by the fireplace. Something private." He aims that last part directly at me, like an assassin.

Worth leaves and we are alone on the sidewalk in front of the restaurant in silence. I look at Prescott and can't comprehend how close I was to believing him. To trusting him. "I don't want to keep you from your date," I say with disgust.

"Danny, wait. It's not a date. Let me explain," he says.

"I can't believe it. You tricked me. Again. How stupid you must think I am, stalling outside while your date with Worth is just minutes away. You tell me you never want to see him again when you have a date with him tonight?" I'm so devastated that I can barely put the sentences together. The words just fly out of my mouth in a reckless attempt to attack him and protect myself. "You and Worth. I just can't... How could you? How am I supposed to believe your explanation or anything you say?"

Prescott blinks and I don't know if it's a result of the cold air or trying to fight back tears. "I can't believe *you*. Again you don't give me a chance to explain. You just jump to your own conclusion. Trust has to start somewhere and if you aren't willing to do that then you're the one who doesn't want to get serious," he says slowly, turning my words back on me.

Whatever thaw we felt a few seconds ago has halted. It feels like we are back where we started making assumptions and insulting each other. I can't stand here on the sidewalk while Worth is sitting at some cozy table waiting for Prescott. It's just too painful.

"I need to go and you don't want to keep Worth waiting," I say and turn and walk away from him as quickly as I can. He's made his choice. A sharp wind snaps around the corner and suddenly the tears that have started down my cheek are blown away. I feel like the frozen tundra—cold, uninviting and lonely.

# Chapter Thirty

*Prescott*

"Prescott, I'm so glad you could make it tonight. You look handsome as always," Worth says as I enter the bar area of La Petite Fête. My head is still swimming. I'm angry, sad and hurt all at the same time. Before I came to this town my emotions were something I was able to control. Now they just spill out like Niagara Falls over a Limoges teacup. I have to use all of my effort to contain them.

Worth is sitting by the fireplace in a burgundy wingback leather chair. I can tell immediately that it's a reproduction. I try to focus on the chair and not the person sitting in it. I'm good at doing that, at least. I hate having to meet with him but I'll be able to do what I should have done in the first place.

As I take off my coat I think for a second that I see Danny entering and my heart leaps into my throat but it isn't him.

A waiter brings a charcuterie board that Worth must have ordered while my mind was elsewhere. "Press, are you alright? I've been going on and on and you've been staring at the fire and haven't said a word."

I snap back to reality and push thoughts of Danny out of my head. "I'm fine," I say and order a drink while Worth takes a phone call. I never drink but I hope the alcohol will help me forget about Danny.

"Here's your beer," the waiter says, handing me a frosty mug. I grab it and take a sip. The bitterness of what I am assuming are the hops attacks my tongue sharply.

"A beer?" Worth says with scorn. "What's next? An order of wings or nachos?"

Danny eats nachos for lunch on Fridays. That was one of his things. I'll admit that at first the smell was a bit much but now I'd do anything to share a plate of chips and guac with him. I know he lied to me and I thought seeing him would make me furious but it didn't. It made me miss him. It made me miss what I thought we could have. I look at my beer and think about how close we've gotten and how much I wanted to get even closer. I hate being deceived, but even knowing what he did I can't help myself from saying what I'm about to say. It's the right thing to do. I'm listening to my heart for one last time and then shutting the door.

"I just want to be clear. You said that if I agreed to help you and met you here tonight you would save one of the buildings?"

"Yes, of course. I told you that," he says acting annoyed by my question.

"Good because it's the bank. The First Bank of Bucks. I want you to spare the midcentury building." I admire and respect the Yardley House but Danny *loves* the First Bank of Bucks. I could never tell Worth to destroy it.

Worth is frozen. He finally takes a sip of his cocktail slowly and then puts it down and snaps at the waiter. He points at his glass to order another. He pauses and then a small manufactured giggle comes out of his mouth. "Press, you know I hate jokes. Stop it."

"It's not a joke. I couldn't be more serious. I want you to save the bank. You said you only need one lot and they can be separated so save the bank."

Worth looks at me like he's just found out the Dow Jones dropped a quarter. "That bank is hideous. How could you not want to save the beautiful one?"

I know he won't understand and I don't owe him any explanation but I tell him the truth anyway. "Beauty isn't just how something looks. It's how it makes you feel and this building makes someone I know feel a great deal of joy."

There is a silence and then Worth starts laughing. Loud. He can barely stay seated on his chair. I'm not sure if it's the cocktails or my pronouncement. He finally gets a hold of himself and then says through the remaining giggles, "That was a very lovely thought. You should use that on an Insta account to inspire the ugly or something, but I'm afraid I can't save the bank. Good lord. The bank?"

"Why not? You said I could save one. Why not the bank?"

"Enough about that preposterous bank. It's too late."

The waiter attempts to put down his next drink but before he can reach the table Worth grabs it and finishes half of it. "Do you want to know a secret?" he asks and I can tell the liquor is having quite an effect on him. I don't say anything. I am steely cold. "Aww, c'mon. I'll tell you anyway. No one's going to touch the Yardley House. It was never in any real danger. I mean, at first we were going to destroy both of them but once the engineers figured out how to keep the supports in place we realized we only had to flatten the bank. We'll build taller, it'll be cheaper and I've already signed the papers so we get a tax abatement." He finishes the rest of his drink.

"Are you serious? You already saved the Yardley House. When did you find all this out?" I can feel the blood rising to my head. My heart is pounding.

"Right after that ridiculous city council thing." Worth gestures like he's swatting a fly.

"So tonight is a setup. You knew this when you met me at the shop?"

"Guilty," he says making a pretend frown like a little boy. "I've been a bit naughty, but you're even sexier when you're angry so where's the harm?"

"Stop it," I say. What a complete and total jackass. He lied just to manipulate me. I think about accusing Danny of lying to me and by comparison it doesn't seem like the same thing at all.

"What's the big deal? You got what you wanted and I should get what I want."

In a flash he moves his face closer to mine and without warning puts his hand on my leg. Without thinking I throw him off me with so much force his arm slams against the table.

"What's wrong with you?" he asks.

I stand up and the words tumble out. "To be honest with you I have trouble trusting people and it's difficult for me to open up. Other than that I'm fine." I grab my coat from the back of my chair.

"Fine, run off to that Dan person and his grotesque big-foot T-shirts." He spits the words out like bitter seeds.

I think about Danny at the city council meeting all passion and determination in his favorite T-shirt. I turn back to Worth with pure venom.

"It's Chewbacca on that shirt, not Sasquatch. Chewy is a Wookie from the planet Kashyyyk, you moron." The phrase comes out of my mouth and I have no idea how I know that. I've listened to Danny go on about Chewy while we were at the store, but I had no idea I was actually listening so well.

"Tell Dan and all your other friends out here that they should say goodbye to the bank because the bulldozers will be there tomorrow morning and a little protest won't make a difference."

I walk away from Worth without looking back. I can't believe what a mess I've made of everything.

## Chapter Thirty-One

*Prescott*

I walk past the shop but keep my head turned away from it. I can't bear to look inside. I'll see him everywhere in there and it would be too painful. I keep my head down staring at the slushy sidewalk when I bump into someone.

"Prescott, quite a chilly night to be out studying slush piles," Arthur says and I look up.

"Oh, sorry. Hi, Arthur." I wonder if I am the only one who didn't know how rich Danny is. I assume Arthur knows that I have been played for a fool but I need to find out. "Arthur, did you know about Danny?"

"Yes, of course."

"Why didn't you tell me?"

"I didn't tell you that Danny is such a warm, kind and open person because I wanted you to find out on your own."

I did find that out. I found out he's the best person I've ever met but that is nullified if he doesn't want to be honest with me.

"No, not that," I say. "The family stuff."

"Oh, that," Arthur says rolling his eyes and letting out a puff of air that immediately makes a small cloud in front of his face. "You mean the money?"

"Yes," I say quietly, knowing that I must be the only dunce who doesn't know. "Why didn't you tell me who he is?"

"I just did." Arthur steadies himself with his cane, grabbing the silver dog's head. "He's warm, funny and open."

"Not that. I know that. Now. I mean..."

"Prescott, that's who he is. Yes, he comes from a wealthy family but that's only a part of who he is. It no more defines him than your background defines who you are."

"But he didn't tell me the truth," I say.

"You mean he isn't warm and funny and open?" I know Arthur is being intentionally obtuse. "Maybe he wasn't completely direct about his background but maybe he didn't want to be judged for it or maybe he liked being seen without all the trappings of his family so he avoided the truth a bit. Maybe he was scared. I don't believe he was trying to trick you."

I look down at the ground to gather my thoughts. Arthur is right. Danny wasn't really trying to trick me, not like Worth. Worth is a liar, a manipulative brat. What Danny did is nowhere near the magnitude of Worth's mendacity. He didn't purposely manipulate me into believing something for his own gain. Danny would never try to trick me to get something out of me. He was protecting himself. I've been protecting myself from the world my whole life so I can understand that. I also finally understand what it means to open up a bit and connect with people and community and I'm not ready to give up on that.

"What's important is how you feel about him," Arthur says and puts his hand on my shoulder. I think about how I felt waiting for him at Gaspo's last week or when we sledded down the hill together or anytime the shop is empty and he insists on having a Disco Dance Break.

Arthur smiles at me gently. "Danny is sweet, sometimes too sweet and he goes overboard. That means people take advantage of him. But I knew you wouldn't do that."

"Never," I say. "Wait...what do you mean you knew... did you..."

"All I'm willing to admit on the record for now is that Danny never lied to you about who he is. Not who he really is inside."

I think about the Danny I have known and come to love these past few weeks and an uncharacteristically goofy smiles moves across my face.

"It looks like you've got it bad too," Arthur says.

"What?"

Arthur starts walking away and then sticks his cane in the snow and turns back to me. *"L'amour. L'amour. Toujours l'amour."* He laughs and walks away.

I'm feeling restless and confused. I don't want to go back

to my empty apartment so I just keep walking. My legs take me to the corner with the Bank of Bucks and the Yardley House. I stand between the two buildings and marvel at how wonderful they both are. The thought of one surviving without the other makes me deeply sad.

I walk over to the First Bank of Bucks as if I need to apologize to it. I put my hand on one of the deep brown stones and bow my head. Then I put my other hand out like I'm almost hugging the building and when I look down I notice something I hadn't seen before. The cantilevered stone wall is supported by shaped concrete. I don't know why I hadn't seen that detail before and if I did I certainly didn't see it this close. Shaped concrete. I examine the structure carefully and try to remember everything I know about architecture in the twentieth century. I start reviewing the relationship of the parts to the whole as I would any fine antique and that helps me develop a hunch. A very important hunch.

I quickly look to the cornerstone of the building to check the date. Just as I suspected. Shaped concrete and the date of the cornerstone make the synapses in my brain start firing. Maybe I can make things right. Maybe I can find a way to show Danny how I really feel about him, and this wonderful building can help me.

# *Chapter Thirty-Two*

*Danny*

I'd set my alarm extra early for the morning of the protest. I knew once it went off I'd want to go back to bed and forget that the day I'd been looking forward to for so long with Prescott was now something where I'd have to avoid him at all costs. My Bugs Bunny alarm clock rings and I slam my hand over the carrot. I can feel the cold early morning air on my nose and pull the comforter over my head. I don't want to face the world.

Lizard knocks on my door. "We have the protest thingy this morning," she says from the hall. "We better get going."

I rip the covers off, hoping the cold will motivate me but it only makes me want to have Prescott put his arms around me and snuggle. I get out of bed, take a shower and do a terrible job of not thinking about him. Before I leave I make a plea to Lizard.

"Maybe I should stay home?"

"This will be good for you. You'll be a part of something bigger than your own misery."

"There are entire countries that are smaller than my misery. Besides what's the point? That guy Worth is just going to do what he wants anyway."

"Danny!" Lizard says like a slap in the face. "We make our voices heard together. You know a protest is about building the community and coming together. You are the one who taught *me* that. You've been telling everyone to never give up. You can't let everyone down."

She's right and even though the thought of having to leave the house is almost more than I can bear, I gather all of the signs I made and head out with Lizard. I'm hoping to firmly establish a spot to stand in so that Prescott will see where I am and not come within ten yards of me. I can avoid him for at least a few more hours. Eventually we have to go back to working together in the shop. I have no idea how I'll be able to handle that. The truth is I miss him terribly, and what's worse than missing someone who is seated a few feet away?

As I approach the block where the protest is scheduled to take place I see a huge crowd and it temporarily energizes me. There are maybe three or four times the number we were expecting. They are all holding signs and have already begun chanting, "Don't be a dope. Save New Hope." I walk closer but the crowd is so big Lizard and I aren't able to get that close to the actual buildings. Considering Prescott might be on the front lines I'm happy hiding in the back.

I hear something in the distance in the direction of the river. The entire bridge is rumbling and I see three huge bulldozers driving across the bridge like some yellow army of destruction. I'm sure they are pushing the weight limit on the bridge and it causes the transom to vibrate in a way that almost sounds like crying. The crowd starts chanting louder and louder as the bulldozers ready themselves directly in front of the bank in the area that is cordoned off.

A car behind me honks its horn repeatedly. I turn and see a black SUV flashing its lights. Lizard and I jump onto the sidewalk but the car stops just next to me and the window rolls down. "Come to see your bank go boom? You know a lot of people record things like this. You should get out your phone."

"Shut up Worth-less," I snap back.

I hear his phone ring from inside the car. I hear him answer it and say, "What do you mean the bulldozers have been halted? Some crazy person is climbing the fire escape to the roof? Well pull whoever it is off of there and tear that building down! I want to see fireworks!"

"Not as easy as you thought, is it, Worth-less?" I hold my New Betta Hope poster above my head and join the crowd's chant. "Don't be a dope! Save New Hope!" I can't imagine who was brave enough to scale the building until in the distance on the roof of the bank I see the figure of a man with blond hair wearing a tweed sport coat and holding a book.

*Prescott*

There was no way I was going to get everyone's attention from street level. The crowd was too big to have my voice heard. Then I remembered there is a rickety old fire escape at the back of the building. I broke from the crowd and ran behind the building. I wasn't thinking; I was just doing. It was my only chance to make everything right. I grabbed the rusty edges of the first ladder with one hand and held the most important book I've ever needed in the other. I got to the very top of the building and walked to the edge. Now I'm standing on the roof of the bank and I can see all of New Hope and the striped awning of our shop, and as I get closer to the edge I can see the street below. Rather, I can't see the street below because it is covered with people holding signs and chanting in protest. It's a much bigger crowd than I thought from street level.

My presence on the roof has halted the bulldozers at least temporarily. "Stop!" I yell as loud as I can. People below stop chanting and a few are pointing at me. I'm used to working in quiet libraries and hushed auction houses so shouting at the top of my lungs from the roof of a bank is way, way, way out of my comfort zone but I don't care. I need to make this work. The greedy claw of the bulldozer is only a few yards away from the building and the guy driving it looks both confused and annoyed. Maybe he's about to bury me under the rubble after the explosion.

I see Worth holding a megaphone and parting the crowd like it's the Red Sea. "Get out of the way! The bank goes and you get to save the historically significant one."

"Not so fast, Worth," I warn him. "I can put all of this to end right now with what I have in my hand." I hold up over my head the book I carried up. "But not until Danny Roman joins me up here. Danny, where are you? I know you're out there. Danny? Danny?" I shout. The crowd picks up my cry and starts chanting: "Dan-ny! Dan-ny!"

"Are you out of your mind?" I hear Danny shout from the street. He is just below me on the sidewalk looking up.

"Maybe, but get up here. I want to show you something."

"But I'm wearing my good Crocs!" he shouts up to me.

"I don't care," I shout back down and I really mean it.

Danny makes his way to the back and climbs up to join me as the crowd keeps chanting his name. "Dan-ny! Dan-ny!" When he appears on top of the building my heart swells.

I grab Danny's hand and pull him toward the center of the roof so we can have a bit of a private moment. "Last night I noticed that the bank uses shaped concrete. I thought that was very peculiar because I know that detail is specific to a particular architect and time. I had never noticed it before because I always saw it from a distance. But when I was hugging the bank…"

"You were hugging the bank?" he asks like I just told him I flew to the roof we are standing on.

"Yes, but that's a different story. Anyway, I spent hours looking through the archives at Princeton's art history library. I've never been more grateful it's open twenty-four seven because I was able to find this." I open the book I have been holding and take out the papers I stuffed in it.

I walk toward the edge of the roof and shout to the crowd. "Here in my hand is the original architectural plan for the bank. One architectural firm finished the building but the actual blueprint was created by another firm. This book and these documents verify everything."

"So what? Let's get this building down," Worth shouts from his bullhorn and he signals to the bulldozers.

"The original blueprints were created by Marcel Breuer!" I shout.

"Who?" Worth asks, like I just said Mickey Mouse made the building. People in the crowd who understand the importance of that name gasp just a bit.

"*The* Marcel Breuer?" Danny asks me. "The guy who built the original Whitney Museum in New York and the IBM building in France not to mention the UNESCO world headquarters?"

"Exactly," I say looking into Danny's eyes. Finally I think I understand the feeling that you can get when you really connect with someone and start to see the world through their eyes. I want to kiss him so bad but we need to get rid of these bulldozers first.

I turn to the crowd again: "Marcel Breuer is the original architect of this building. I'm sure once we bring this to the attention of the state planning board they'll be able to certify this as historically significant. You are aware of the fine that goes along with destroying this property?"

"You don't have any legal document. Where's your stop work order?" Worth asks through the megaphone, but I can tell he knows he's lost this round.

"We don't need one," Danny shouts. "Legally you now have prior knowledge and intentionality which is all that is needed to be in violation of the zoning ordinance." Danny rattles off the string of legal terms without missing a beat.

I give him a look of confusion and he says to me, "In full disclosure I went to a semester of law school but didn't like it. You have to be called on to speak and that didn't work for me. I want to make sure you have the full picture."

"So noted," I say smiling because I love his ability to mix humor into this whole mess.

"This isn't over," Worth says. He makes a call, screams at someone and within a few minutes the bulldozers go back across the river like cockroaches retreating from the light. The crowd cheers. I turn to Danny and speak to him quietly.

"I'm sorry," I say. "I know meeting with Worth was asinine. I shouldn't have done it. I thought I was doing the right thing, but I should have talked to you about it at the very least. And then last night I was still so upset because I thought you lied to me."

"I did lie to you. I mean I wasn't completely honest about my background and family."

"But you didn't lie to me about who you are. Not really. I realize that now," I say. I'm so glad we are talking this through even if we are standing on the roof of a building that was about to be destroyed with a hundred people or so watching us from the street below. "You didn't tell me about your background but that's not who you are or it's only a part of who you. You are the most honest person I've ever met because you share yourself wholly and completely with the people around you. What in the world is more honest than that?"

"I'm sorry I assumed the worst of you with Worth," Danny says. "I thought we were having this connection and when I thought you might be sharing a connection with Worth I overreacted."

"It's easy to assume the worst with Worth and probably a good idea. I couldn't stop feeling the feelings I have for you. I kept thinking about how the town had come together and how you and I had come together to save these two buildings that we both love. I realized I had to find a way to show you how I really feel." I put the art history book and documents in his hand. "Now we can save the bank. I know how much you love it."

"I do," he says with a big smile.

"I never thought that I would appreciate a building like this but seeing it through your eyes has changed how I see the world. Danny, you've changed me. You've shown me that being honest about how I feel makes it easier to be part of the world. To connect to it." I'm smiling so brightly I think it will melt the snow.

"Well since we are being completely honest, I have a confession," Danny says.

My smile drops and I look straight ahead, bracing myself for whatever he's going to say.

He looks at me sheepishly and asks, "The Yardley House?"

"Yes," I say cautiously.

"I've always thought it was beautiful. I've always loved that roof. I mean it's gorgeous. And that bird fan in the shop that I told you looks like something that flew into a ceiling fan—I love that too. I might actually have purchased one for myself a few weeks ago. And, this one is big. I hate truffles. I despise them. They taste like something a pig digs up with his nose because, well, that's what they are. I hate them." He says this all quickly and without stopping. The absurdity of it and the fact that it's so Danny makes me laugh out loud.

"Danny you embrace everything. Even when you don't like something you go all out. You follow your heart no matter where it leads. I just hope it always leads you to me."

"Prescott, when you stormed in to the shop that first day I thought I was going to have to taxidermy you in your tweed blazer but when you went all the way to Harrisburg to replace my cookie jar, I knew exactly where my heart was leading no matter how much I tried to have it go in a different direction."

"Danny," I say as softly as I can so that the words just float from my mouth to his. "I think you're beautiful."

He smiles and floats the words back to me. "I think you're beautiful too."

Our faces lean toward each other and I have entirely forgotten that we are standing on the roof of the bank until the crowd that is still gathered below begins to chant: "Kiss. Kiss. Kiss." We walk closer to the edge to see everyone. The entire street is filled with people looking up at us and chanting in unison. "Kiss. Kiss. Kiss." I grab Danny in my arms and we do exactly what they want.

# Epilogue

*Arthur—three months later*

The bells to the shop ring as I enter, both a familiar lullaby and a trumpet to arms. I take a few steps inside and remind myself that I'm not responsible for opening the till or drawing back the curtains. Sometimes I miss it but only on days like today when the trees outside Toula's bookshop are blossoming and the sweet warm air promises a procession of shoppers to fill the spring afternoon.

"Be with you in a minute," I hear Danny say from the pantry. I'm grateful to have some time alone in my old shop. It takes only a second to notice the sweeping changes that have taken place. Where once there was an intransigent boundary now no such limitation exists and the transformation is joyous. I see a purple bean bag bear sitting in a makeshift hammock between two ornate Gothic door locks, a fine collection of pewter serving utensils displayed inside a *Charlie's Angels* lunchbox and an entire festival of Smurfs playing up and down a Victorian stick and ball secretary desk with fine maple spindles. It's like a potluck at the United Nations and it's delicious.

The curtain to the pantry parts and Prescott sees me. He rushes over to give me a warm hug. "Uncle Arthur, when did you get back?" he asks as Danny takes his turn hugging me hello.

"Did you love Acapulco? Was the honeymoon bungalow as pretty as in the pictures? Where's Serilda?" Danny peppers me with questions.

"We loved every second of it. The bungalow was on the beach and each night they brought us these fruity drinks that looked like sunsets in a glass," I say holding on to the memory of our lovely week in Mexico. "Serilda is still unpacking. They seem to have an outfit for every hour of the day."

"They looked so lovely in the images you sent of the ceremony. Absolutely diaphanous in that gold chiffon on the beach," Prescott says.

"And if I was seeing things correctly," Danny adds, "you even went shoeless for the ceremony in the sand. Who would have believed it?"

"Love can make you do a lot of things you never thought you'd do. Like elope to Mexico," I say raising an eyebrow as I look around the store.

"We did some reshuffling recently. It's been getting a

great response except…well, someone is having a problem letting go," Danny says tilting his head toward Prescott.

"I am not," Prescott says. "Well, maybe a little. I'm not going to sell those Smurfs to just anyone. Toothy needs a good home and the buyer didn't look like she would take the responsibility seriously."

"Babe, she was seven," Danny says.

"Good stewardship can begin at any age," Prescott says and walks over to Danny and grabs his hand. Their interlocked palms swing for a moment between them and then Prescott says, "Should we ask him?"

"Sure," Danny says, a radiant smile appearing across his face.

"What are you doing Labor Day weekend?" Prescott asks me, his smile matching Danny's radiance and perhaps surpassing it.

"Are you? You mean?" I'm too excited about the potential news to get the words out.

"Yes, yes, yes," Prescott blurts out with an enthusiasm that might have been uncharacteristic a few months ago. Danny pulls Prescott close to him and they share a tender kiss.

"He asked me just before you left and we thought Labor Day weekend would be perfect for a wedding. Just before the fall season starts," Danny says giddy with excitement.

"But we have a question for you, Uncle Arthur…" Prescott starts.

Danny finishes with, "Which one of us are you going to give away at the wedding?"

The question makes me laugh and the thought of them

spending a lifetime together fills me with joy. I grab my cane and begin to head out the door. The answer to their question is easy. I stop and turn before leaving the shop. "I'm not going to give away either of you."

"What?" they ask in unison.

"I can't. You don't belong to me. You belong to each other."

I walk out of The Beautiful Things Shoppe and once I'm on the sidewalk I look back through the window and see Danny and Prescott embracing tightly. Two *beautiful things* have become one.

★ ★ ★ ★ ★

*Reviews are an invaluable tool for spreading the word about great reads. Please consider leaving an honest review on your favorite retailer or review site.*

*To purchase and read more books by Philip William Stover, please visit his website at* philipwilliamstover.com.

*Available now from Carina Adores
and Kim Fielding!*

**Some people search their whole lives to find love.
He just wants to avoid it.**

Teddy Spenser spends his days selling design ideas to
higher-ups, living or dying on each new pitch. Stodgy engineer
types like Romeo Blue, his nemesis—if you can call someone
who barely talks to you a nemesis—are a necessary evil.
*A cute necessary evil.*

*Read on for a sneak preview of what happens next in*
Teddy Spenser Isn't Looking for Love…

# Chapter One

Passersby grumbled as they detoured around Teddy Spenser and his scooter, but he remained on the sidewalk outside the cosmetics store window, silently critiquing the display.

*This is all wrong.* There were no winged cupids and, worse, not a single heart. Just a blue-haired mannequin in a silk bathrobe and above her, like a 3-D thought bubble, the word *LOVE* crafted with shiny silver ribbons arranged in an elaborate cursive font. The colors were wrong too: all winter whites and frosts. Even kindergartners knew that red and pink were the go-to hues for the holiday.

If the designer was trying to be avant-garde, they'd missed the mark and ended up with boring and pointless. Nothing about the display made Teddy want to buy cosmetics for himself or anyone else, and it certainly did nothing to put him in the holiday spirit. Not that he wanted to be in the mood. Valentine's Day was stupid.

It wasn't a real holiday. Nobody got the day off from work. The mail arrived just like always, full of bills and grocery-store circulars and reminders that eye appointments were overdue. And all that crap about True Love? Nothing but a marketing ploy. He knew Valentine's Day was a big moneymaker in certain industries, so he couldn't fault them for trying to make the most of it.

With a sniff of disdain, Teddy got back on his scooter and, narrowly missing a burly guy in a construction vest, continued on his way to the office. It wasn't an especially cold day, as February in Chicago went, and bits of dirty snow were the only vestiges of the last storm. The sky was a washed-out gray that seemed to begrudge any thoughts of spring, and Teddy shivered despite his parka, ski cap, and gloves. His ancestors, who'd spent possibly thousands of years surviving winters in England and Scandinavia without Gore-Tex or central heating, would probably consider him a wimp.

Soup. He was definitely going to have soup for lunch today—something thick with butter and cream and potatoes and maybe even cheese. A meal that would act like a layer of insulation for his freezing inner self. He might even have chocolate for dessert. Not Valentine's Day chocolate. He refused to eat any of that—at least until it went on clearance.

Reddyflora, *where beauty and technology meet*, occupied a suite in a nondescript building on LaSalle, just a couple of blocks from the Daley Center. Teddy dragged his scooter up the three flights of stairs since the ancient, creaking elevator always sounded as if it were ready to plummet into the pits of hell. The office was in the back of the building, where tiny windows looked down on an alley clogged with garbage bins, and dropped ceilings made everything feel claustrophobic. As far as Teddy was concerned, the building's only advantages were on the ground floor: a Mexican fast-food joint and a sandwich place.

Shortly after he was hired, Teddy had asked the founder and CEO, Lauren Wu, why she hadn't set up her HQ in the suburbs. For the same money, she could have leased a spacious suite in a modern office park, and employees would have benefited from cheaper nearby housing.

"The 'burbs?" Lauren had been incredulous, using the same tone she might use to describe something scraped off the sole of her designer shoes.

"Sure. Hinsdale, maybe, or Wilmette."

"The Loop is cutting-edge, Teddy, and that's where we want to be. Because Reddyflora is cutting-edge too, right?"

He squinted at the flickering lights in the hallway before stashing his scooter in a corner of the sizable warren of employee cubicles. Lauren had an office of her own, of course, which included a couch she sometimes slept on. The only other coworker with a private space was Romeo Blue, the company's software engineer.

"Romeo Blue," Teddy muttered as he hung his coat and scarf on a wall-mounted hook. No way that was his real name. It sounded like a porn star or indie musician, not a guy who got paid to tap away at a keyboard all day.

"Hey, Teddy!"

Teddy waved at Imani Wallace. The job title on the nameplate for her cubicle was Fiscal Analyst Extraordinaire. Right now she was frowning and motioning him over. "I've been waiting for you forever," she said when he arrived.

"It's not even eight yet."

"I've been here since six."

He tried not to make a face. He'd known when he accepted the job that Lauren expected her employees to put in long hours, but he wanted to see at least a glimpse of sunlight. Imani wasn't likely to, at least not today. She rarely headed home until almost seven.

"Is there an emergency, Imani?"

She peered at her screen. "No. But I've been pricing out the base model, and the figures are not looking good. Unless we can cut costs, we're not going to turn a profit."

"We could raise the price."

"Uh-uh. We're maxed out already—your own reports say so."

Although he knew she was going to say that, he sighed anyway. "Send me the numbers. I'll see if I can find a way to cut some corners or sub some cheaper materials."

"Yeah, okay, fine." Her attention was back on her computer screen.

Teddy navigated to his own cubicle—his nameplate announced Design & Marketing—sat down, and booted up. He'd done as much as he could to brighten the space: reproductions of tourism posters, patterned adhesive paper on the metal drawer fronts, and vintage desk accessories he'd unearthed at a thrift shop. His chair cushion matched the drawer fronts, and the soft glow of a real lamp somewhat successfully battled the overhead fluorescents. A small rug covered the ugly floor tiles, despite it being an annoying trip hazard. He might not have a view, and the air always smelled like floor cleaner, but plenty of people toiled under far worse conditions.

He made his way through the overnight accumulation of emails, most from vendors trying to sell things Reddyflora didn't need or couldn't afford. Imani's spreadsheets had arrived, so he turned his attention to examining them. He didn't like numbers, at least not when they were arrayed in soulless columns, but cozying up to them was part of his job.

Within an hour, the suite was bustling with activity. Conversations, people walking around, printers spewing paper, phones ringing. It was like the soundtrack of an office, and it made Teddy smile. He could almost imagine himself as an actor in a musical, as if at any second he and Imani and the others might burst into song. Something with clever lyrics about how they were toiling away as they chased their dreams.

"Hey."

Teddy hadn't noticed anyone come up behind him, and he startled so violently that he almost knocked over his coffee. He spun the chair around and discovered Romeo Blue looking down at him, stone-faced.

"What?" Teddy knew he was scowling and didn't care.

"Can we speak in my office, please?" As usual, Romeo's voice was low, his words clipped. As if he refused to spare much energy to speak to Teddy.

"I'm busy right now."

"As soon as you can then." Romeo spun and marched back to his office, leaving its door slightly ajar.

Teddy could have followed him; Imani's numbers weren't so urgent that they couldn't wait awhile. But he remained stubbornly at his desk even though he could no longer focus on the computer screen. Romeo Blue. Teddy had googled him once, just for the hell of it—not at all to dispel lingering notions that his coworker was a spy working under a really stupid alias. It turned out that Lenny Kravitz used Romeo Blue as a stage name back in the eighties, and that was more than a little weird since *this* Romeo resembled a young Lenny Kravitz, albeit with a darker complexion and a different clothing aesthetic. Kravitz probably didn't wear suits from Zara. And to be honest, although Kravitz was gorgeous, Romeo was even more so, with perfect eyebrows, velvety eyes, and a mouth that—

"Nope!" Teddy stood abruptly and grabbed his coffee mug. He needed a refill.

He finished off that cup, visited the depressing bathroom he'd been fruitlessly begging Lauren to redecorate, and chatted briefly with the cute copy-machine repairman before finally knocking on Romeo's open door and stepping inside. And then, as always when he entered this room, Teddy glowered.

It was a fraction of the size of Lauren's office, with barely enough room for a desk, two chairs, and a computer stand. Despite that, it was a real office instead of a cubicle. But what truly annoyed Teddy was that Romeo hadn't even bothered to decorate the space. There wasn't a single knick-knack or picture, and the mismatched office supplies—a black stapler and taupe tape dispenser—appeared to be from the discount bin at Staples. The only touches of personality were the three computer monitors—*three* of them, for God's sake—and, of course, Romeo himself.

Maybe Romeo thought himself so decorative that his mere presence sufficed. Or he didn't want any other objects to detract from his glory.

Also, he smelled like sandalwood, bergamot, and vanilla. Dammit.

"You could put a nice landscape print there." Teddy pointed at an expanse of bare white wall. "A palm-tree beach or snowy mountains. If you framed it right, it would even look a little like a window, and your office wouldn't be so claustrophobic."

Romeo squinted at him. "I have screen savers."

Teddy didn't point out that the only visible monitor displayed a massive block of tiny text that was probably programming code. He stared pointedly at Romeo instead, eyebrows raised. "You commanded my presence?"

"I asked you to come talk to me, yes."

"Here I am."

"Right." A flicker of emotion, which Teddy couldn't identify, crossed Romeo's face. It didn't seem like a particularly positive emotion, but then he'd rarely seen Romeo crack a smile. He was probably too full of himself to be caught feeling happy with the peons, ordinary-looking people who worked in cubicles and attempted to put together interesting outfits from resale stores and vintage clothing shops.

Romeo grabbed a tablet—apparently three monitors weren't enough—and came around the desk to stand beside Teddy. He didn't quite loom, but compared to Teddy's five-eight in his Bruno Magli boots with the thick heels, Romeo was closer to six feet. In loafers.

"I put something together for the midrange model." Romeo tapped at the tablet a few times before handing it over.

The mock-up was rough, but it was clear enough to make out details. There was the vase Teddy had spent so many hours designing: a simple powder-coated steel frame around a cylinder of clear glass, and, in front, a gently curved video screen. He'd worked really hard with other Reddyflora employees to make sure the screen would be durable, affordable, water-resistant, and—most important—attractive. The results were excellent, production costs weren't as challenging as with the base model, and consumers would be able to program the screen to match their mood and décor. Even when the screen was blank, the vase looked nice. Teddy had made sure of that.

But now he furrowed his brow and enlarged the image. "What the hell is *that?*" Something dark and bulky was just visible at the back of the vase, butted up against the metal frame. He swiped a few times until the tablet showed the back of the vase. "Is that your unit?" He was too upset to blush over his unintended double entendre.

"Yes."

"But it's really big!"

"It has to be. It needs to house a processor and battery and USB port, and it needs to be waterproof. Plus there's the sensor." He pointed at a plastic prong that extended from the unit into the bottom of the glass vessel.

"You didn't tell me it would be this big."

Romeo blew a puff of air. "I did my best. I can't bend the laws of physics."

"Scale it down, then. Get rid of some of the bells and whistles."

"Which bells and whistles would those be? The ones that give it power? The ones that make it think? The ones that provide input from the flowers, which is the entire raison d'être for the unit in the first place?" For once, Romeo's voice was raised.

Well, Teddy was pissed off too. "Your unit is fugly! Who's going to want to buy a vase that looks like ass? And not good ass either."

"Find a way to camouflage it."

Teddy growled. "*Find a way to camouflage it.* Do you think I have a magic wand? Good design takes time, Romeo, and you can't just throw stuff together on the fly. God, and we almost have the specs worked out on production costs. But if I start adding more pieces, Imani will eviscerate me. Slowly."

"I can't help any of that." Romeo took the tablet and moved back toward his chair. "This is what we're going to need to make the software operate." His jaw was set and his eyes flinty.

Teddy opened his mouth to argue but couldn't think of anything convincing. He didn't know squat about programming or about the hardware needed to make gizmos run properly. He designed and marketed, making things look pretty and convincing people they couldn't live without them, all without blowing the company's budget. He had no idea how to work that now.

Through gritted teeth he managed "Send me those files," before marching out of Romeo's office and into the cubicle area. His imaginary upbeat show tune had been replaced by a wailing lament. Crap.

Time to find some lunch.

# Chapter Two

"Jennifer Murray had another baby. I saw it on the Facebook. Very cute little girl."

Teddy slumped a little deeper into his couch and considered switching to speakerphone. If he did, would his grandmother hear the crinkle of waxed paper as he snacked? "That's great, Gram. I'm happy for her."

"Do you remember Jennifer Murray? You used to play with her when you came to visit. She had strawberry-blond pigtails, but now I see in the photos that she dyes it auburn."

What Teddy mostly remembered about Jennifer Murray was an altercation at the playground, during which she'd demanded that he relinquish the swing. When he'd refused, she'd punched him so hard in the stomach that he'd fallen, skinned his knees, and ended up with bark splinters embedded in the palms of his hands. For the remainder of his two-week stay at his grandmother's, she'd called him Dead Ted.

Instead of reminding his grandmother about that unpleasant summer, he used his free hand to pull another Ritz cracker out of its sleeve. He'd munched through the better part of a package during this call, and when he was done, he was going to need to vacuum away the crumbs.

"Maybe her hair has changed shades naturally," he offered.

"No, it's dyed. I can tell. It's a good dye job, though. She probably has it done at a salon. Although now with two little ones at home, I don't know if she'll have the time for that."

"Hmm." He nibbled the cracker as quietly as possible.

"I think it's a good idea to have your children as close in age as possible. I had three boys in four years, you know. It wasn't easy, but I'd rather that than have one in diapers and one learning to drive."

"Gram, if this is a subtle hint that you want grandkids, you're wasting your time with me. Talk to my brother."

She made a *pfft* sound. "I'm never subtle, sweetheart. You know that. If I wanted you to have children you'd know it." She was quiet for several beats. "But do *you*, Teddy? Want kids, I mean."

He ate another cracker, this one very fast. Now he was thirsty but lacked the courage to walk the few feet to his kitchenette for a glass of water. He might freeze along the way. He'd just have to suffer his parched throat while staying cocooned in three fleecy blankets and a cashmere scarf around his neck.

"I like children, but I doubt I'll have any."

"Lots of gay couples adopt, sweetie. Or they have surrogates."

"They do, but I'm not a couple. I'm just me. And I'm not brave enough for single parenthood." This time he ate two crackers at once, which didn't help with his thirst but did stop him from blurting out anything rude to his grandmother. She loved him. She cared about him. It wasn't her fault that he found relationship-related discussions toxic.

"Teddy dear, you're young. You have time for your life to go all kinds of unexpected places. Don't rule things out so easily."

"But I don't want unexpected. I have everything mapped out. Our vases are going to be really successful." He hoped he sounded more confident than he felt. "I'll send you one of the first ones off the production line."

"And I'll pimp them to everyone in my garden club."

His grandmother's unexpected choice of words made Teddy spray cracker crumbs across his blankets and probably halfway across the apartment. "Pimp, Gram?"

"I'm on the Facebook. I know all the hip new terms."

They chatted for a few more minutes, mostly about her upcoming trip to New York City, organized by her local senior center. She was going to see three Broadway shows while she was there, and she promised to send him the playbills.

By the time the call ended, Teddy was out of crackers and so dehydrated he worried his skin would begin to crack.

His landlord would come searching when the rent wasn't paid, and find him in a desiccated heap on the couch, surrounded by crumbs and blankets. At least he'd look stylish in his Burberry scarf.

Maybe Reddyflora's next project should solve dilemmas such as his: a person alone in his apartment, wanting something fetched but too cold to get it himself. What if someone could figure out a way to give a robot vacuum arms and a smidge of artificial intelligence? That would be ideal—then Teddy could use an app to send it for a glass of water, and it could clean the floor as it went. The gadget could have a cutesy, friendly name—Bobby the Butler Bot, perhaps—and come in bright colors to match various décors.

Teddy rubbed his chin thoughtfully, wondering if Bobby could be manufactured at a viable price point and, more importantly, how feasible the software would be.

But that turned out to be a mistake. His runaway thought train went straight from software to software developers, and that meant it headed directly to Romeo Blue. Such an aggravating man, all smug in his dumb boring office with his ugly unit.

Damnit. Teddy didn't want to think about Romeo's unit.

The next morning, Imani flew at Teddy before he even had his scooter stowed away. "What the *hell* is up with those new specs, Teddy?"

Well, it wasn't as if he hadn't known this was coming. He shot her a long-suffering look before stripping off his outerwear and hanging it up. "I need coffee before this conversation. Do we have coffee?"

"Second pot just brewed."

She hovered impatiently while he filled the humongous three-dollar clearance mug he'd found at Target. It had a cute little rainbow design, but more importantly, it held enough coffee to caffeinate a small army. Or at least enough to fortify him through a discussion with Imani.

She wheeled her chair across the floor to his cubicle and waited with crossed arms as he got himself situated. "Well?" she demanded at last.

"It's Romeo's fault." Okay, perhaps not the most mature response, but it *was* absolutely accurate. "He claims the electronics housing has to be big to fit everything, and it is capital-U ugly. I had to make some design changes to camouflage it."

"We can't afford those changes. Look what they did to the price per piece! You gobbled the profit margin right up." She waved a paper at him, which was an especially bad sign. Like everyone else at Reddyflora, Imani did the majority of her work electronically, but when she thought something was crucial or terrifying, she printed it out. Quite possibly so she could brandish the bad news theatrically, as she was doing right now.

"We can't afford not to make the changes," Teddy replied glumly. "Nobody in their right mind would buy the vase otherwise."

She heaved a heavy sigh. "I don't want to be a narc, but I'm gonna have to tell Lauren."

"Yeah. I figured."

"You sure you and Romeo can't work this out somehow?"

Teddy imagined himself trying to reason with Romeo, who'd only glower back at him and shake his head. Maybe Romeo would throw in some obscure technical jargon for good measure, or spout physics equations to support his arguments. "Not without a magic wand."

"We haven't budgeted for those."

For the next hour or two, Teddy buried himself in writing ad copy and sending emails to press representatives in hopes of enticing them to write articles about Reddyflora. Usually he enjoyed these activities, but today he kept getting distracted by activity outside his cubicle. He was all too aware when Romeo arrived and attempted to make a beeline for his office before getting waylaid by Imani. And Teddy noticed too, when Imani emerged from Romeo's office a short time later, grumbling at the papers clutched in her hand.

She skulked until Lauren click-clacked into their presence in her Jimmy Choos, at which point Imani insisted, "We need to talk, Lauren."

Teddy was staring at his desktop, but he could practically hear Lauren wince.

It was nowhere near lunchtime, so Teddy tried to fabricate another reasonable excuse to escape. It was too early in the season to hope for a tornado warning, and Chicago was generally lacking in serious seismic activity. Could he manufacture a wardrobe malfunction, perhaps? But today he wore a pair of 1940s pleated trousers that he adored far too much to damage, even in the interest of avoiding conflict.

In his upper right-hand desk drawer, behind the extra packs of staples, paperclips, and pens, Teddy had a secret weapon. It didn't look like much from the outside: just a small square box covered in a pale turquoise velvet. The kind of box you might use to present a ring, which had in fact been its original use. It had once contained a band of black titanium edged with rose gold. Not the Tiffany version, which Teddy couldn't afford, but a nice, less-expensive rendition. The engagement ring had looked so good on Gregory's finger that he'd said he might want to use it as a wedding band. Now it sat somewhere at the bottom of the Chicago River, where Gregory had thrown it when they broke up.

But Teddy still had the box. And inside was a tiny rectangle of some cheap metal—a zinc alloy, he suspected—stamped with four letters: *LOVE*. He'd found it on a curb a week after Gregory left, and he'd picked it up and saved it. He didn't know why. He could probably buy a full gross of identical tags for twenty bucks on Amazon. Yet he'd tucked it into that stupid box and taken the box to work, and every time he peeked inside, he felt better about life. It was as if the little charm was a promise that difficult times would eventually pass. Happiness, the letters implied, waited just around the corner.

Today he didn't believe that, but the tag improved his mood anyway. Even faux cheer was better than nothing.

He'd just tucked the box back into the drawer with a sigh when his phone buzzed. A text from Lauren: Come see me.

Shit. He wondered whether it was the profit margins on the base model that had her agitated, or his blowup with

Romeo. Neither would be fun. And he couldn't procras-
tinate with her as he had with Romeo yesterday.

Teddy cast a longing look at his desk drawer, stood, and
trudged a path through the cubicles. He knocked on Lauren's closed door and waited for the invitation to enter.

Lauren, her hair pulled into a neat bun, wore a black
sheath dress and a white cropped jacket with black floral
embroidery. She stood next to a massive glass-topped desk
with a base of reclaimed hardwood and metal train rails.
Her aesthetic was definitely minimalist, and the desktop
held nothing but her laptop and a small arrangement of dry-
stacked round stones. A small gray couch sat unobtrusively
in a corner. Elegantly framed black-and-white photos of
single flowers hung on the wall—a tulip, a lily, a rose, an
allium—each with a bare stem, as if they awaited the perfect vase. She'd replaced the overhead fluorescents with a
modernist chrome-and-crystal chandelier, and a geomet-
ric area rug in grays and faded blues covered much of the
floor. Her chair had a tall back but delicate lines.

"Have a seat." She gestured at one of the three chairs
in front of her desk, low-back things that looked nice but
felt uncomfortable no matter how you sat in them. Teddy
nodded and obeyed, and she smiled warmly. "I tried that
Indian place you mentioned, and it's amazing. Thanks for
the rec."

"Glad you liked it."

"You're right about the décor there too. It's fresh enough
to surprise without being jarring or distracting."

Her praise came off as genuine rather than an attempt
to soften the blow of whatever was coming next. Partly

because, all her aspirations of innovation aside, she was the type of person who let you know exactly what she was thinking and feeling. If she didn't like something, she said so plainly. But she was also forthcoming with compliments, which made working for her much more bearable, despite the questionable choice of office building. Plus she had vision and drive.

"Their drink menu needs more imagination," Teddy said. "I mean, it's okay, but…"

"Nothing new. Yeah. It'd be good if the chef took a quick glance beyond the food."

He scooched his butt on the seat in vain hope of a better perch. "Their dessert choices, though—" But before he could wax rhapsodic about the rose chai cheesecake, someone knocked on the door.

"Come in!" Lauren called.

Teddy's heart sank when Romeo walked into the office. He'd really been hoping for Imani. The only solace was that Romeo looked as unhappy as Teddy felt. Lauren, on the other hand, appeared entirely cheery as she waved Romeo to a seat. "We were discussing Indian food."

"I already had lunch. And I'm allergic to some curries."

She chuckled. "Not to eat now, Ro. Teddy told me about a new restaurant, and I was just letting him know how much I liked it."

"Oh." Romeo ducked his head and stared at his hands. His tightly curled hair was always perfectly shaped. He had long, broad-tipped fingers with very neat, clean nails. He probably booked manicures and other pampering treatments at regular intervals.

Lauren crossed her arms atop her desk and her expression grew serious. "I have bad news and good news."

Teddy clamped his lips to avoid blurting out any double entendres about Romeo's unit, and Romeo simply looked bewildered. "News?"

"Mmm-hmm. As I'm sure you're both aware, we're inches away from starting production—but cash flow is tight, tight, tight."

"Imani just gave me the new numbers this morning," Teddy said, feeling a little frantic. "I'm working on it. And Romeo and I are in conversation too." That was an exaggeration, perhaps, but not quite an untruth.

She waggled her hands. "I know, I know. You're all busting your butts on this. I've noticed the long hours you've been putting in, and I super appreciate you. But you can only squeeze things so much, right? And we all want quality products. We want Reddyflora to shine. And...guys, we're in trouble here."

Teddy's throat felt too thick for words, so he was grateful when Romeo asked the obvious. "How much trouble?"

"Layoffs. I've already cut my own salary to the bone, and there's not much more I can do except shrink the payroll." Lauren stared at a spot somewhere over Romeo's shoulder.

Teddy struggled to appear stoic. He'd been unemployed before and he could survive it again. But dammit, he'd really hoped this job was going somewhere. He'd believed in Reddyflora. A quick glance showed Romeo cool as ever, but of course he knew that his job was safe. Nobody could make smart vases without a software guy.

"You mentioned good news?" Teddy asked.

And Lauren's demeanor changed instantly, her eyes sparkling and her shoulders twitching with excitement. "Yes! I'm so psyched over the newest development."

Teddy and Romeo exchanged confused glances. "What's the development?" Teddy asked, not sure he wanted the answer.

"A potential investor! She believes in us and is almost ready to pump a whole lot of money into our production. She'll get fully behind our marketing too, which is important because she has all the right connections. With her on board, everyone can keep their jobs." She tapped her fingers on her upper arms. "And you know who she is? Joyce Alexander!"

With difficulty, Teddy suppressed a squeal. "*The* Joyce Alexander? Seriously?"

"Yes!"

"That's incredible! How did you even—wow, Lauren, this is huge!"

"I know!" she sang. "I just found out less than an hour ago, and I had to take some time to calm down before I could even talk about it to anyone. I mean, it's not just a fat bank account we're dealing with here, but celebrities. Media! With her help, I can see us splashed all over the major décor mags and lifestyle blogs. Reddyflora vases could be the must-have accessory. Like those Brno chairs and furry cushions everyone was buying a few years back."

"Like ubiquitous succulents," said Teddy, who was way over that trend, especially since all of his plants had promptly died.

"Exactly! We are the succulents of the future!" Lauren

and Teddy leaped to their feet and high-fived with such enthusiasm that they almost toppled the little stone cairn.

"Who's Joyce Alexander?"

Both Lauren and Teddy gaped at Romeo, but it was Teddy who spoke first. "The fashion goddess?"

Romeo shook his head. "I don't really know fashion."

That was news to Teddy, who thought Romeo always looked well put together, but Romeo seemed sincere. Teddy collapsed into his chair. "Okay. So, she first hit it big in the seventies with these floral dresses with strong Victorian influence. Lots of lace and taffeta and full skirts. She hit the right price point too—girls in the 'burbs could afford them for prom and other special occasions. Eventually she branched out into men's fashion, and she got away with selling retro looks even in the eighties and early nineties when everyone else was doing those godawful neons and boxy blazers and acid-washed jeans." He shuddered.

"The eighties were a long time ago." Romeo still looked puzzled.

"Right. But she evolved. Managed to keep her brand strong right through grunge and then hit it even bigger with goth. She was doing jewelry and cosmetics and fabrics and furniture. She became a lifestyle brand."

"She had a resort in Vermont," Lauren chimed in. "And a line of interior paint colors."

Romeo didn't look impressed. "You're using a lot of past tense here."

Teddy slumped melodramatically. "She's...moved on to another plane."

"She's dead?" Those delicate eyebrows shot upward.

"If she were dead she couldn't really offer to back us, could she? Unless Lauren's been negotiating via Ouija board."

Lauren shook her head emphatically. "Nope. I never do business with the deceased. You can't trust 'em."

Repositioning himself in his seat, Teddy suspected this might be the strangest workplace conversation he'd engaged in. This year, anyway. "She's stepped away from most of what she used to do. Sort of retired. In fact, she's a bit of a recluse nowadays. But she remains a grande dame of fashion, a doyenne, and she pops up every now and then to put her seal of approval on something she especially likes. And when she does, everybody suddenly has to have it. Last year it was brightly colored vegan snakeskin boots with kitten heels."

"Kittens?"

Teddy groaned and was thankful that Lauren stepped in. "Don't worry about it, Ro. Take my word for it: she's still a huge big deal. And if she backs us, we'll also be a huge big deal. No layoffs. Capital for future projects."

Although Romeo didn't look nearly as excited as Teddy felt, he asked a pertinent question. "Okay. But why do you need us? Money's Imani's gig."

Teddy had become so caught up in the whole idea of Joyce Alexander, he'd forgotten that Lauren needed something from them. He cocked his head and waited.

But Lauren didn't answer right away. She sat in her tall-back chair and straightened the laptop on the desk. She adjusted a stone or two on the sculpture and then sat back, looking as if she desperately wished she had something more to fidget with. She cleared her throat. "Well. Joyce hasn't made up her mind yet. I need to make a really convincing pitch. And *that* means you two need to get your shit together."

All the Joyce Alexander giddiness fled Teddy like helium escaping from a popped balloon, and he wasn't cheered up by Romeo's expression, which resembled that of a man who'd accidentally swallowed a bug. "We're trying," Teddy ventured.

Lauren nodded. "I know. But ticktock, guys. I head to Seattle in three days, and I need an answer before then. Tell me how we're going to make this work."

★★★

*Don't miss*
Teddy Spenser Isn't Looking for Love *by Kim Fielding,*
*available now wherever*
*Carina Press ebooks are sold.*
www.CarinaPress.com

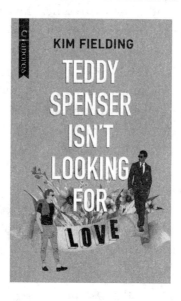